carly phillips

hot stuff

Recycling programs for this product may not exist in your area.

ISBN-13: 978-0-373-77432-6

HOT STUFF

This edition published by arrangement with Harlequin Books S.A.

www.HQNBooks.com

Printed in U.S.A.

hot stuff

PROLOGUE

YANK MORGAN WAS A BACHELOR, a gambler, a ladies' man and completely unprepared for the sight sitting before him. Three little girls in descending height and matching dresses stared at him with wide eyes and expectant expressions. Ages twelve, ten and eight, they were his sister's children. Nieces his assistant Lola bought birthday and holiday gifts for, signing his name to the cards. Kids he saw a few times a year for an hour at a time. That was about to change.

Thanks to a chartered plane crash in the Andes, his sister and her husband were gone, leaving Yank as guardian of their three girls. Frustrated by the notion and emotionally devastated by the loss, Yank balled up the note left by the attorney and tossed it across the room, not even aiming for the garbage can.

The oldest girl, Annabelle, shot him a scowl, then quickly schooled her features into an unreadable expression. He wondered if she was afraid of him but before he could ask, one of her sisters chimed in.

"Mama was right about him. Uncle Yank's a pig," Sophie, the middle one, said.

"Shh." Annabelle placed a hand over her lips.

"Don't be rude. He's the only relative we got left." Her eyes, big and wide, showed all the fear inherent in those words. So much so that he was determined to do his best by all three of them.

The youngest, whose name he thought was Michelle, bent down and picked the paper up off the floor. Before she tossed it into the trash, Yank caught sight of her white panties beneath her short dress.

"Well I'll be damned. You've got a bow on your butt," he muttered aloud.

His niece turned. "You have a foul mouth, Uncle Yack."

"That's Yank and you're darned right I do. Any of you got a problem with that?" he asked all three girls.

Annabelle immediately shook her head. She obviously understood the value of staying on his good side. He liked her intelligence in a bad situation, but worried about how he'd handle her as she got older. It wouldn't do to have a kid smarter than him living in the house, he thought wryly. Maybe the other two weren't as swift.

"If you can curse, does that mean I get to do what I want, too?" The youngest faced him, hands on her hips, a determined tilt to her chin.

She obviously had gumption. "That depends. What do you want to do?"

"Ditch the dress!"

Yank chuckled. Maybe this parenting business wouldn't be so hard after all. "I think that can be arranged. You're Michelle?" he asked.

She nodded. "But you can call me Micki."

"Nobody calls you Micki and besides that's a boy's name," her middle sister complained.

"Micki it is," Yank said, thinking of his idol, Mickey Mantle.

Sophie rolled her eyes. "Tomboy," she called her sister.

"Barbie doll," Micki yelled back.

With each word, their voices escalated and Yank cringed. Annabelle jumped between them and stamped her feet. "You two behave," she said, but in trying too hard, the words came out just as loud and whiny as her sisters'.

And that was Yank's introduction into the world of little women. He had no clue what to do with any of them.

CHAPTER ONE

"THE MEETING WILL come to order." Yank Morgan slammed the gavel against the rubber plate, calling The Hot Zone weekly meeting to order. His dark, wiry hair liberally sprinkled with gray was full and shaggy on a normal day, but after continually running his hands through it in frustration while he waited for his nieces to settle down, it was considerably more disheveled.

As president of their sports agency/PR firm located in a high-rise in midtown Manhattan, Uncle Yank liked to assert his authority. He used the gavel, an engraved birthday gift given to him by Judge Judy, often and with zeal. Unfortunately the gavel didn't change the fact that he was a man outnumbered by three women. Four if he counted Lola, his personal assistant, who liked to tell him what to do and when to do it.

Annabelle Jordan glanced at her sisters who also studied their uncle with fond amusement. As teenagers, they'd paid little attention to Uncle Yank's rules, mainly because he didn't have any. The older the girls became, the more their uncle searched for a way to pretend he hadn't let his personal and professional life go to hell in a handbasket, as he liked to say. The gavel seemed to give him a measure of pride and confidence, and was a small price to pay for him to feel in control with his new partners.

He'd continued the sports agency, but on Annabelle's graduation from business school, he'd allowed her to make her dream of a family business into reality. None of the sisters wanted to be sports agents, but they'd all desired to get into public relations. It was Annabelle who'd seen a means to tie the agency to PR and expand the reach of Uncle Yank's clients beyond their limited career on the field.

Her vision had been a success. The PR side of The Hot Zone specialized in handling professional athletes both in the prime of their careers and into retirement, forced or otherwise. And as each niece had graduated business school, Uncle Yank had rewarded them with a position and piece of his firm. Together they'd created a family business which fed Annabelle's need to keep her siblings and small family together.

"So let's go through today's agenda," Lola said, pen in hand to document the meeting. As usual, her attitude indicated she was ready to do business, even if her longing gazes toward Yank spoke of something entirely more personal. Lola, with her business demeanor, buttoned-up dress and raven hair pulled into a bun, was in love with Uncle Yank. Everyone knew it.

Everyone except Uncle Yank. Neither was over the hill and Annabelle felt bad for Lola. After all, the other woman had wasted most of her life waiting for the ultimate bachelor to notice her as something more than a prize assistant and a surrogate mother for his nieces.

"First order of business. Our annual summer party is scheduled for the third Saturday in July. Does everyone have it on their calendar?" Lola asked.

All nodded. Annabelle already had the date jotted on her agenda. The annual Hot Zone party was as much a family event as a business one.

"Okay then. On to the clients," Lola said.

"Micki? What's going on with Roper?" Uncle Yank asked of their star baseball player. Even when he was questioning the girls about their social lives, Uncle Yank always started with Micki, the youngest and worked his way up to Annabelle, the oldest.

Her youngest sister rolled the pen between her palms. "I'm trying to counter some bad media. He'll be fine. He just needs to watch what he says to the press," she said in a soothing voice. With her blond, curly hair and deliberately casual dress, Micki always presented the epitome of relaxed confidence.

"Admitting to having his nails done and a full body wrap at St. Lauren's spa on his day off will definitely put a kink in his reputation as a ladies' man," Annabelle murmured.

"He isn't gay, he just likes the finer things. He needs to learn discretion," Micki insisted. "I'll stick by his side for a few weeks and he'll learn how to handle the media. We'll spin things in his favor," she assured them.

"He'd be better off pulling a Hugh Grant than acting the part of a sissy boy," Uncle Yank said. "Handle him, Mick."

Sophie snickered and Micki shot her a dirty look. "Don't worry. I will."

Annabelle had no doubt her sister would accomplish her goal. All three of them usually did. Although each took on a client as their own, they worked as a team, brainstorming and formulating a PR plan together. The only division occurred in how they assigned clients.

As every guy's friend, Micki preferred to tackle the difficult athletes. She enjoyed cultivating trust, smoothing ruffled feathers and keeping an athlete looking good to the media. Sophie, the brains in the family, thought, dressed and acted above it all. Her hair was always perfectly set, either professionally blown-dried or pulled into a conservative updo and her designer suits complemented the appearance she sought to present. Not surprisingly, photo shoots and an athlete's upscale ventures were more her terrain.

Annabelle preferred the guy's guy. The sweat-soaked, masculine football player who made a female look and feel feminine in comparison to his size, bulk and scent. She enjoyed being on the field and in the company of jocks, a weakness that tended to land her in trouble, starting with the high school captain of the football team who'd dated her, but then broken her heart when he'd cheated on her with her best friend.

Her bad luck with men had continued with the star quarterback at the University of Miami, who it turned out had only screwed her in order to have a pretty woman on his arm and get closer to her uncle Yank at the same time. After her first real broken heart, she'd decided since men desired arm candy, she'd darn well give them arm candy and enjoy herself at the same time. With her emotional walls firmly in place, she'd graduated with honors, received her MBA and come home to New York. Expanding the agency had been a real accomplishment and she took pride in working in its luxury offices with views of the East River, located in the heart of Manhattan.

Life had been great until Randy Dalton, linebacker for the N.Y. Giants, had slipped past her defenses. For the first time since college she'd allowed herself to think a man could care for more than what he saw on the outside, more than what her family business connections could bring. She'd indulged in an affair, knowing her heart would likely follow, and it had.

Since Randy was one of the wealthiest, most eligible bachelors in New York City, their romance had played out in public, dominating the media. When he'd moved on to a younger actress, Annabelle had been left behind, her heart hurt once more and the gossip rags only too eager to report the story in their unique way. In the six months since, Annabelle sometimes wondered if her ego had taken the bigger hit, but the end result was the same. She was finished with men. She was going to focus on her job, period.

"Sophie?" Uncle Yank barked, snapping Annabelle out of her daydreaming, philosophical funk.

"What's on your agenda?" he asked, moving along to the middle sister.

All the information was on the pages in his hands, but since he seemed to want more frequent face-to-face meetings, the sisters agreed to humor him.

"I'm just trying to keep the peace between Dalton and O'Keefe," Sophie said, of Annabelle's ex and the Giants' new owner.

Randy was the type of jock client Sophie would normally avoid, but after Annabelle's public breakup, Micki had been tied up so Sophie had been all too willing to take over representing Randy Dalton. Annabelle didn't envy Randy.

"Like I told Dalton, he's too stupid to understand discretion and the fact that he's got contract negotiations coming up," Sophie said, confirming Annabelle's hunch that her middle sister enjoyed making the man feel like an ass day in and day out. "He's also too much of a jerk-off to remember that he broke Annie's heart and nobody in this family cares about anything more than the bottom line," Sophie said, defending her sister.

"Mouth, Sophie," Uncle Yank muttered. "Watch the mouth."

All three sisters rolled their eyes. "We learned our words from you," Annabelle reminded him. "And thanks for treating Dalton like the jerk he is, Soph." Still, Annabelle understood that business held sway and The Hot Zone would continue to represent the louse until either Dalton fired them or they could contractually cut him loose.

"Annabelle? What's going on in your end of things?" her uncle asked.

Annabelle looked forward to the twinkle in his eye when he glanced at her. Despite his grumbling, Annabelle knew just how much he adored her. "I just wrapped up overseeing Ernesto Mendoza's Nike commercial and put him on a plane back to Dallas. Last night I accompanied the chairman of NYCT's son to a charity gala. I made sure they know we've got the stars they want to support their cause. They'll turn to us before they look to Atkins for sponsors," she said, winking at her uncle.

Despite his long-standing friendship with Spencer Atkins, they were business rivals of the deepest sort, Annabelle knew. And she always looked out for Uncle Yank's best interest.

"That's my girl," Yank said in a voice infused with warmth and pride.

"Did you wear the Louis Vuitton dress?" Sophie asked, referring to Annabelle's newest acquisition.

Annabelle grinned. "You know it, sister." The dress, with its low vee in the back was perfect for keeping a man's attention on her, especially when his hand lay on the small of her bare back.

The banging gavel startled Annabelle and she jumped in her seat.

"Back to business," Uncle Yank grumbled and all three sisters laughed.

"Well besides all that, I've got the usual insanity waiting for me in my office," Annabelle said, wrapping up her summary.

"Micki?" Uncle Yank asked. "Got any openings for a new client?"

Micki shot her uncle a regretful glance. "Not right away. My schedule's booked. Armando's got the United Way shoot coming up and he made me promise

I'd be there myself. And until the *Post* backs off the gossip and innuendo on Roper, I'm busy 24/7."

Uncle Yank rolled his eyes. "Hire him a hooker and book a photographer to take pictures of him in the act," he muttered. "Sophie?" Uncle Yank asked.

She spread her hands wide, also indicating there wasn't much she could do. "My schedule's pretty tight, too. Besides I'm not sure I can deal with another dumb jock ogling my boobs and trying to get into my pants while I'm attempting to book him for charity work."

"You need to lighten up," Micki said, offering her usual refrain. "You're such a stick in the mud, it's no wonder you haven't had a decent date in ages." She ribbed her sister and Annabelle awaited the fallout.

Sophie scowled. "I've dated plenty. Just not someone who rather smack another guy's behind than a woman's."

Micki let out an exaggerated sigh. "There's no way I'll ever buy that those intellectual types you go for do anything for you," she said as the two sisters launched into their typical bickering.

"Would you two save the personal stuff for after work?" Annabelle asked.

"Annie's right." The sound of the gavel broke the argument. "No sex talk in the boardroom," Yank said, his face beet-red as it always was when his nieces got on a roll.

The problem was, the girls never took him seriously. Not about the opposite sex, anyway. How could they when he'd never married and never tried to hide his string of women from them as they'd grown up?

From the time they'd moved in with their bachelor uncle, he'd used them to pick up women—until Lola had gotten wind of his chick-magnet scheme and taken over, joining them on trips to the park, the mall, and the playground, making them appear to be one big happy family. And putting a serious dent in Uncle Yank's social life in the process. The sisters loved Lola as their surrogate mom and Uncle Yank couldn't function a day in his life without her. He was just too stubborn to see how much he needed and loved her, too.

"Lola and I can handle whatever business comes up until Micki and Sophie's schedules clear," Annabelle said, returning them to the discussion at hand.

"But I think we should consider bringing in new publicists," Micki said. "We've discussed expanding before and I think we're getting close to having no choice."

Sophie and Annabelle murmured in agreement. They were getting too successful to handle everything themselves.

"We'll talk about it," Yank promised.

"Next meeting?" Annabelle insisted, knowing he'd avoid it otherwise. She would, too, for much the same reasons. Annabelle hated to lose the family atmosphere that now dominated The Hot Zone.

"Next meeting," he agreed. "You always did know how to lead this group," Uncle Yank said, chuckling.

"That's my job." Annabelle forced a laugh but his words sobered her as the past came back all too clearly. Little did Uncle Yank know, she'd *had* to take on the role of leader and peacekeeper.

As the oldest sibling when their parents died, the fear of being separated from her sisters lived in Annabelle's heart. She was the only one who'd heard the social worker's threat to the lawyer. If Uncle Yank, the bachelor, balked at taking the girls or if he screwed up in any way, they'd end up in foster care. Nobody would have wanted to adopt kids their age, especially all three of them. Keeping the family together had become Annabelle's obsession. So any time Sophie and Micki argued, those words came back to haunt Annabelle.

"So, on to discussing the potential new client?" Lola asked.

Annabelle was grateful for the subject change. "Who?" she asked.

Sophie and Micki exchanged looks, a sure sign they already knew.

"Brandon Vaughn," Micki said, practically jumping out of her seat to be the first to tell.

"The Heisman winner and Dallas's franchise player until he blew out his knee," Sophie said, proud of her ability to spout from memory.

"A Hall of Famer and Uncle Yank's prize client until the guy bailed on him after his injury," Lola continued to enlighten them.

As if Annabelle could forget. She'd been away at school at the time of his departure. But that hadn't been the end of Brandon Vaughn.

"We were introduced at a charity event a few years ago," Annabelle murmured aloud. His blue eyes were mesmerizing and when he'd looked at her, it was as if no other woman existed. Not even the bimbo on his arm.

He'd also carried a cocky air, the one that informed her *I know you want me, baby, and every other woman in the room does, too.* Unfortunately he was the exact kind of man that drew Annabelle the most. She admired his kind of sexy self-confidence. Too bad it was always her undoing.

As were his looks. Silky black hair, chiseled features and he filled out his tuxedo like no man she'd seen before or since. She remembered thinking it was a good thing he was no longer involved with her uncle or she'd be in big trouble. Just the very thought of him caused swells of anticipation and lust to flow through Annabelle's veins like honey. And oh how she loved the silken smooth taste of honey, she thought.

Annabelle swallowed hard. "What does Vaughn want after all this time?"

Her uncle let out a low, threatening growl. "It'd better be to kiss my ass. The only reason I'm even seeing him is that Lola here insisted I take the appointment." He jerked his pencil Lola's way.

"Rumor has it his ex-wife was calling the shots in the old days." As usual, Micki offered the voice of reason and understanding, defending the ball player no matter what.

"I've met the man," Annabelle said. His rugged features and come-hither grin were now firmly in her mind again. "And somehow I can't imagine any woman pulling him around by his ba—er, jock strap," she said, catching sight of Uncle Yank's scowl and moderating her choice of words accordingly. "He's a jock through and through."

Sophie nodded. "Which makes him good for one thing only."

"Amen," Annabelle said, knowing exactly what her sister meant. She'd been drawn to Vaughn back then, and considering the sexual drought she'd been in for the last six months—eight if she counted the dwindling days of Randy Dalton's interest—Annabelle found herself longing for that one particular thing Brandon Vaughn had to offer.

"How soon did you two say you could wrap up your current clients?" she asked her sisters, hopefully. She had no desire to take on Uncle Yank's newest client alone.

Sophie and Micki eyed each other knowingly, a conspiratorial glimmer in each of their eyes. "We didn't," they said at the same time.

Annabelle had seen that glimmer when they were kids. She'd seen it again at the mention of Vaughn's name. It wasn't often those two grouped together, but when they did, Annabelle was usually the target.

"Neither of us is free now. And we won't be for a while." This from Sophie.

"A long while," Micki added.

Annabelle rolled her eyes. It figured. For once, and at her expense, the bickering duo decided to agree.

CHAPTER TWO

BRANDON VAUGHN HATED EATING crow. He hated admitting defeat even more. So as he stood outside The Hot Zone offices for his meeting with Yank Morgan, he was in a stinking foul mood, even if seeing the old man was exactly what he needed to set right both the past and his future.

"Mr. Morgan will see you now." Lola, the same assistant Yank had had since the old days, gestured toward the closed office door.

Her assessing brown-eyed gaze followed him as he rose from his seat. "You look good, Brandon." She was one of the few people other than his parents to call him by his first name.

"Not that you couldn't stand to get some more sleep, judging from those dark circles under your eyes, but you're still a handsome devil," she said with a warm smile and a wink.

Obviously she didn't hold a grudge over his leaving all those years ago, but Vaughn doubted Yank felt the same.

"You're looking mighty fine yourself, honey." In fact, though likely somewhere in her mid- to late-fifties, Lola didn't look a day over forty. "I hope the old man's treating you right?"

Lola shrugged. "He hasn't changed a bit."

Vaughn accepted her cryptic answer. He'd learned if he didn't pry into other people's lives, they tended to leave his secrets alone.

But obviously Yank still didn't see the prize that was right in front of him, and as Vaughn passed Lola's desk, he couldn't help but pause. "Maybe if you loosened things up around here, Yank would do the same." He tugged playfully on the collar of her blouse.

"You may have a point." Lola's eyes narrowed, as she mulled over his words. "The girls have been telling me the same thing."

The *girls.* Wrong damn word, Vaughn thought. Yank's nieces were all women. Three beautiful women, but he'd only be willing to work with two of them. Micki knew her way around a locker room like any guy, and Sophia was an expert with numbers and PR. Both enjoyed stellar reputations in the business. So did Annabelle, but he had his reasons for not wanting to work with Yank's oldest niece.

The blond-haired, blue-eyed, sexpot was hot stuff. She made headlines as often as he had and her tendency to appear more like a groupie than a professional made her bad business in Vaughn's mind. As was getting involved with Yank's niece. And if he worked alongside her, he'd be tempted to do just that.

He'd met Annabelle once before when she'd been on the arm of her client of the moment. Their eyes had met, held and the hit had been harder than any he'd taken in the field. He'd known then just as he did now, Annabelle Jordan meant trouble.

Without warning the intercom buzzed. Lola pressed the button and Yank roared, "Well, is that son of a bitch coming in or is he gonna make me wait until I'm old and gray?"

"You're already gray," Lola shot back, then glanced at Vaughn and spoke, lowering her voice. "No need to tell him he's already a crotchety old coot," she said laughing. "I guess he's ready to see you, Brandon."

Vaughn treated Lola to one of his cocky grins. Nobody had ever seen him sweat and he refused to start now. Even if he'd rather deal with the physical agony of destroying his knee again than face the old man.

Vaughn strode inside. Yank Morgan looked as imposing as Vaughn remembered him, with just a few extra gray hairs sprinkling his wild hair and thick beard.

"Hey, Pop," Vaughn said, using the nickname he'd adopted for Yank.

The other man scowled. "Pop's reserved for family and friends. Not lowlife, back-stabbing—"

Vaughn rolled his eyes. Plenty of players left their agents and moved on. It was a fact of the business. "I don't blame you for being pissed, but lowlife snake? You can do better than that," he said, pushing Yank's buttons on purpose. At least this way the old guy would get it all out of his system and they could move forward.

"How about damn stupid, dumb-ass jock who let a woman lead him around by his—"

"That'll do," Vaughn muttered. The cold, hard truth

still hurt. "Now are you going to forgive me or do I turn around and walk out the door for good?"

As Vaughn waited, his heart pounded hard in his chest while the deafening silence gave him too much time for unwanted memories to return. He'd missed the older man and suddenly even his professional reasons for returning to Yank's agency weren't as important as the man's forgiveness.

From the first day they'd met, Yank had provided all the praise and pride Vaughn's own parents had withheld.

Vaughn's Heisman Trophy, two Superbowl rings, and Hall of Fame induction meant nothing to Theodore Vaughn. In his embarrassed father's mind, Vaughn was still the pathetic son who'd only graduated high school then college because his teachers had looked the other way in deference to the school's athletic program. And his mother had stood by her man, to hell with her child. All Estelle's efforts went into the superficial. Creating the perfect-looking home, becoming the perfect-looking wife, and cementing the perception of...well, perfection.

Yank had not only represented Vaughn's interests in the first Dallas deal, but had cared about him, too. He'd straightened Vaughn's ass out in all the ways that counted. And he'd been repaid with Vaughn's betrayal.

"I heard you kicked your wife to the curb," Yank said, finally breaking the oppressive silence by mentioning the woman who'd caused the trouble.

"Yeah." Laura was a lesson Vaughn had learned the hard way. Before her, he'd kept all women at a distance, sticking to quickie sex and leaving right after. He never believed a woman would accept him, flaws and all.

Then came Laura, a high school teacher who'd convinced him to trust her, but after his injury, he'd quickly discovered she wasn't the soft-spoken woman he'd thought understood him. She'd changed into a money-hungry, self-indulgent, control freak and Vaughn had never seen it happen. He'd been too caught up in the game, because the game was all he'd had to define himself.

So while Vaughn was laid up in the hospital with a concussion and a potentially career-ending hit to the knee, Laura had made a deal with Spencer Atkins, Associates, Yank's PR rival. She'd talked Vaughn into leaving Yank at a time when he was out of his mind with painkillers and fear. She'd claimed she'd had his best interests at heart and so he'd stood by the deal she'd made in a stupid attempt to believe he had both a marriage and a career. In reality the two had already ended.

"Laura got the bars I opened in D.C., N.Y. and Dallas and I got my freedom," Vaughn said with no small amount of satisfaction.

"How do I know you've learned your lesson?" Yank asked. But the rough timbre of his voice told Vaughn he was softening toward him.

"Would I be here groveling if I hadn't?"

A smile lifted Yank's mouth. "So tell me what you're doing here."

Vaughn knew that was as much of an *I forgive you* as he was likely to get from Yank Morgan.

He'd take it. And now they'd gotten to the heart of

the matter. "I'm this close to opening a lodge in Greenlawn, my old hometown upstate."

Yank leaned closer, squinting. "And why the hell would you want to do that?"

He understood Yank's question. With all the recent aggravation, Vaughn often needed to remind himself of why it was important for this venture to succeed. "It's going to be a winter retreat for affluent adults and a school/summer camp for special kids." Kids whose education fell short, who slipped through the cracks, and who couldn't read as well as others.

A silent moment of understanding passed between them. Because Yank knew Vaughn's secret, the weakness he never showed or shared, he had no doubt the other man would understand Vaughn's reasons for the lodge without him having to go into detail.

Sure enough, Yank nodded slowly. "So what's the problem then?"

"The shit started hitting the fan."

Yank raised an eyebrow and leaned back laughing. "I assume you don't mean that literally?"

"I'm renovating an old hotel. Problems started with incomplete deliveries, then some missed orders altogether. Finally a few of the construction crews failed to show on time. In each case they claimed I'd called to reschedule."

"Did you?" Yank asked.

"Hell no! We're already behind. I'd announced a Thanksgiving opening and the way things are going we'll be lucky to have guests by Christmas."

Yank grimaced. "Any chance your assistant or secretary made the changes?"

"Not if they wanted to live," he said with certainty. Besides he'd already grilled the entire staff over the possibility. "Nobody rescheduled. Just like nobody who works for me started the rumor that there're termites in the building when there isn't a bug to be found."

He slammed his hand on the desk, his frustration returning. "I need good publicity and quick, or I stand to lose my entire investment. If I don't get paying guests in time for this winter, I'll lose the funding for next summer."

Then the kids would miss out. Not just on fun but on the opportunity to work with qualified teachers who'd help them with their educational problems in time for the school year.

Yank rubbed his hands together in thought. "You need Annabelle."

"Sophie," Vaughn said at the same time, thinking of the jock-hating sister.

Yank laughed, his eyes glowing with pride now that the subject had turned to the nieces he adored.

"Hey, I saw what Sophie did to turn Contreras's PGA amusement park from a kiddie snack shack into a high-class establishment," Vaughn said, pressing his case.

"Sophie was darn good for Contreras but only because she doesn't consider golfers athletes. She wouldn't touch you with a ten-foot pole and besides she's busy making sure my biggest moneymaker and pain in the ass behaves going into his next contract negotiation."

At Yank's declaration, Vaughn knew Sophie wasn't

an option. "I'll take Micki, then. The folks in town will like her."

No small consideration. Whichever sister took this job would have to spend time in his small hometown of Greenlawn. Get to know the people. Be in close contact with Vaughn. And Annabelle was too much, too *everything,* to do his lodge or his reputation any good. At this point, his success was tied to both.

"Besides from what I've read this is right up her alley. She knows how to turn a bad situation into a golden one."

"Yessiree, Micki can handle any jock. You've got my niece's numbers," Yank said. "Only problem is Micki's already busy doing just that. The only one who's free to take care of your problems is Annabelle."

Vaughn broke into a heated sweat.

"Annabelle's a real people person," Yank continued, his voice not leaving room for argument. "She's smart, she's savvy, and she can handle herself in a big city or a small town. She thrives on crisis management and can turn any bad play into a touchdown." Arms folded across his wide chest, Yank looked him in the eye, then went for the kill. "You trust me, don't you? That's why you came back, isn't it?"

All the guilt and betrayal Vaughn had lived with for years came flooding back. He owed Yank Morgan for treating him with respect and caring. If working with and placing his trust in Annabelle was the way to repay him, then Vaughn had no choice.

"Okay," he said, decision made, even if his stomach was now in knots. "Annabelle's the one for the job."

Without warning, Yank's office door swung open

wide. As if summoned, Annabelle breezed inside and Vaughn's gut churned with sudden, burning need. She hadn't changed. She was a blond-haired, blue-eyed beauty who had really grown into her looks. Her features were patrician but her attitude and swagger were all New York chic.

Without sparing him a glance, she placed an obviously designer bag, not that Vaughn knew which designer, onto her uncle's desk. "You'll never guess what I've got in here."

She glanced up then, and stopped short, meeting Vaughn's gaze. Her porcelain-like skin flushed a damned attractive shade of pink and he was glad he affected her, too.

Her gaze darted to Yank. "Lola wasn't at her desk so I just let myself in."

"Not a problem. We were just talking about you. You're just in time to meet your newest client. Vaughn, meet Annie," Yank said.

The childhood nickname didn't suit the elegant woman, but did provide him with an intimate glance into her personal life, and the heat pulsing through him increased.

As she stepped back to appraise him, Vaughn watched closely, deciding he'd take his cues from her.

"Everyone in the business knows Brandon Vaughn," she said, obviously playing to his ego. "But I think I told you we've been introduced before."

If she was flustered, she no longer showed it. Instead she stepped toward him. "Nice to see you again." She extended her hand in greeting.

He gripped her soft palm in return. What should have been a brief, businesslike handshake was electrified by a sizzling connection instead. He might have sucked in school but he knew chemistry and theirs was just as strong as it had been at their first meeting.

"Nice to know I still have a reputation to speak of." He forced a laugh.

"So we're working together," she said, her voice a touch hoarser than before.

"Your uncle thinks we'll make a good team."

"I'm sure you were mistaken," she said, her eyes suddenly twinkling with challenge. "Uncle Yank knows I work solo. Any client I take on has got to agree to play by my rules and follow my cue. Otherwise I can't promise results."

"I'm sure we'll find some middle ground," he assured her, not glancing at Yank who merely watched from the sidelines, leaving Vaughn to deal with his last choice of Yank's nieces. "So what's in the bag?" he asked.

She unzipped the top and pulled out a mutt that was nothing short of a ball of frazzled fluff. The white dog looked like an oversize cotton ball but for the patch of black hair over one eye.

"What the hell is that?" Yank leaned forward for a closer look, squinting as he examined the dog.

"According to the shelter, he's a coton de tulear."

"A *what?*" Brandon asked.

"A coton," Annabelle explained. "Like a bichon frise," she said, as if that made any more sense.

The dog squirmed restlessly until Annabelle cradled

him beneath her breasts in a move that left Vaughn breathless, speechless and with a complete hard-on while wishing he could trade places with the pooch.

Oblivious to his reaction, Annabelle went on to explain. "I was doing my shift at the shelter when I met the newest arrival. I mean who abandons a sweet dog like this, papers and all?" She pressed her lips to the top of his fluffy head. "But the kennel is overcrowded and if nobody adopted him by next Sunday, they'd have to put him down. And I couldn't handle the waiting and not knowing, so—"

"You took him yourself," Yank finished for her. "The kid's been hiding strays for as long as she's been with me. She was afraid I'd turn them out in the cold and—"

"Vaughn doesn't want to hear any old childhood stories," Annabelle said, cutting off another unexpected glimpse into Annabelle Jordan.

He shifted his weight and sat on the edge of the desk. "Actually I don't mind at all."

"Well I do."

Yank cleared his throat. "You'll have plenty of time to get to know one another while you're working on the problems at Vaughn's lodge. You have electricity? Fax and phone service?" he asked.

"Most of the time," Vaughn said.

"Great, because we can't spare anyone to tag along with Annie right now. So you go on up to the lodge, assess the damage and we'll work things out from there. Lola's always around if you need her."

Annabelle sighed. "We've had two assistants on maternity leave, the temp agency keeps sending us duds, and the good ones get experience and move upward," she explained to Vaughn, agreeing with her uncle.

Though from the uncomfortable shifting of her feet, she didn't seem all that happy about accompanying him alone.

"Which reminds me. Micki's got a point," she said to her uncle. "We need extra help."

"Finish this assignment and we'll talk about everything. Hell, maybe I can steal an agent from Spencer Atkins, the client poaching dirtbag," he said, shooting a direct glance at Vaughn.

He refused to flinch.

Annabelle rolled her eyes. "We need more publicists, not agents. So where's the lodge located?" she asked in an obvious subject change.

"Upstate. About an hour and a half from the city," Vaughn replied.

She shuffled the dog around, but didn't move him from the snug spot beneath those luscious breasts. "Give directions to Lola. I'll wrap things up around here, leave in the morning and be there midday tomorrow. Once I get up to speed, I'll comprise a game plan," she said.

She seemed to have a no-nonsense way of directing things around her. Well, she would soon learn he was finished being directed, manipulated, or puppeteered in any way, by any woman.

"Since I'm staying overnight in the city, I'll pick you up whenever's convenient and drive you upstate myself," he countered.

Her jaw clenched and her body stiffened, enough to

have the dog wriggling to escape her confining arms. She soothed him with a pat on the head, then turned back to Vaughn. "I'd rather have my car."

And he'd rather not have her zoom into town in the flaming red Porsche she'd been photographed in numerous times. The last picture had shown her tearing out of The Waldorf after an argument with her ex-boyfriend, the quarterback.

He opted for a diplomatic approach. "I don't want to call attention to your presence. It's a small town and I don't want anyone thinking I'm into the flashy or frivolous. I need their trust and I want them to line up for employment and to recommend the lodge to relatives."

"Are you insinuating I'm loud and flashy looking?" she asked in a deceptively sweet voice, latching on to the one nondiplomatic part of his speech.

"He ain't insinuating nothing, Annie. He's outright telling you to leave the hooker mobile at home." Yank burst out laughing, and judging from Annabelle's furious expression, making the situation one hundred times worse.

She clenched her jaw. "Fine, you can pick me up in front of my building at three. Meanwhile, may I ask what people will think I'm doing there? Acting as your assistant? Your secretary? Or can we just call me your publicist?" she asked with obviously feigned sweetness.

He shook his head. "Nobody needs to know my business."

"Then why not just call Annie your girlfriend?" Yank suggested, grinning like an idiot at his idea.

"No," both Annabelle and Vaughn said at the same time.

It was probably the only time they'd agree, he thought. On anything.

CHAPTER THREE

LOLA BEGAN HER RITUAL of straightening the office for the night. Although she could leave the drudge work for the cleaning staff, she usually enjoyed the suddenly quiet time when she stayed. But most of all, she liked being around to take care of Yank, even if he didn't always deserve or appreciate it.

"Do you really think you can play with Annabelle and Brandon's lives?" she asked as Yank passed by her desk, treating her to a wink that never failed to send swirling spirals of warmth through her body.

He paused. "I'm not playing. I'm deadly serious. All three of those girls have been messing up their love lives and I'm sick of watching from the sidelines."

"Look who's talking," she muttered. "They're young. They're entitled to make mistakes. What's your excuse?" she asked him.

He rolled his eyes and as usual ignored her jibe. "Annabelle's picked real losers and because of that, she wouldn't know a decent man if he bit her in the ass."

"And suddenly Brandon Vaughn's a decent man? Just yesterday you called him a lowlife, blood-sucking snake."

He chuckled. "Any man with the balls to grovel is

okay in my book. I missed the kid. Besides he and Annie have a lot in common. More than either of them know," he said.

"Besides picking *losers?*" Lola asked wryly.

"Yep. You got tomorrow's schedule?" he asked her.

Having anticipated his request, she picked up a sheet of paper she'd printed earlier. She let it dangle between her fingertips, unsure of whether to hand him the page or—

"Read it to me, will you?"

She sighed, wondering when he'd admit to having a problem. He'd either have to take himself to a doctor or she'd be forced to make the appointment for him.

"You have your weekly breakfast with Spence Atkins, a conference call with O'Keefe and Sophie regarding Randy Dalton, and then, nothing."

She hesitated, then decided to assert her authority and if he didn't like it, tough luck. "I was thinking Dr. Lenkowitz could fit you in for that eye exam you canceled last month. You really shouldn't put it off any longer."

Yank scowled, the frown doing nothing to detract from his good looks. "I'm fine and since I have the afternoon off, I'd rather go to the track than waste time sitting 'round with blurry eyes waiting for him to use those machines on me."

She raised the newspaper from the desk and asked, "Which paper am I holding?"

She knew good and well he couldn't tell if it was the *Post* or the *News* without moving closer and she dropped the section back to the table before he could answer. "I'm making an appointment. I'll let you know when it is," she informed him.

"Damned bossy woman," he muttered.

"Then find one who isn't," she said, rising from her desk.

He stormed back into his office and shut the door behind him, ignoring her.

She suppressed a smile, wondering if he knew how predictable he'd become. He counted on her enough that he'd never fire her. If she wanted out, she'd have to quit.

The thought made her queasy. Until now, she'd been content to remain at The Hot Zone with Yank. Especially since he'd mellowed, his days of dating different women every night behind him. Her feelings for the man ran deep or she wouldn't have put up with him on any level for all these years.

Contrary to what the girls' thought, she and Yank had had their affair, right before the girls' parents had died and left them with their bachelor uncle. Lola had hoped that, over time, he would come to see her as more than his assistant or even another woman he'd taken to bed. Then the girls had arrived and the passion of their early affair had given way to the priority of settling his nieces and comforting their grief. He'd needed her for that and she'd fallen in love with the three little girls. She'd already been head over heels for Yank Morgan.

Unfortunately, becoming an instant parent had scared Yank, so much so that instead of settling more, he'd gone wild. He'd been the doting uncle by day, but moved from one willing female to the next by night—all in the hopes of proving to himself that just because he'd become the girls' guardian, his lifestyle didn't have to change.

Lola had put a quick end to his using the girls as chick-magnets by turning them into a family. For the children, her scheme had worked. They'd had as normal an upbringing as possible with Yank as their surrogate father. But Lola had put her own life on hold to help him. She'd done so without being asked and she'd requested nothing in return.

She liked to think that if not for the girls needing a female influence in their lives, she'd have long since moved on from Yank Morgan and his unwillingness to commit. It was too late to really know. But it wasn't too late to acknowledge the ever growing restlessness she was feeling. The lack of comfort in the routine she used to love. And she was too smart not to understand why.

The girls were grown women and didn't need either of them the way they used to. Although Yank was certainly no longer the youthful prize he once was, it hadn't changed *her* feelings one bit. Though the girls didn't yet realize he was having vision problems, Lola did. She'd have no difficulty remaining by his side throughout whatever life had in store, but not with things the way they were now.

She wanted more from Yank Morgan than he'd given thus far, or for the sake of her self-esteem and her future, she'd have no choice but to walk out on the man once and for all.

ANNABELLE WAITED for Vaughn to pick her up and thought longingly of her car locked in the New York

City parking garage below her building. It wasn't that she loved the little sports car. She'd bought it in a fit of pique, when she'd realized her then twenty-nine-year-old body couldn't compete with Randy's eighteen-year-old girlfriend's. It was the freedom the car represented that she would miss.

She liked being in charge of her own destiny and being stuck up in Greenlawn with no means of escape frazzled her already shot nerves. Nerves that were on edge for one reason only—Brandon Vaughn, his sexy gaze, hot body, and the disdain she sensed smoldering just below the surface.

She'd been standing outside her uncle's office and she'd overheard him ask for Sophie, then Micki. He'd all but begged for anyone but her, actually. He was settling for her as his publicist and she resented the implication that she wasn't as good as her sisters.

She didn't know what the jock had against her, but she planned to do the best damn job she could and then hightail it out of the small town. Because despite it all, he was just the kind of macho ladies' man who could seduce her body and wreak havoc with her heart. But considering he was pushing her away as hard as she was running, they ought to survive their time together just fine.

A black Lincoln Navigator SUV pulled to a stop and Vaughn stepped out. Shades covered his eyes but she could sense him staring at her as he strode around the back to help with her bags. Though it was early summer and she expected to be hot, the sizzling spike in her body temperature had nothing to do with weather and everything to do with the man staring at her from behind his dark lenses.

Sammy, the aging doorman in her building, attempted to assist with the luggage, bending over, then grabbing his back as if he'd pulled a muscle. Annabelle groaned. He loved this charade, faking an injury in a bid for a pity tip.

"I can handle it," Vaughn said, lightly slapping the older man on the shoulder. "The knee's bad but you wouldn't want me to feel like a complete has-been by helping, would you?"

"You're as good as your reputation, Mr. Vaughn," Sammy said, obviously recognizing him.

Annabelle was used to being with self-absorbed stars and Vaughn's attempt to use his own injury as an excuse to protect Sammy's pride was so unexpected, a suspicious tingling warmth rose in her chest.

Vaughn palmed a ten-spot into Sammy's hand, falling right into the old man's con. Annabelle shrugged. She wasn't about to ruin Sammy's fun.

As the doorman walked off, Vaughn took one look at the animal bag hanging from her shoulder, and slid his glasses down on his nose. "No frigging way."

Annabelle grit her teeth. "I am not leaving him behind."

"You're only going to be gone a few days. Isn't there a neighbor who can take it?" he asked, looking pained at the thought of bringing her pet along.

"Not *it. He.*" She didn't think he'd noticed the rabbit cage behind the biggest suitcase, at least not yet. "And *he's* still skittish from being on death row. He needs the certainty of knowing I'm not going to abandon him." And since Annabelle knew exactly what that fear felt like, there was no room for compromise here.

Vaughn set his jaw and opened the back door of the truck. He hefted her large suitcase, laptop and duffel, which held her toiletries, into the trunk. That was when his gaze fell onto the rabbit's cage.

"Oh, for the love of—" He bit back a curse. "Why don't you just live on a farm?"

"What do you have against animals?"

Vaughn raised his gaze heavenward and drew an even breath. What had he done to deserve this torture? "I have nothing against them."

"Do you have a pet?" she asked, standing up for herself and arguing right back. He admired her grit but she was really pushing every button he had.

"No pets. Not since I was ten."

"It was probably a dog. A big old nasty rottweiler," she muttered. "I'll bet you had matching personalities."

"Actually it was a fish." He'd won it at a school carnival throwing a football through an old tire.

He'd named the fish T.D., short for touchdown, and brought his prize and a small container of fish food home with him. Of course no one had even noticed the fish, so it had been up to Vaughn to feed him. Unable to read the directions and afraid to underfeed, Vaughn had poured a hefty amount of food into the bowl. He'd repeated it three times the first day and when T.D. had consumed it all, he'd increased the amount the day after that. The fish hadn't lasted more than a couple of days before it had gone belly up.

When he'd explained to his parents, his father had called him an idiot while his mother had been relieved nobody would have to clean a fish tank in her pristine house. Vaughn's feelings had never entered the equation.

It hadn't been his first lesson in dealing with his dyslexia, but it had been a lasting one. One cemented in his adult life. *Don't get close to anyone and don't take responsibility for anything other than yourself.*

Unaware, Annabelle waved a hand, dismissively. "Fish aren't anything like real, live furry pets. These kind get under your skin," she said, blowing a kiss at the mongrel he'd met yesterday.

Vaughn didn't hold the comment against her since she didn't know his history. Yet once again, he couldn't help noticing the contradiction between the warm, loving woman who showered animals with love and affection and Miss Hot Stuff in the stilettos and short skirt. With all the construction going on back at the lodge, he hoped like hell she'd brought sneakers.

"Look," Annabelle said, shooting him a pleading glance. "Many hotels allow pets so it shouldn't be hard to keep these guys out of your way."

Her words brought him back to reality. "Hotel?" He let out a laugh.

"Motel, then."

He shook his head.

"Bed and breakfast?" she asked hopefully.

"Honey, would I be building a lodge if the town didn't have the need?"

She shrugged. "I just got this assignment, remember?

I'm not yet up to speed. But I will be." She patted the laptop he'd just hefted on top of her large suitcase at the same time his hand came to rest on the computer.

A jolt ricocheted through him, shaking his equilibrium. She sucked in a startled breath and withdrew her hand fast. Apparently she'd felt the connection, too.

Vaughn quickly grasped for the thread of conversation they'd suddenly dropped. Hotels, motels and where she would stay. Not exactly the safety net he'd been looking for. But obviously Yank hadn't given her any facts on this subject.

Vaughn had always found that truth was best served cold and hard. "There's no B and B, either. The nearest hotel is a solid forty minutes away. You'll be staying at my place."

One delicate, finely shaped eyebrow rose warily.

"Trust me, it's not a come-on," he said, reading her mind.

Or maybe it was his own mind he was betraying, since he couldn't stop imagining her in his king-size bed, the normally cold sheets hot from the friction of their bodies having sizzling sex.

"Are you sure about that? Because I know attraction when I feel it and this is obviously mutual."

Swallowing a groan, he met her gaze. "What my body wants and what I want are two different things." He slammed the trunk shut.

"No sense sugarcoating it," she muttered, a glimmer of hurt in her voice.

Well hell, it wasn't like he didn't desire her or find her attractive. He just didn't need or want the involvement. But, he reminded himself, he cared about her uncle and he certainly didn't want to hurt her feelings, either. He walked around to hold the passenger door open, hoping good manners would make up for the verbal slap.

"Since I'm staying with you and you don't want to make a flashy scene, what exactly are we going to tell people I'm doing?" she asked him.

They'd never settled this question yesterday and he'd spent last night thinking this through. As he'd tossed and turned, thoughts of the beautiful blonde pervading his mind, her sexy scent forever in his memory.

"We'll tell people you're an old college friend with a background in hotel management. Nobody in town will know any better and in the meantime, you'll get an inside look at the lodge and I'll get you a rundown on the problems," he said, repeating the scenario he'd concocted.

She stared at him without saying a word. He took that as agreement.

"You'll be my spin wizard, decide what kind of ad or whatever to take to fix things, and be on your way. And that, as they say, will be that." He slammed the door shut and hoped like hell he was right.

VAUGHN'S HOME TURNED OUT to be a huge, modern monstrosity built in the midst of traditional suburbia, Annabelle thought. If he was seeking to make a statement, something to say *I've arrived,* he'd done it in a grand way.

She didn't have a problem with the house itself,

but the lack of shrubs, trees, plants and flowers gave the white stucco an austere, unwelcoming look. The best thing Annabelle could say about the place was that she'd be guaranteed breathing room and space away from the hot-blooded athlete to whom she was so attracted.

Though how she could be hot for a guy who didn't want to want her in return was beyond her. Damn her hormones anyway. She'd chosen to confront the sexual currents head-on by acknowledging them and, with any luck, neutralizing their power. Hah. If anything, she thought as she watched him unload her suitcases from the back of the truck, muscles flexing beneath his shirt, he intrigued her even more.

As she followed him up the stone steps, she focused on the reason for this trip. Damage control for the lodge, which Vaughn intended to use as a summer place for underprivileged kids. She shook her head, still unable to reconcile that altruistic part of the man with the gruff guy who disliked animals. She wondered if the charity bit was for show and she pursed her lips in thought.

Somehow she had to get a handle on the man and assess this situation and its players. Otherwise she had no way of handling his crisis. So far Vaughn wasn't cooperating. Since she had yet to meet his friends or family, or get a sense of who he was and what image he wanted to convey for the lodge, she had only this house to go by.

The large and lonely dwelling didn't bode well for her vision of a PR damage control plan. Neither did his notion of keeping her in the background for too long. She could lay low for a while, but to fix this situation, she very much intended to make her mark.

"I love your house," she said with forced enthusiasm.

"Really? I hate it." He paused at the door and dug into his pocket for the keys.

Now there was a comment worth exploring. "Then why live here?"

"Because I wanted to move back to my hometown and this was the only place that fit my needs." He flung open the front door and lugged her belongings inside. Her laptop hung from one shoulder, a large suitcase trailed behind him from one hand and he hefted her toiletry bag in the other.

He'd left the animals up to her and she held Boris and Natasha in each hand as she stepped inside. "And what needs were those?" she asked, picking up their conversation.

"Peace, quiet and space."

She nodded as if she understood. She didn't, of course. She'd lived life afraid of being separated from her loved ones. Even now, as an adult, she lived across the hall from Sophie and Micki, needing to hear their voices and feel them close by. She even filled her apartment with things, breathing and otherwise, so she'd never really feel alone.

"So which wing is mine?" she asked, only half joking.

"The house is huge, but I only reopened one part," he explained. "I didn't need the rest and didn't see the need to have it cleaned out or fixed up."

Odd for a man who'd just claimed he needed space, Annabelle thought.

He walked her through the hallway, which had been painted white, and pointed directly in front of her. "That's the kitchen," he said, showing her a state-of-the-art room with stainless steel appliances, white cabinets and white walls.

Then he started down a long hallway and halted halfway. "This room has a double bed for friends who come by. My room's that one there." He gestured to a closed door and a room with which hers shared an adjoining wall. "You have your own bathroom, so you should be fine," he added.

She choked back a laugh. A bed in a sterile white room, and a bathroom with shower. "All the comforts of home." Or a prison cell.

"I thought so."

"What's up the center stairs?" she asked of the grandiose circular staircase she'd seen when she'd walked in.

He shrugged. "More rooms I don't need."

Upstairs probably held a huge master bedroom and a variety of other larger rooms, while he chose to stay downstairs, in an area originally designated for staff. Strange and stranger, she thought. Looking at the bright side, this area was small and cozy, or would be if it had been decorated at all.

"Down the stairs behind the kitchen, there's a gym in the basement, and a hot tub and sauna. Make yourself at home," he said, turning away.

She glanced at her watch. "It's almost dinnertime and I still haven't seen the lodge."

"Hang on." He disappeared into his room and returned with a stack of files in his hand. "I thought you could go through notes on the problems we've been having. Tomorrow you can see things for yourself." He handed her the large pile of papers. "I'll go get your luggage."

She narrowed her gaze at his retreating back. "Is it my imagination or is he being deliberately distant and businesslike?" she asked, unzipping the dog bag so Boris could pop his head up and lick her cheek. The rabbit could take care of business in the crate, but the dog needed a walk.

She hooked him on to his leash and headed back into the hall just as her host was returning, suitcases in hand. No room on either side, she attempted to slide past him, her back flat against the wall. Her maneuver forced Vaughn to do the same and their bodies brushed evocatively against one another.

Chest against chest, thigh against thigh. Nothing could disguise the instant heat they generated. Even the impassive look on his face disappeared, warmth replacing his steely resolve. His sexy blue gaze deepened, darkening to sapphire pools she wanted to dive into.

Annabelle inhaled, trying to fight the pull, but his potent masculine scent that had surrounded her for two and a half hours in the truck suddenly enveloped her again. And this time she was face-to-face with temptation.

His full lips beckoned to her and her entire body waited for the touch of his mouth on hers. She darted her tongue out, moistening her lips. Waiting, hoping...

Until the dog barked loudly, shattering the silken silence surrounding them and startling Annabelle out of the ridiculous spell holding her captive. She let the dog, who weighed less than twelve pounds, pull her away from Brandon Vaughn.

As she headed outdoors for fresh air and sanity, she wished she could have left the burning desire behind as well.

CHAPTER FOUR

"SHE'S HOT STUFF, Vaughn. Are you sure you aren't doing her?" Nick Gregory, Vaughn's lifelong friend, asked.

Nick was also an investor in the lodge with as much at stake as Vaughn. Nick had been recently laid off from his job at CNT Sports Network and had wanted in on the project. Vaughn hadn't needed the money but he'd agreed anyway because there was no one he felt closer to than Nick.

Vaughn and Nick had grown up together in Greenlawn, New York. They'd rebel-roused throughout high school varsity football and as a result, the people in town remembered them as a collective pain in the ass, even if both had returned as hometown heroes, Nick from his stint for Detroit and Vaughn for Dallas.

"Earth to Vaughn. I asked if you were doing the lovely Miss Jordan."

It was Nick's best friend status that kept Vaughn from strangling him now.

Vaughn paused from lifting free weights, and with Nick spotting, put the 380 pounds back in their holder. "Hell yeah I'm sure." Not that it stopped him from wanting to bury himself inside all that lush femininity.

"I wouldn't need to release all this pent-up energy if I were."

He vividly recalled the moment in the hall when he'd almost pinned her against his rock-hard body, lifted her tiny skirt and taken her right there against the wall. Vaughn sat up and let the blood rush out of his head. It had already permanently settled in another body part and would remain there as long as Annabelle stayed in his home.

He shot Nick a warning glance. "You'd better not be thinking of touching her, either, or her uncle will come after you with a shotgun." Reminding Nick that Yank would be pissed served as an important reminder to himself. Screwing Yank's niece would put him back in the doghouse he'd just crawled out of.

"Considering she's way over eighteen, I don't think Yank Morgan would be all that upset. You on the other hand—" Nick barked out his trademark laugh.

Vaughn merely frowned. "We have enough business problems without adding a woman to the mix. Let's just try to get things sorted out and back on schedule."

"Good by me. I'm outta here. I'll meet you at the site tomorrow 10:00 a.m.?" Nick asked.

"Yeah."

"You coming upstairs?"

Vaughn eyed the treadmill. Though his knee prevented him from playing ball, he still kept in shape. "I'm going to run a mile or so first."

"No problem. I think I'll stop and say goodbye to your houseguest on my way out," Nick said, a wicked grin crossing his face.

Vaughn scowled, pushed the safety key into the treadmill and joined Nick as he headed up the stairs.

ANNABELLE SAT ON THE BED in the guest room, paperwork, laptop and documents around her. "Micki, are you still there?" She adjusted her cell phone so she could hear her sister's voice more clearly.

She and Micki often hashed out problems and potential solutions. She was bringing her sister up-to-date on what she'd read so far in Vaughn's files so she could figure out a methodical plan.

"I'm here. I'm just thinking. You mentioned there've been missed deliveries on materials. From the same company?" Micki asked.

Annabelle curled her legs beneath her. "No, that's what's so strange. Different companies, different times, nothing consistent here to go on. But it seems beyond the usual construction and work delays. Then there's the occasional subcontractor who suddenly doesn't show up and messes with the schedule. Add the heavy rains in May and June, rumors that make no sense, and things are backlogged and screwed up like crazy."

"Bad PR," Micki murmured.

"If they don't open by Thanksgiving or, the latest, Christmas, they'll lose an entire season's worth of bookings, which are intended to help fund the camp Vaughn is planning. Another thing he never mentioned to me. I read it in the paperwork." She exhaled hard.

"He's a real mystery man, huh?" Micki asked.

"A contradiction is more like it. On the one hand, he's an athlete and you know how they thrive on attention. On the other, he keeps his secrets buried deep." She shook her head. "You'd think he'd be proud of the camp and want to publicize it all over. But who knows what goes on in that thick skull of his."

Micki chuckled.

"Anyway, people already know there are problems and Vaughn's been stalling cancellations with promises he may not be able to keep." Annabelle tapped a pen against the clipboard.

"What's your preliminary plan?" her sister asked.

"Counter the bad publicity with good, of course. Make sure anyone who's booked knows that there are problems due to reasons they can relate to or misunderstandings that will be cleared up. And assure them that the resort will be even better in the end."

"What do you think is really going on up there?" Micki asked.

"Either someone is deliberately sabotaging the lodge or someone's a huge idiot. Either way, we have to make the resort and Vaughn look good."

"I take it that's not an issue?" Micki asked.

"Heck, no. The man always looks good," Annabelle said, laughing. "And to do the same for the lodge, I was thinking of offering premiums to already confirmed customers. If the opening is stalled and they have to be rebooked later in the year, we'd have to give them something tangible in return anyway."

"Maybe you could promise them one free night?"

"Sounds like a possibility." Annabelle smiled and jotted down Micki's suggestion. "More importantly, though, I need to publicize Vaughn's contribution to the community. The camp is one thing that will undoubtedly play well to the public. I need an angle to hook people in and keep them trusting in Vaughn and this project while he works out the kinks. And I'd like to find out *why* he's doing this. I might be able to use that information in the campaign."

"Sounds like you need to do some digging," Micki murmured.

"Especially since he's been so closemouthed about himself," Annabelle agreed. "I need to see the lodge, meet the workers and get a genuine feeling for the people in town."

"Gauge their reaction to the place being built," Micki said.

"Better yet, I need to gauge their reaction to Vaughn."

"What's *your* reaction to the man?" her sister asked.

Annabelle had always been closest to Micki, not only because they understood each other so well but because with their parents' deaths, Annabelle had seen it as her duty to always be by her littlest sister's side and make sure she felt loved and cared for. The fact that Annabelle desperately needed those emotions in return always made her feel a bit guilty, as if she were using Micki to fill her own needs. But then what were sisters for? All three sisters had their strengths and weaknesses that made the business and the family work.

She didn't hesitate to confide in Micki now. "He's incredible, Mick. So innately sensual, and sexy as hell."

"He sounds delicious," Micki said, dreamily.

She laughed at her sister's description, a pathetic

attempt to cover the all over, tingling warmth that made her feel like Vaughn was in the room with her right now. "Well I've learned my lesson and I'm staying clear of the man. How's your baseball player?" she asked Micki.

"He isn't mine and he's fine. I'm about finished here and ready to come home. Oops," Micki said, obviously catching her slip.

Annabelle laughed. "Like I didn't know you and Sophie were setting me up when you claimed to be too busy to take on Vaughn as your new client?" She piled the folders and papers and moved them to the nightstand. "I'm over Randy, the jerk. And, thanks for the thought, but I don't need a man to help me forget about him, especially another self-absorbed guy who's got a history of bedding jock bunnies. And since I've just described Brandon Vaughn, rest assured I can handle him just fine. From a nice, long distance."

A slow round of applause startled her and she jerked her gaze toward the door. Vaughn stood there with a man she'd seen while she was walking the dog earlier.

A hot, embarrassed flush rose to her cheeks. "Gotta go now. Bye." She snapped her cell phone shut and glared at the two intruders. "Ever hear of knocking to announce your presence?"

Vaughn grinned and began a lazy, deliberate *knock-knock-knock* on the door.

"Too late." She jumped up from her seat on the bed to meet them on even footing. The dog followed, hopping up and down on his hind legs to get their attention.

"Hey Q-Tip, heel," Vaughn said to the dog.

Annabelle scowled at him, which did nothing to distract her or alter his effect on her. Both men's sheer size, strength, power and masculinity overwhelmed her but only Vaughn's did so in a blatantly sexual way. That damned attraction again.

The other man, a blonde whom many women would find good looking, stepped forward, hand extended. "Nick Gregory," he said. "Vaughn's partner."

"I've been reading up on you. Especially since Vaughn never told me he had a partner in this venture." And she'd wondered why a man with business problems had failed to mention his partner.

Nick laughed, apparently finding the omission amusing. Annabelle didn't. How could she help if Vaughn left out information? She made a mental note to dig deeper into Nick and Vaughn's relationship.

"That's Vaughn's ego for you. Can't ever admit he needs anyone."

"I don't need anyone but myself," Vaughn said.

A warning Annabelle knew she ought to heed. "Now that we've established that, anyone care to tell me what you're both doing here?"

"Just came to say good-night, babe." Nick winked at her.

"I'm nobody's babe." She caught Vaughn's smirk and wondered what the man was thinking.

She glanced at both men as she deliberately shifted her long jersey that covered her shorts, drawing both men's attention to her bare legs. She wasn't surprised when their gazes traveled up to her low-cut vee-neck top.

"Sweet dreams, fellas," she said, hoping they tossed

and turned all night long. It would serve them right for eavesdropping.

Especially Vaughn, whom she knew would star in her erotic dreams, all night long.

THE NEXT MORNING, with an hour to spare before they were to leave for the lodge, Annabelle took Boris for a long walk. Summer had already hit the upstate town and the heat and humidity were in full swing. The heaviness in the air did nothing to help her wake up after her sleepless night.

Vaughn's house was on the outskirts of the small town and everything was within walking distance. She paused at the window of Cozy Cups, a quaint storefront decorated with pinups and children's drawings. The aroma of brewed coffee assaulted her senses and her stomach growled, reminding her she hadn't had her daily dose of caffeine. Besides a good PR person never passed up an opportunity to learn the lay of the land and the slant of the people who inhabited it.

Decision made, she bent, picked up Boris and headed inside. The shop was a countrified Starbucks and a comfortable warmth settled around her. She got a renewed jolt of much-needed energy just by inhaling.

A pretty brunette who appeared to be about Annabelle's age stood behind the counter. "Hi. Welcome to Cozy Cups. What can I get for you?" she asked with a large smile.

"That's more of a welcome than I ever get at my regular place in the city and I've been going there for the last two years," Annabelle said, laughing. "I guess there really is a difference between the city and the country mouse."

The woman grinned. "I didn't think you were from around here. I know most people who walk into this place. I'm Joanne Walsh."

"Annabelle Jordan. Nice to meet you." Since the woman had a genuine smile, Annabelle decided she'd reach out. Not just because she was on a fishing expedition but because she was naturally drawn to her warmth. "I'm visiting a friend," Annabelle offered by way of information.

"First tell me what I can get for you, then tell me this fella's name," she said, petting a squirming Boris who was obviously dying to sample all the delicious aromas for himself. "And then, you can fill me in on who you're visiting."

Annabelle liked Joanne's outgoing personality immediately. "Light coffee, Grande, Boris and Brandon Vaughn. In that order."

Joanne shook her head, her brown eyes sparkling with laughter. "You do like things big and strong."

Annabelle wasn't touching that comment but she couldn't suppress a grin.

With a wink, Joanne turned and poured a large cup of coffee with a touch of regular milk, then slid the cup across the counter.

Annabelle took a minute to inhale the fresh aroma before taking a sip. "Mmm. You make a good java."

"Thank you. So tell me how you know Vaughn."

"We go way back," Annabelle said, keeping her cover story in mind.

"Do tell." Joanne propped her head in her hands as she leaned across the counter. "Vaughn and I go way back, too. High school."

"Boyfriend and girlfriend?" Annabelle asked, too eager for information on the man.

"Yep, but don't remind my husband. The only way those men can coexist in this town is to ignore the past."

Annabelle rolled her eyes. "Men and their egos. I understand only too well," she said thinking of her many clients ruled by their pride and nothing else. She sensed there might be more to Vaughn, but without proof, she was afraid she was running on pure hope. "Prom King and Queen?" she asked only half joking.

"*Naah.* We didn't last until June. A short fling and Vaughn was ready to move on. Good thing for me since I hooked up with Teddy. He's my husband." Joanne's voice melted with warmth at the mention of his name.

Envy for the relationship she'd never have swelled in Annabelle's chest. Joanne obviously didn't hold any grudges or have any long unrequited feelings for Vaughn.

"Vaughn's not exactly the relationship type, is he?"

Joanne shook her head. "Since high school he's stuck to the same M.O. with women. Love 'em and leave 'em. It's sad for him since he's such a great guy and doesn't know what he's missing. Instead he puts all his free time into either the lodge or the high school kids he volunteers with."

Annabelle's PR brain immediately picked up on information that would help her use his reputation to further the lodge's image. "I'd love to hear more."

"Vaughn really gives of himself to the kids in this town."

So that altruistic streak went deeper than Annabelle had originally thought. Inside she warmed at the possibility that Vaughn was really more than pure ego. "He's so stubbornly silent, I know practically nothing about his life," she told Joanne, in a not so subtle attempt to pump the other woman for information.

Joanne shot her a sympathetic glance. "I hear you. I don't think even Nick knows what goes on in Vaughn's head and he's his best friend."

"Speaking of Nick, I was wondering about his relationship with Vaughn. They seem close."

"As brothers," Joanne said, nodding. "They watch each other's back. On the field in high school and in every other way you can imagine now."

"No jealousy?"

Joanne burst out laughing. "Aside from basic male one-upmanship, no way. You see, Nick's house was Vaughn's escape from parental pressure growing up. Nick's folks were like surrogate parents for Vaughn. Everyone in town knows Vaughn's mom and dad are elitist snobs."

"And Nick never cared that Vaughn's career was just that much bigger than his?" she asked.

"Not that he lets on." Joanne swiped the counter with a damp rag. "Look, it's fact that Vaughn's just pure magic, a legend in his own right. Nick's come to terms with it. It's not like he hasn't had his own great career and all."

Annabelle digested the information and knew

Joanne spoke from the heart or at least told it the way she saw it. Still Annabelle wondered if Nick had truly made peace with coming in second to Vaughn in all things, or if he nurtured a grudge deep inside.

"That's good to know," she said to Joanne, not divulging her doubts.

"Why do you ask?"

Before Annabelle could reply, a group of workmen strode into the store, giving her a reprieve from having to explain her motives.

Joanne sighed. "I'm sorry. But if you're in town and want to talk more when I'm not working?"

Annabelle nodded. "I'd love that," she said, meaning it. With her sisters in the city and Vaughn not exactly a talkative housemate, she knew she'd need to hear a friendly voice every now and then.

The men filed in behind her and Annabelle shifted Boris in one arm and held her coffee in the other as she dug in her purse for money.

Joanne waved a hand. "Friendship's my price for a cup of coffee," the other woman said, treating Annabelle to a brief smile before turning her attention to the new group of customers.

"Thanks."

"Hey, pretty lady," one of the men said to Annabelle. "I get off work at five. You free?"

Annabelle glanced down at her sweats and knew her face held not a trace of makeup. She decided either the town had no single women left or he was blind. "No, thanks," she said.

He stepped closer. "Come on. I can show you a

good time," he said, deliberately bumping his hip against hers.

"So can Vaughn," Joanne piped in. "And if he catches you horning in on his territory, you'll be out a job and probably a couple of ribs. Go back to your wife, Roy." Joanne chuckled. She obviously knew the man well.

He grumbled and the men behind him snickered, offering a few choice comments at his stupidity.

Roy cast Annabelle a sheepish look. "Why didn't you say you was with Vaughn?" he said, his voice filled with awe and respect. "I'd never move in on his woman."

"I'm not—"

Joanne made a slicing motion across her throat, indicating Annabelle should shut up while she was free of Roy's advances.

Joanne poured the men's coffee without them putting in a request and Annabelle guessed they were regulars. All the while, Joanne continued to talk. "Roy's got his faults, but we put up with him because he's got his good points. He's an excellent father and he respects Vaughn."

"Everyone likes Vaughn," Roy said, ignoring Joanne's other comment.

Murmurs of assent grew around him. Vaughn was obviously a popular town legend.

"He's brought employment to town and he's helping my kid stick with school so's he can get his football scholarship and do better than his old man."

Annabelle was grateful for the insight into Vaughn through the townsfolk's eyes. They perceived her client not just as a businessman but as a human being. So far, he rated top notch. All boded well for the lodge.

"Well don't you worry, Roy. Your mistake will stay just between us," Annabelle promised him.

Annabelle placed Boris back on the ground and he took off at a run for the grass across the way. She couldn't stop thinking of Joanne, Roy, and the other men who admired Vaughn, all with good reason. Despite his reputation as a womanizer, she had to admit, she was beginning to admire him, too.

AS ANNABELLE RETURNED to Vaughn's house, Boris finally decided he'd found the appropriate spot and squatted to pee on Vaughn's front lawn.

Of course her host chose that exact moment to step outside.

He wore black nylon sweats and a gray shirt, ripped at the sleeves. He hadn't shaved and he was still sexy as hell.

"Couldn't you take him somewhere else?" Vaughn asked as he strode down the front steps.

Annabelle forced a bored shrug. "Boris picks his own time and place. Don't all men?"

Vaughn's gaze fell to the dog who'd started to kick up the grass on the lawn with his hind legs. Annabelle tried not to groan.

"That brings up another interesting question. Aren't male dogs supposed to *lift* their legs to mark their territory?" Vaughn asked.

"Maybe he doesn't consider your home his territory. You certainly don't act like you want him here."

"I don't. But don't try to convince me he's smart enough to squat here because of it." Vaughn laughed then, the sound taking her off guard.

"Would you believe that when Boris was at the shelter with other male dogs, he did lift his leg. Go figure. I guess there are times he wants to be one of the boys." She shook her head, still shocked at the dog's actions.

"Locker room behavior," Vaughn said. "Now that I can relate to." He leaned down and patted Boris on the head, harder than Annabelle would have liked but she wasn't about to interrupt the unexpected, bonding moment.

His hand was large compared to her mutt's smaller head and the contradiction, added to Vaughn's attempt to make nice to the animal, showed a completely different side to the man. One she knew he hadn't intended to reveal. And one he wouldn't want her to see any more than she wanted to like him. But she did.

Without warning, he paused, his hand midair and glanced up at her. Her gaze locked with his. She wanted to thank him for the glimpse into his soul because that's exactly what she thought she'd just seen.

"Brandon!" a shrill voice said, shattering the beautiful morning silence and destroying their moment.

He rose to his feet, squaring his broad shoulders, stepping away from her and withdrawing. Annabelle felt as if she could see the walls being erected around him with each movement, and wondered what had caused such an abrupt change.

"Hello, Estelle," he said, his expression hard and unyielding. The ex-jock who took no crap from anyone had returned.

Annabelle narrowed her gaze, curious as to who this woman was, and why she had the ability to turn off anything soft inside Brandon Vaughn.

"That's no way to refer to your mother, especially in front of strangers," the woman said, answering Annabelle's silent question.

Annabelle stared at the immaculate woman in the pants suit. Her slacks were pressed, her heels high, and her sweater jacket screamed *St. John's,* a high-end designer. Annabelle ought to know, since she and Sophie often wore the suits to work. She'd never have pegged the elegantly dressed female as Vaughn's mother. She was too pristine looking, too uptight, too severe. At a glance it became obvious that mother and son had no more in common inside than out.

Annabelle wondered why Brandon would turn to ice around his mother and she was dying to find out. Since being orphaned, studying other people's families had become her favorite pastime. Watching and figuring out what kind of parental relationship people forged was practically an obsession.

When Vaughn remained silent, his mother stepped forward. "I see your manners haven't improved. Since you aren't you going to introduce me, I'll do it myself. I'm Estelle Vaughn, Brandon's mother," she said to Annabelle. "And who may I ask, are you?"

"She's an old college friend and she's visiting for a few days," Vaughn said, obviously resigned to the introduction. "Annabelle Jordan, meet my mother."

"It's a pleasure." Annabelle wrapped Boris's leash tighter around her hand to prevent him from jumping on the perfect-looking woman.

"I wish I'd known you were bringing company," Estelle chided her son as if he were a child.

But there was nothing childlike about Vaughn anymore and he bristled at his mother's tone. "Why? So you could bake a cake?"

Annabelle winced as did Estelle. Any mother would want to be spoken to with respect yet Vaughn had denied Estelle the basic courtesy. Annabelle couldn't understand. How many times had she wished her mother had lived so that they could bond, or fight and makeup again? Yet Vaughn had two living parents that he easily dismissed. Didn't the man understand the importance of family?

"Oh I know. You'd have thrown one of your infamous dinner parties," Vaughn continued. "Well you don't need to bother yourself. Annabelle's a guest in *my* home. I wasn't planning on bringing her into yours."

Feeling like a guilty eavesdropper, Annabelle took a step back. Neither mother nor son seemed to notice.

"Now that's a pity," Estelle said, her voice seeming to be earnest. "Any friend of yours would be more than welcome. But I'm sure you two already have *plans* of your own." This time innuendo suggested that more was going on between Annabelle and Vaughn than mere friendship.

Which led Annabelle to wonder if Vaughn often brought women—sports groupies in particular—home with him. She immediately discounted the idea, recalling his reaction to her red car, his unwillingness to let her call attention to them, and his need for peace and quiet. Vaughn might be all show when he was on display, but in his hometown, he was about privacy. If he wanted the lodge's perception turned around, that would have to change.

But at the moment, Annabelle was all about ending this uncomfortable discussion between mother and son.

CHAPTER FIVE

ANNABELLE GLANCED at Estelle Vaughn, the desire to make peace between the woman and her son overwhelming. “Oh we have lots of plans,” Annabelle said, jumping into the conversation and deliberately taking over. “I’ve just taken a job as manager at a N.Y.C. hotel and Vaughn and I decided we could help each other out.”

Vaughn shot her a warning look. A look that said don’t mess in my life.

She glanced at him and shrugged in return. If he didn’t seem inclined to make this meeting any easier, she did and part of her PR plan entailed more openness on his part.

“To what do I owe this visit?” Vaughn asked his mother.

Estelle brushed an imaginary strand of hair off her perfectly made-up cheek. “I just came over to remind you that the President of Greenlawn College is coming for dinner tomorrow night and he’d like to talk to you about that coaching job. And since members of the Board of Trustees will be attending, it’s important that you be there.”

“Important to Theodore, you mean.”

"Any dinner party involving the college is important to your father." She batted her eyelashes in an obviously practiced move designed to silently sway him.

He merely glanced heavenward, dismissing her.

It struck Annabelle, not for the first time, that this woman didn't know how to work her son to get him to do her bidding. Every move she made seemed to strike Vaughn the wrong way.

"It's also important to you, dear. Especially with their job offer on the table."

Vaughn shook his head. "I already told them and you, I'm busy with the lodge and the volunteer work I do at the high school. I don't want their job."

Estelle looked at Annabelle, treating her to a pleading, woman-to-woman glance. "Would you please tell him that it's more respectable to take a paying job as a football coach at a Region One college than to work for free with the juvenile delinquents who don't want to study hard enough to pass their classes?"

And now Annabelle understood what Joanne meant when she'd called Vaughn's parents elitist snobs. She tensed, waiting for Vaughn's reply.

"Those *delinquents* are kids that the system ignores." Vaughn's voice rose in anger. "Sports is their only chance of getting into a decent college, and if I can help them see that academics are important too, then I'll have accomplished something," he said, gritting his teeth so hard the muscles bulged in his neck.

She didn't know why these kids were so important to Vaughn, but at least now she understood his goals.

From a business angle at least, Annabelle could come down on Vaughn's side.

"Actually from a public relations perspective, volunteer work is much better than work for hire," she said to Estelle. "Vaughn obviously doesn't need the coaching job to make a living and if he's giving back to the students and to the community, it's admirable." Her defense of Vaughn came too naturally for her peace of mind and she told herself she admired his goals, nothing more.

"Yes, well you're merely a hotel manager, dear. You wouldn't understand the world of academia that Brandon comes from." Estelle studied her from behind her large-framed sunglasses.

Annabelle suffered the subtle put-down in silence. Apparently her men's-style plaid pants and white T-shirt hadn't passed Estelle's inspection. The thought had her biting back a grin. She chose to shut her mouth and let his mother continue.

"Vaughn has the opportunity to make his father proud and it's time he took it," Estelle continued, oblivious to the fact that she'd long since lost her audience.

"A Superbowl ring wasn't enough for the old man," Vaughn explained to Annabelle in a bored voice she didn't buy for one second.

His father didn't find the biggest accomplishment in Vaughn's career enough? *That* had to hurt, Annabelle thought.

"Let's not revisit old drama again," his mother said. "You know how I hate airing family business in public. Just tell me you'll be at the dinner. Please."

"I agree with your mother," Annabelle chimed in, seeing the opportunity as a golden one.

"Like that's going to sway me." He folded his arms across his chest and stared stony faced.

She sighed. Whatever Vaughn's reasons for not wanting to attend this dinner, they couldn't be as important as the PR reasons for him *to* attend. College events would bring visitors who would need a place to stay. Though Vaughn didn't yet realize it, he needed the University President and Board Trustees on his side, referring guests to his lodge.

And since Vaughn was paying Annabelle to do her job, she damn well intended to push harder and explain her reasons to him later. "Your mother's right. I wouldn't understand academia," she said, neglecting to mention her college degree and her MBA. "But even a dinner party would be a nice diversion from this small town with no nightlife." She grasped his arm and squeezed tight. "Can't we go, please?" she asked him in a whiny, girlfriend voice.

His mother already thought them a couple. She saw no reason not to reinforce the notion.

He cleared his throat. "I don't think—"

"Oh, please? I brought a nice dress and I'd love an excuse to wear it."

Estelle remained silent, obviously weighing her options. Her son at the dinner party with his inappropriate girlfriend or no son at all. "Annabelle's right, Brandon. Give the young lady an excuse to get out of her sweats and dress up for a change."

Annabelle shot Vaughn a triumphant grin. Damn

she was good at reading people and gauging their reactions. Estelle had played right into her hands.

"Fine. We'll be there," Vaughn said, patting her hand in a way that felt more like a slap than a love tap.

"I can't wait to tell your father." Estelle jiggled her keys and began to walk away.

Annabelle knew she'd pay later, but for now she was darn proud. She'd just performed her first duty as his publicist and garnered him an important public appearance with her by his side.

Now all she had to do was keep things as superficial as the "jock bunny" label implied. Which shouldn't be a problem considering Vaughn's distant attitude. It was her own growing desire she had to keep in check.

VAUGHN WANTED TO KILL Annabelle. Short of that he'd settle for strangling her and that fairy pooch that didn't know how to pee like a man. Instead he'd driven her to his resort and handed her over to Nick for a tour. Meanwhile he'd headed to his on-site office to get some work done.

He needed the time to deal with the fact that she'd just put herself smack in the middle of his family hell. Add to that she was forcing him to show up at one of his parents' ridiculous cocktail parties in the name of good PR for the lodge.

If he'd known he'd have to make that kind of sacrifice, he'd have sold the entire place to Nick and been done with it. Nothing was worth subjecting himself to his father's boring speeches intended to impress the

Board of Trustees and, Vaughn was certain, to remind him of all the so-called brain power his son lacked.

Yet as frustrated and angry as he was with Annabelle, he was forced to admit her reasoning made sense. He'd figured the lodge as an upstate getaway for kids during the summer and a cozy lodge resort in the winter. He'd never even thought about local colleges. He should have. But now thanks to Annabelle, he'd tap into a brand-new market. It was brilliant, he thought, as long as he didn't have to admit that to his new publicist.

He ran a hand through his hair and turned to the stack of paperwork in front of him. Thanks to the delays, the plumbing installation was behind schedule, but they'd made up good time in other areas. He hoped they could continue on such a smooth path.

Calmed somewhat, he headed to meet up with Nick and Annabelle. He found them near the lake where they had spread out a blanket beneath a tree. Annabelle and Nick sat side by side, laughing and eating from a picnic basket. The dog hopped up and down on his hind legs begging for attention and when that ploy failed, he ran laps around a nearby bush.

From Vaughn's perspective, the son of a bitch who called himself Vaughn's best friend had decided to romance Annabelle.

Vaughn came up to the oversized blanket they sat on. "I thought we were here to work."

Annabelle glanced up. She hadn't expected to see Vaughn so soon and her adrenaline shot up a notch.

"We did work," Nick said as he shot Vaughn a

sidelong glance. “I gave Annabelle the grand tour and we came to find you, but Mara said you weren’t to be disturbed.”

Annabelle grinned at that. Mara was a woman who spoke her mind about business and a whole lot more. She’d been in Nick’s face, flirting, but Nick had deliberately ignored her blatant interest. When he’d asked her to call a local restaurant to deliver a lunch picnic for himself and Annabelle, Mara had nearly flung the telephone at his head.

Oh, those two were interesting, Annabelle thought. As was this picnic, which had taken her by surprise. Then there was Vaughn, who looked ready to grind either their lunch, or her hyper dog jumping at his feet, into dust.

She grabbed Boris away and spoke to Vaughn. “Actually your assistant said you bit her head off and ordered no interruptions unless she wanted to lose her job.”

Vaughn ran a hand through his hair. “It’s been a long day.”

“It’s only eleven.” Nick chuckled. “I hear you’re going to the university fund-raiser after all. Plan on giving that coaching position a shot?”

Vaughn shook his head. “I told *you* to apply for it. They’d be damn lucky to have you.”

“As second choice. I’d rather manage this place like we talked about.”

Annabelle listened to the discussion between the two men with interest. Nick was Vaughn’s best friend, but despite Joanne’s assertions of loyalty, he was obviously runner-up to his pal, both in the lodge and in coaching choice. Could there be jealousy there? Enough to cause Nick to sabotage his own investment? The notion didn't seem likely but she couldn't afford to overlook any possibility.

"I was hoping we could go over some things," Annabelle said, glancing at Vaughn.

He nodded. "I have time now."

She rose and brushed stray grass off her Juicy sweats. With all the dirt and construction, she'd decided to dress down to visit the lodge.

"I'm going to go over the end-of-construction schedule and make sure the inspectors are lined up," Nick said.

"Ask Mara if she confirmed the electrical inspection. I want to get the drywall up," Vaughn reminded him.

"Will do. You two don't kill each other while I'm gone." Nick treated Annabelle to a teasing wink that had Vaughn clenching his jaw.

"We'll try not to," Annabelle replied in her best sugary-sweet voice.

Nick took off for the lodge and Annabelle turned to Vaughn. "Friend or foe?" she asked him about Nick.

"Friend." He spoke without hesitation. His steely-blue gaze met hers, ice in his eyes. "And who the hell are you to even ask?"

Okay so Vaughn's loyalty ran deep. She'd suspected as much. But could she say the same of Nick's? "I'm the person you're paying to fix things around here."

"I'm paying you to fix the lodge's perception with the public, not question my best friend's loyalty."

She shook her head. Vaughn was a typical layman who didn't understand how PR was connected to every aspect of his life. "You're right," she said, opting to calm him down first. "But I can't do that if I don't know what's going on or who wants to prevent you from opening."

"And you think Nick's sabotaging his own investment?" Vaughn let out a loud laugh of disbelief.

"It's not impossible. And he is jealous."

"Of what? The man's a legend in his own right—"

"Who lost his last job because he wasn't pulling in ratings and who comes second to you in ownership of the lodge as well as a coaching job at the local university. I'm just saying he has reasons to undermine you."

"But he wouldn't. End of discussion." He glanced around at the remnants of their lunch. "So did you enjoy yourself?"

Deciding to test the jealousy theory, she answered him in a low, seductive purr. "As a matter of fact, I did have fun with Nick. He's a great guy." She began to clean the trash and put it inside the basket. "Charming, entertaining..."

She deliberately baited Vaughn even if, despite appearances, her get-together with Nick had been all business, something she intended to tell Mara at the first opportunity. She and Nick had shared a few laughs and he'd explained the workings of the lodge's construction, the foremen in charge, and who supervised each department.

"You had fun," Vaughn repeated.

"Yes. F-U-N. Which part of the word don't you understand?"

He clenched his jaw tighter. "Fun's a word I can handle just fine, honey." He stepped closer and her breath caught in her chest.

He towered over her, a big, strong, sexy man who made her skin flush hot and her body heat with the distinct rush of arousal flowing through her. Being practical flew out the window around this man and Annabelle knew it. Her heart might be warning, *look out,* but her body screamed *go for it.* And she remained on edge, wondering how far he'd push the issue.

Vaughn couldn't stand to hear how much *fun* she'd had with his best friend. "I can show you a lot better time than Nick ever could." Even as he spoke, he recognized that he was being absurd.

Vaughn knew Nick wasn't intending to seduce Annabelle. Intending to make Vaughn crazy? Yes. But romancing her? Not a chance. The man had feelings for Mara even if he was fighting them, not that Vaughn knew why. So his own reaction to Nick and Annabelle was over the top.

"I thought we'd reached the end. As in the end of any discussion about Nick." Her lips twitched in a knowing grin.

Already on edge, her words nudged him even closer to the precipice. "Ending *any* discussion sounds damn good to me." He stepped forward, and she stepped back, until she came up against the tree.

She glanced up at him. Her eyes were wide, but by no means uncertain. She straightened her shoulders, which had the effect of pushing her breasts against the flimsy tank top. Her nipples hardened beneath his gaze, tight peaks of aching need just begging for his touch, his mouth and he knew damn well he was going to kiss her. She obviously knew it, too, and she wasn't about to stop him.

God, he had to taste her or go insane. His gaze never left hers as he lowered his mouth, touching his lips to hers.

Sizzling heat sparked between them, electricity that traveled directly to his groin. Yet as much as he wanted to satisfy the ache she'd inspired from the first time they'd met, he wanted to kiss her more. To devour her sweet, warm, moist mouth in a completely primitive display of possession.

That's how this woman made him feel. Aggressive and hungry for her. So when a soft moan of acquiescence escaped her throat and her lips opened wide, he indulged his desires. He slid his tongue inside her welcoming mouth, filling, learning and savoring each seductive movement she made, her tongue mating with his, matching him thrust for eager thrust. Her hands cupped first his cheeks, then traveled until her fingertips ran through his hair and tugged on his scalp. Just when he didn't think they could get any closer, she somehow managed.

If it was possible to make love to her with his mouth, that's exactly what Vaughn did. The instantaneous reaction and spontaneous combustion was more than even he'd bargained for.

He tasted her sweetness and he wanted more.

Needed more. He thread his fingers through her hair and felt the silken strands sift through his fingertips in a waterfall of sensation. He tugged on one long lock, pulling at the nape of her neck.

With a sensual moan he hadn't expected, she twisted against him, easing her body against his and he responded. His groin hardened, seeking a home between her legs and he ground against her, damning the barrier of clothing separating them.

His hands reached for the waistband of her sweats when a yapping bark brought him out of the haze of desire and allowed reality to resurface.

"Boris," she murmured, almost drowsily.

"I'm not Boris, I'm Vaughn."

She laughed and leaned her forehead against his.

He savored the intimate moment, which was quickly ruined when Q-Tip squatted and peed on Vaughn's favorite pair of Nike's. Nothing could have killed the moment faster. Nothing could have been more welcome.

"Boris. Bad!" Annabelle said sternly. "I'm sorry."

The lodge was his whole world right now—it gave him a sense of purpose and he needed it so he could help the kids.

He'd had everything to lose and nothing to gain by kissing her.

Annabelle groaned. "Boris might not think your home is his territory, but he's obviously decided to make his mark on you."

Most importantly, Vaughn was out of the doghouse

with Yank, and another bonehead move like this would put him right back in.

"You aren't laughing," Annabelle continued rambling and cringed. "You're ticked. I guess I'd be ticked, too."

He slid his tongue over his lips and swallowed a groan when he tasted Annabelle and the tidal wave of desire washed over him once more.

"And you aren't listening to a word I've said," Annabelle said, reinforcing her words with a kick of her foot against his with an admirable amount of force he couldn't ignore.

"I heard you," he muttered.

"Then what'd I say?" She slipped away and began to straighten her shirt and smooth her disheveled hair.

He'd tangled that hair, he thought and his fingertips tingled all over again. Damn, this woman was one potent package. She distracted him and caused way too much havoc with his mind and body.

"I asked you to repeat what I said." She swung her foot back and perched her toe against the grass. "Did you hear me? Or do I need to kick you again?"

He scowled. "You said you were sorry and you'd have the dog put down if he peed on my feet again."

She glanced at him, horrified. "I said nothing of the sort. I—"

"You said that Q-Tip here's decided to mark me as his territory." Just as Annabelle had obviously marked him. Vaughn shook his head, frustrated with himself and her ability to make his every thought turn to her.

"Something like that." She touched her lips with her fingers.

Whether idly or on purpose, she had him thinking about kissing her again. And for the reasons he'd just listed in his head and would permanently emblazon on his brain, *that* couldn't happen again. Ever.

CHAPTER SIX

OH YEAH, BABY. Those were the only words floating through Annabelle's mind as she sat in her room, jotting down notes on the people she'd met today. Those somehow related to Vaughn by either work or friendship.

She started a diagram but couldn't concentrate, so she moved on to the press release. She needed Vaughn to make a public statement about the lodge and send a letter to those who already had bookings. Unfortunately she couldn't concentrate on anything but that kiss.

A kiss like the one they'd shared could make her reevaluate her decision to remain celibate. Judging by her swift reaction to Vaughn, it'd been too long since she'd been in any kind of relationship and she obviously needed the physical contact.

Desperately.

And only one man would do.

She and Vaughn were alone in this big house, nothing between them except the memory of that kiss. How could she not reevaluate her perspective and give herself permission to act on her desires?

True, she'd challenged herself this same way before and lost, but she'd learned her lesson and this time, she wouldn't be hurt. This was a situation of limited duration with a man she knew up front wasn't interested in anything serious. She'd only be in this small town and large house for a short time. Too short to invest her heart in Brandon Vaughn. But her body was another story.

Besides, if she didn't give herself permission to seduce Vaughn, she'd never get any work done. Taking his wary reaction into consideration, she needed to start slow. But she'd absolutely decided to go for it with Vaughn.

Her stomach growled, interrupting her thoughts, but not her work, which just wasn't flowing. Time to prepare a meal and feed the mind and the soul. She could cook for both herself and her missing housemate, who'd dropped her off and disappeared for parts unknown. Probably looking for more of that precious space he always seemed to need. She could just leave a plate warming in the oven for him later.

She decided to make use of his state-of-the-art kitchen and rummaged through the cabinets and fridge, coming up with steaks in the freezer, baking potatoes and some salvageable green stuff for a salad.

An hour later, she had both steaks defrosted, marinated and sizzling on the downdraft cook-top grill. She'd found a bottle of Merlot, and was flipping the steaks and pleasantly buzzed when Vaughn finally returned.

"Annabelle, are you here?" he called out loudly.

At the sound of his deep voice, her stomach churned

with excitement. As she waited for him to stride into the kitchen, she tried to force a nonchalance she didn't feel.

He entered just as she decided the steaks were finished. She placed them on the table along with the rest of the meal before glancing up. Looking at him was a feast for the senses. Vaughn wasn't an athlete who'd let his body go to hell after retirement. On the contrary, his T-shirt, cut off at the abdomen and the sleeves, showcased well-toned muscles and tanned skin. No man should look so good.

"Of course I'm here. Where else would I be?" she asked, forcing herself to focus and answer his question. "You insisted I not bring my car, then you took off, not to be seen again for hours."

He had the good manners to look embarrassed. "Sorry. I needed—"

"Space," she finished for him.

"Right." He shot her a sexy grin. "So, something's cooking." He shoved his hands into his back pockets and peered over her shoulder at the meal on the table.

"More like someone's been cooking."

"For two."

Caught, her face heated with embarrassment. "I thought if I was going to be using your food, I should at least include you in the meal. Just in case you were hungry."

Vaughn stared, surprised at the dinner on his table. He'd been a real bastard to her and she'd thought about including him anyway.

"Thanks," he said awkwardly. He wasn't used to people doing things for him.

"You're welcome. You might as well sit. Unless you've already eaten?"

He shook his head. He'd been out in a pathetic attempt to outrun thoughts of the steamy summer kiss they'd shared.

No such luck. Seeing her again brought back hot memories of her sweet mouth and the way those luscious curves had felt pressed against him. With a groan, he settled into the chair across from her, resigned to the fact that she was with him, whether physically or emotionally, and would be until their working relationship ended.

"Wine?" she asked.

He nodded. "Why not."

She added to his glass, then leaned forward in her seat. "So you've been out running."

He ran a hand through his windblown hair. "That obvious?"

She shrugged. "Only to someone who's looking." Her heavy-lidded gaze met his and held, until he couldn't mistake her meaning.

He had to laugh. "I need to ask you something."

"If I can ask a question in return, I'm more than happy to answer."

He nodded. "Are you always this direct? Sexually I mean."

She steepled her fingers and paused in thought. "I suppose that depends. I generally say what I think. I can't see any sense in hiding my feelings. As for what's going on between us, I'm focused on two things."

"And those are?"

"One," she said, raising a finger. "I need your cooperation to fix the problems with the lodge and so far you're not giving me any, and two," she said, raising a second finger, "I believe in bringing things out into the open and our attraction is there whether either one of us likes it or not. So instead of letting it get in the way of work, I choose to acknowledge and deal with it, so we can move forward."

He blinked, staring at her in amazement. "Are you saying you got the attraction out of your system and can move on?" Because he sure as hell wasn't able to do any such thing, no matter how badly he wanted to.

"I said move *forward.*" She emphasized her point with a shake of her head that had her ponytail falling over the shoulder of yet another of those jerseys she favored.

He stabbed his steak and let the fork remain. It was one thing to acknowledge the attraction, another to contemplate doing anything more about it. Moving on seemed smartest. Safest. He wasn't sure what she meant with her semantics, but she was directing the conversation and he decided to see where she was headed.

"So while we're eating, I thought we could deal with my first point and talk business."

She'd obviously decided to drop the more heated subject and he exhaled a hard sigh of relief. The knot in his stomach eased, as did the tension lodged inside him.

He cut into the steak and began eating. "Delicious," he said, between bites.

"I'll let the cook know." She spoke with laughter in

her voice but he couldn't mistake the glow of pleasure in her cheeks or the warmth in her eyes at his compliment.

Just watching her, his skin flushed hot with wanting.

"Tell me about your reasons for building this lodge. I'm sure it has something to do with the kids you want to bring in for the summer. And I already know you volunteer at the high school. So, what gives?" she prodded and not too subtly, either.

Her pointed questions froze everything that had been thawing inside him. He was drawn to her yes, but he didn't trust her. Not enough to divulge his deepest secret and thus expose his biggest fear—that no woman would ever love the real Brandon Vaughn. The man beneath the trophies, money and rings.

"I thought we were going to talk business." He cleared his throat before continuing. "My reasons for the lodge are personal."

"So you say." Leaning back in her seat, she drained the last of her drink. "But I answered your question and you said you'd answer mine," she reminded him.

Her eyes had glazed with the effect of the wine. Her deep vee-neck plunged a bit too low, revealing soft white skin and plump cleavage he'd give anything to taste. Her allure had never been more potent.

Too bad he was about to douse the flame. "As I recall, I said you could ask. I never agreed to answer."

Dismay flickered in her eyes but she covered it with a casual wave of her hand. "You disappoint me, Vaughn."

"I'll have to live with that." But he suspected it

wouldn't be as easy as he claimed. He didn't like coming up short with her and he wasn't sure why.

"Just don't underestimate my determination," she warned him. "In the meantime, tell me more about this house."

At least that answer he could give her.

She rose and began collecting dirty plates.

"Leave them. The cleaning lady comes in the morning." He stopped her, catching her wrist in his hand. The petite feel took him off guard. For a woman so sure of herself, she seemed fragile in his grasp.

He wondered if he'd have to be gentle with her when they made love, then discounted the notion. She was stronger than she looked and tough as nails. And he was an idiot even thinking about having sex with this woman.

He quickly released her. "I bought this place because it fit my needs," he said, answering her question.

She lowered herself back into her seat. "So you said. But it's a contradiction. You say you need space and you buy a huge house, yet you only open and live in a fraction of it."

"So? It's far enough from the residential sections of town to give me the privacy I want."

"Mmm. I guess that makes sense."

He narrowed his gaze. "You don't sound convinced."

She pursed her lips in thought. "Well when your mother was here earlier, I picked up on some of what you two were saying. And the dynamics were pretty obvious."

He clenched his jaw tight, hating any conversation that involved his mother or father. He'd long since come to terms with the man he'd become or so he thought until thoughts of how his parents viewed him resurfaced.

"What does that have to do with anything?" he asked Annabelle.

"I think you came home to show your parents how good you've done in your life."

"When did you become a psychiatrist?"

She shrugged. "A publicist has to be good at reading people and dissecting situations. And right now I sense I'm making you uncomfortable."

"You're just pushing too much. As you've seen for yourself, my parents don't think I've accomplished a damn thing with my life, so hell yes, I wanted to show them a thing or two."

"And buying this monstrosity accomplished that?"

"No," he admitted. "It just brought me back to all the crap I left behind." He'd intended to give her a short, one-sentence explanation so she'd back off. Instead he'd given her more insight into himself than he allowed most people.

"Then why stay?" she asked, still prodding for answers.

"Because this town is my home," he bit out.

She ran her tongue over her lower lip. "Now *that* I can understand." She hesitated, then drew a long, deep breath, causing her chest to rise and fall.

Though he watched and his body responded, he held his own, wanting her to explain. That sexual tension she'd stopped discussing remained alive and smoldering just below the surface. "How so?"

"You and Uncle Yank are close, or at least you once

were. So you must know he took us in when my parents died." Quivering emotion laced her voice.

Vaughn reacted without thinking. One minute they were adversaries, the next he reached across the table and grasped her hand in his. "I'm sorry about your folks."

She nodded in gratitude. "Thanks."

"You were lucky to have Yank."

"Yeah we were." She spoke softly. "But for a while I wasn't even sure he'd take us in. I was so afraid the three of us would be separated and—" She paused and hiccuped, an obvious attempt to swallow her emotions. "Anyway, my point is, I can relate to the need for that feeling of home. But home isn't the same as family, you know?"

A low growl rumbled deep in his throat. "Not everyone can have Ozzie and Harriet parents."

"And I just told you I didn't have any parents. I'm just saying that for whatever reason, you and your folks don't connect. But you feel that connection to this town anyway. So much so that the lodge is the home this house will never be."

She understood him and that scared him even more than the sizzling kiss. "Your point?" he said too gruffly.

"I'd like you to let me use that emotional connection to this town in order to reach out to the people, and not just those around here. People in Greenlawn already love Brandon Vaughn. But I'd like to reach your extended public. The people you want to come and vacation at your lodge." She leaned closer. "Let them see the man inside the athlete and want to help you as much as you want to help the kids."

She squeezed his hand tight and he glanced down. He'd almost forgotten they sat hand in hand, making a personal connection.

There was now a subtle understanding between them. He drew a deep breath. "I'll think about it." He told himself he was responding to her business sense.

Still he hated the idea of exposing something he did from the heart and using it as a media ploy. Then again, he wasn't stupid. If he wanted the summer camp to become a reality, he needed the funding the winter lodge guests would provide. That was, after all, the reason he'd hired Annabelle in the first place.

Their hands remained intertwined. Her gaze met his, soft and understanding. Nothing businesslike in her expression or in the depths of those blue eyes now. This time if he acted on impulse and kissed her again, more than just sexual desire would be at work. At the moment he didn't care.

A loud knock sounded at the back door of the kitchen. Vaughn turned and glanced over. A familiar figure stood outside, one of his workmen who often came by uninvited. "I wonder what he wants."

"Who?"

He jerked a head toward the back entrance. "Roy Murray. My electrical foreman."

"Why doesn't he use the front door?"

He rolled his eyes. "He decided back doors are reserved for friends, and according to him, that's what we are. But he really does mean well." Vaughn rose and opened the door.

His foreman stood there in his jeans and white work

shirt, tool belt on and a grin on his face. Vaughn caught sight of his son behind him.

"Hey, Roy, Todd. To what do I owe this visit?"

Roy stepped inside and Todd followed.

"We don't mean to interrupt, Coach. But Dad and I were out for a walk and he wanted to stop by."

"Not a problem, Todd." Vaughn held out his hand and exchanged a handshake with the kid. They'd developed the gesture as a means of bonding during practices.

Roy looked on. "Hope it's all right we've come by. I was told your back lights need fixing and I thought I'd help you out."

The guy was the ultimate do-gooder but a complete pain in the ass sometimes. Still, he was an ace electrician and Vaughn saw shades of his old self in Todd, who also struggled in school.

"Who could've possibly told you my lights were out?" Vaughn asked.

"One of your neighbors."

Vaughn wasn't buying. "I don't have any neighbors. It's one of the reasons I bought this place."

"Oh jeez. Come on, Dad. Let's leave Vaughn alone."

"I always enjoy your company, you know that."

Vaughn slapped Todd on the back, meanwhile Roy laughed. "Okay, okay, I confess. I was out taking a walk last night and I noticed it myself. You're so busy with the lodge and hopefully thinking about coaching at State, you don't need home improvement things to worry about. So here we are." He grinned at Vaughn.

"That's awfully nice of you to try and help me out,

but I have a handyman coming by later in the week to handle things."

"I also wanted to thank you. Todd told me you ran plays with him the other day. He's grateful and so am I. I told you he's got a good heart," he said, speaking to Annabelle behind him.

"You two know each other?" Vaughn asked, surprised.

Roy stepped forward, his shoulders squared. "We met at Cozy Cups this morning. She was talking to Joanne, and mano to mano," he said to Vaughn, lowering his voice, "I think the women were exchanging bedroom secrets about you. One ex-lover and another present one. Dangerous info there, if you know what I mean." He winked at Vaughn and darted another glance at Annabelle.

Beside him, Todd shuffled his feet, uncomfortable with his father's frank talk.

"How are you, Roy?" Annabelle asked, ignoring his indiscreet words.

"Just fine. This is my boy, Todd."

Annabelle remained seated but waved to both visitors. "Nice to meet you. Your father and Vaughn have said great things about you."

The teen actually blushed. Vaughn understood. Annabelle had that effect on people.

"Uh, Dad, I think Mom will be wondering what's taking so long if we don't get going," Todd said.

The foreman nodded. "Yep. Women like to keep us men on a short leash."

Personally Vaughn thought Roy needed an even

shorter one. "Well thanks again for your offer and Todd, I'll see you soon. We're ready for the electrical inspection?" Vaughn asked as he opened the door for Roy to leave.

"Ready, boss. And keep in mind, the college boys need you if any of them are going to go pro."

"That's why I'm helping them now, Roy." Vaughn slammed the door closed behind the other man, then turned to Annabelle. "The man's a piece of work."

"He sure is."

"But Todd seems nice."

Vaughn grinned. "The kid has so much potential it scares me sometimes. He's got raw talent."

"And you're so sweet to coach him."

He shrugged. "Kids like him need the extra attention, if not on the field, then off it."

"Which brings me back to what we were discussing earlier," she said, pointedly.

He laughed and let it go. "I'm going to turn in for the night. If you want to go to the lodge with me in the morning, I suggest you do the same."

"And I'll take that to mean any serious discussion we were having is over."

He grinned. "You're perceptive."

"And smart and determined. We covered a lot of things we may need to revisit again."

"We'll see."

She crooked her finger and as if he were connected by a string, he drew inexorably closer until her lips were inches from his. In that moment, he wanted her with a ferocity that rocked his world.

Wanted her more than any other woman at any other time in his life.

"No, *you'll* see. Because the answers I'm looking for could very well determine the success or failure of your beloved lodge."

He glanced at her glossy lips and full pout. Through sheer willpower, he didn't allow his gaze to drop lower, to the enticing vee of her top and the fleshy mounds beneath, but his fingers twitched anyway.

Suddenly she straightened and with a sassy flip of her hair and a smile of female satisfaction on her lips, she reached for the leash she'd left on the counter. "And now I think I'll go take my dog for a walk."

Before he could think, let alone answer, she whirled away, out of reach, leaving nothing but her fragrant scent and the promise of a restless night's sleep in her wake.

LOLA PICKED UP the telephone, then placed it down again. She'd promised Yank she'd keep his secret, but for how long? How could she not tell the girls about the diagnosis on his eyes?

The ophthalmologist's words came back to her with clarity. Macular degeneration could progress slowly or quickly depending on the person. And there were new treatments that could slow or halt its progression, the success rate also depending on each particular case. She and Yank had the written information, but he was refusing to read about it, at least right now. The doctor said denial was normal at first and as soon as he adjusted to his situation, he'd come around. Lola hoped so. By the time he did, she intended to be fully versed on all of his options.

But the girls, they needed to know. She'd just have to give Yank a deadline by which he either told them or she'd do it herself.

As for Yank, while sitting in the doctor's office, she'd glanced at his profile and accepted that he was the man she loved. If he needed a reason to push forward and help himself, she'd just have to give him one.

She glanced at the various shopping bags spread over her room, which contained her new wardrobe. The wardrobe that would hopefully catch the attention of any man, even one with blurry vision and a thick skull.

Now all she needed was the nerve to wear the clothing. But Lola was certain she'd find the courage. Because her future was at stake.

CHAPTER SEVEN

VAUGHN FELT SOMETHING warm and soft lying beside him. Slow, even breathing comforted him. He rolled over, opened his eyes, saw green eyes peering at him and yelled at the top of his lungs. "Annabelle, get the hell in here!"

His loud voice scared what he thought was a cat, causing the animal to dive onto the floor and probably crawl beneath the bed.

Annabelle barged into the room. "What's wrong?" she asked, coming to a skidding halt.

"I woke up with a cat staring me in the face." Vaughn pushed himself back against the pillows and folded his arms across his chest.

"You did, huh?" She lowered her gaze and her stare landed on his chest. "Uh, Vaughn? Are you naked beneath that sheet?" As if picking up where they'd left off last night, a slow, deliberate, sexy smile tilted her lips.

"Don't change the subject." If she didn't notice his body's reaction to her, he wasn't about to point it out.

"Then answer the question," she said, licking her lips, slowly, a woman with an obvious agenda. "What are you wearing beneath that sheet?"

He let out a groan. Why did it seem she was always in charge? And why did he enjoy it so damn much? "Same thing I always wear to bed. Nothing," he replied.

She blinked and her stare lingered on his bare chest. "So you're talking to me now and you're *naked?*"

"The cat?" he reminded her through gritted teeth. "I woke up with a strange cat in my bed."

"Better than a strange woman, I suppose."

He rolled his eyes. "Look, you came here with a dog and a rabbit and now we've added a cat. How, when and for God's sake, *why?*"

No way would he continue to discuss his state of undress. He already had a morning hard-on and that only grew when he looked at his houseguest. Her hair was disheveled from sleep and her face lacked any makeup or artifice. On her luscious body, she wore a short sleeve T-shirt and matching Jockey shorts. She had more coverage than a bikini would provide and yet the morning-after look was so much more provocative. Sexier in a subtle, leave-it-to-your-imagination kind of way.

Without another word, she crossed the room and sat on the end of the bed with a huff, not at all uncomfortable being closer to him, confirming his hunch of an agenda that had nothing to do with sex. The talk of him being naked was a deliberate distraction. His being buck beneath the sheets wasn't an issue for her. His catching her with another animal in his house was.

"Well?" he asked, striving for focus when all he wanted to do was give in to the intense urge to tangle naked between the sheets with her.

She sighed. "I found the cat while walking Boris last night. She didn't have a collar, was purring and obviously hungry so I brought her back here, gave her some tuna and put her in my room. Obviously I forgot to shut the door tight after I walked them this morning so she joined you."

"Well, she can't stay."

She folded her arms across her chest. "Until I find her owners, yes she can."

Her determined tone brooked no room for argument. Yet once again, instead of inciting his anger, she made him laugh. "Anyone ever tell you that you're a stubborn little thing?"

"Not in those words, no. But Uncle Yank always said that as the oldest, I like to assert my control." A soft smile surfaced on her face.

Vaughn stared at her intently. "I think it's more than that." And he intended to analyze her the same way she'd scrutinized him last night. At least then he'd know they were back on even footing.

"What do you mean?" she asked, eyebrows raised, her curiosity evident.

"I think your control issues are a reaction that goes way back to your childhood. You said yourself you were afraid you and your sisters would be separated. You were determined to never let that happen. To do that, you needed to be in control at all times."

She remained silent.

Since she was being unusually quiet, he took advantage and continued. "I think that saving animals is yet another means for you to have control. It lets you to accomplish exactly what you feared you couldn't do for your sisters."

She shivered, not spitting or hissing back at him, confirming his theory. He'd nailed her insecurities the same way she'd nailed his.

Funny though. Evening the score didn't feel as satisfying as he'd thought it would. Instead his stomach churned with the knowledge he'd brought back painful memories for her. Yet he couldn't deny he liked knowing he could read her as well as she could read him.

Annabelle rose and walked to Vaughn's side of the bed. He'd hit the mark, she thought, shocked at how well he understood her and even more stunned he'd bothered to try.

She seated herself by his side and tried to look nonchalant, hard as it was with the heavy weight of the emotions he'd brought to the surface. And then there were those damn pheromones flying around them—the attraction and desire that grew as they got to know one another better, even as they fought against it.

She licked her lips. "Whether or not you're right and I'm not saying you are, the cat has nowhere to go."

"I know." A smug look pulled at those sexy lips.

"Vaughn, you can't possibly turn it out on the street or bring it to a shelter where they might have to put it down."

"I know that, too." He sounded resigned.

She wondered if she dared to hope. "It's only for a short time. I'll try to keep her out of your way. And your bed," she promised.

Which reminded her. The lucky stray had woken up

in bed with a naked Brandon Vaughn. Annabelle had tried without success to keep her gaze averted from that nude body barely hidden by a low-slung sheet. Now she fought to keep her mind from the fact that she was sitting on his bed, so close to all that heated masculinity.

His gaze dilated and a look of pure, seductive need crossed his face, until he, too, moved forward. Their lips were inches apart and only one thing separated them, Annabelle thought.

"The cat?" she asked.

"Stays."

"Thank you!" She knew he'd given in for her and her only. Grateful, she wrapped her arms around his neck and her mouth deliberately grazed his. Tingling excitement rushed through her and she remained there, waiting.

"This is a mistake," he said, not pulling back an inch.

"Probably a big one," she agreed.

But he didn't seem any more inclined to stop than she did. And she'd already decided to push forward with seducing Brandon Vaughn.

Their gazes held and her heart pounded so loud in her chest she thought even he could hear. And then finally, blessedly, he was kissing her. That well-defined, full mouth was hard on hers, taking possession.

He set her aflame and a burning heat rose inside her. His tongue darted into her mouth and the rest of her body responded. Her nipples tightened into hardened peaks. A wave of arousal washed over her and she felt a delicious pulling sensation from her breasts to the fullness pulsing between her legs.

She shivered, trembling with desire and the need to feel his hardened body and warm skin touching hers. She placed her hands on his bare shoulders. His heat and breadth were overwhelming and she was grateful when he took control and rolled her onto her back.

She was in Vaughn's bed, tangled sheets around them and his hard, sexy body aligned with hers. Excitement and anticipation built to a frenzied peak.

"This is heaven," she murmured.

Vaughn had to agree. Her voice had affected him on a gut level and just looking at her made him hard. But touching her silken skin and feeling her stretched out beneath him, soft, supple and willing... Well, he'd never experienced anything this close to perfection.

Glancing down, he brushed her tangled hair off her cheek. She thought she'd seen heaven? "You ain't seen nothing yet, baby."

A low, seductive purr rumbled in her chest and reverberated through him. He trailed kisses over her cheek, inhaling her feminine scent, and as he breathed in deep, the weight of her chest pressed hard and enticingly against his. He needed to touch her. Needed to feel those hot, heavy mounds in his hands.

"Touch me," she said, reading his mind. And in case he wasn't sure what she meant, she grabbed his hand and placed his palm firmly against her breast.

He liked her aggressive nature, appreciated that she wasn't afraid to take what she wanted. Unfortunately the jersey prevented him from really caressing her breasts the way he wanted to. He pulled the oversize shirt up and over her head, then tossed it onto the floor.

He took a moment to savor the sight. She was straight out of his fantasies. Her breasts were large and full, her dusky nipples tight and begging for his attention. Attention he was all too willing to give and he put his hand back on her breast, cupping the full mound completely.

At the first touch of bare skin, she moaned, the sound getting lost in his own low groan of satisfaction. She was a perfect fit, her nipple pressing insistently into the center of his palm, her malleable flesh ready and willing. And if that weren't enough, his groin nestled in the moist, damp vee of her legs as her hips swiveled beneath his. Maintaining focus and taking it slow had never been more difficult, yet somehow he managed.

He cupped her in one hand until he'd branded her skin everywhere, then held her nipple between his thumb and forefinger, rolling gently. Her hands tangled in his hair and she arched her back, seeking more.

The sound of the telephone ringing penetrated his consciousness and he muttered a low curse.

"Don't answer it," Annabelle whispered. At the same time, her lips trailed over his neck, punctuated with enticing licks of her tongue until he trembled above her.

The need to take a woman had never been stronger. The desire to possess her nearly consumed him. The phone rang again and he jerked up in bed.

His bed.

With a half naked Annabelle beside him.

"I have to get it." With the problems at the lodge, he had no choice and reached for the phone. "Vaughn here."

The answering machine picked up at the same time and he had to wait until his voice recording finished before he could talk and hear the person on the other end.

"It's Mara. We have another problem, boss."

He broke into a sweat that had nothing to do with Annabelle. "What the hell happened now?"

"What's wrong?" Annabelle placed a comforting hand on his arm.

He held up one finger and she nodded in understanding.

He listened to the rest of Mara's story in stunned silence. "I'll be right there," he said and hung up.

"Vaughn?"

He blinked, trying to focus on Annabelle's question. "Someone broke into the lodge last night and spliced the electrical wiring in strategic places around the site."

"Preventing you from passing the inspection today." Annabelle caught on to the issues at hand immediately. She grabbed for her jersey and pulled it over her head. "Give me ten minutes to get ready and I'll go with you." Though all business, compassion flickered in her gaze.

He had no choice but to focus on his lodge, but he was shocked she'd thought to do the same. He was impressed with her professionalism considering how they'd been interrupted.

But as much as he cursed whoever was sabotaging his dream of having sex with Annabelle, he should probably thank them for forcing him to come to his senses in time.

BY THE TIME ANNABELLE and Vaughn walked into the office at the lodge, Vaughn had withdrawn into himself. If Annabelle hadn't experienced their intimacy first hand, she'd think she'd imagined the whole thing.

But she hadn't. He'd been as hot with wanting her as she'd been for him. Try as he might to ignore those feelings now, she refused to be a partner to his denial. Work would come first, but she wasn't finished with Brandon Vaughn. She would see to it that they completed what they'd started. And he'd enjoy every seductive moment.

But right now, the problems and delays were an issue they could no longer ignore. So while Vaughn went to round up employees and talk with the police, Annabelle made notes on how to publicize the situation at the lodge in a preemptive strike.

Mara walked back into the office and flung her body into her chair with a weary sigh. Her brown hair, cut in an updated shag, gave her a sexy, with-it appearance that would make a splash in a New York bar. Add to that, she seemed to be genuinely nice, hadn't held the picnic against Annabelle—though she was giving Nick the cold shoulder—and was smart enough to run things in Vaughn's absence. Annabelle's instincts told her to trust Mara.

"Boy, I wouldn't want to be the guys on duty last

night. Vaughn and Nick are ripping them to shreds." Mara shook her head and tossed a pencil across the desk, her frustration obvious.

"Who? The security guards?"

"Mmm-hmm. We hired a private firm with a stellar reputation. But apparently, the guard out front didn't see anything and the guy in the back perimeter slipped out to go to the bathroom without letting his partner know."

Annabelle winced. "I wonder if he'd done it before. If someone had been watching his routine, they could have counted on him disappearing."

"Well, regardless, the inspection's put off until the wires can be fixed," Vaughn said, joining them. Gone was any version of the man she'd been with earlier. Tension radiated from him in waves and anger vibrated just beneath his skin.

Nick followed him inside, looking just as pissed off.

"Who would want to prevent this place from opening?" Annabelle asked, glancing at Nick.

"Beats me." Vaughn shrugged. "I just gave the police a list of anyone and everyone in my life. Let's see what they come up with."

"Speaking of people in your life, you got a phone call," Mara said.

"Who?"

"Laura." Mara glanced at Annabelle. "His ex-wife," she said by way of explanation.

Vaughn visibly stiffened. "What the hell did she want?"

Mara shrugged. "How would I know? I'm merely

hired help. She wanted to speak to you and seemed completely pissed that I wouldn't interrupt whatever you were doing."

"Nothing's more important than what Laura wants, when Laura wants it," Vaughn muttered.

Annabelle raised an interested eyebrow.

"I'll get back to her whenever." He grabbed the paper from Mara's hand and shoved it into his pocket. "I've got more important things to deal with."

Annabelle nodded. "You sure do. While the police are handling the detective work, we need to focus on damage control. I've put in a call to the local television affiliate and a reporter's on his way over."

Vaughn's glare turned icy. "Why would you want to broadcast problems?" he bit out, all his frustration and anger spewing at her.

Nick and Mara looked at Vaughn and Annabelle with interested stares.

"Would you like to take this somewhere private?" she asked Vaughn.

He waved away her offer. "What I'd like is for you to explain."

She shrugged. "You're someone used to being in the spotlight, so you ought to realize the police blotter will have spread this news in no time. Wouldn't you rather we put out our story first and in as positive a light as we can manage?"

Nick cleared his throat. "She's got a point, Vaughn."

"Kiss ass," Mara muttered under her breath. But not low enough to be ignored.

Since now wasn't the time to make love not war

between these two, Annabelle continued before anyone else could comment. "What I'd like to do is focus on your commitment to kids and education in a summer camp environment. Acknowledge that, yes, we've had some difficulties and delays, but we'll do everything in our power to open on schedule. After all, it's for the children, which ought to appeal to the viewers' emotions and make them think twice about canceling."

While she thought, she bit down on the cap of her pen. "I could use a quote from you in there," she said, addressing Vaughn. "Something about why these kids mean so much to you. We'll give the public a positive to focus on."

"This whole thing isn't about me or my reasons for what I do."

She sighed, exasperated. She'd come here two days ago and accomplished nothing professionally during that time because Vaughn refused to take her advice.

She'd give it one more try and then she'd have no choice but to leave him to sink his own ship. Or in this case, his lodge. "Look, you're a celebrity. And if you want people to care about this place and stick with you, they can't think you're in it for purely selfish or monetary reasons. Otherwise they'll pull their reservations from here and head up to Killington or the Poconos or someplace else where they don't have to worry about whether or not their reservations will fall through. So it's up to you," she said, hands on her hip. "Do we do this my way or do I leave you on your own and head back to the city tonight?"

Silence reigned. Annabelle knew he was fighting within himself.

"Isn't it enough that I'm helping children? Do we have to get into why?" he asked in a more neutral tone than he'd used with her so far, obviously biding his time.

"I need a media hook."

"Then tell them I remember what it's like to be a kid," he said in a near growl and stormed out the office door.

"Whatever that means." She raised her hands in the air. "Unbelievable."

Wisely Mara and Nick chose not to comment.

Annabelle then drummed her fingernails on the desk in pure frustration. He'd left her with nothing. Zilch. Zip. Nada.

And if that's all the wisdom and insight Vaughn chose to offer, she'd have no choice but to come to her own conclusions and put the best spin she possibly could on his vague words.

His reaction be damned.

In the silence that ensued, a walkie-talkie went off on Mara's belt and she spoke to the person on the other end. "Be right there." Mara glanced at Nick. "Rocco needs me to sign for something. Don't mess up my desk while I'm gone," she said to annoy Nick, if Annabelle had to guess.

He merely treated her to a quick salute and with a growl of frustration at not having gotten to him, she stormed out the door.

Alone, Annabelle turned to Nick. She couldn't help

but wonder what was going on with these two. "Any reason you don't give her a break?" She pointed toward the exit Mara had just taken. "She's pretty, smart, and she's obviously got it bad for you."

Nick began to pile up papers on the desk, an obvious pretense of being busy. "She'll get over it."

"Why should she have to?" Annabelle shot back.

He frowned and shifted from foot to foot, appearing extremely uncomfortable with the subject of Mara, so much so that his normally friendly, fun demeanor had disappeared. "I have my reasons."

Annabelle glanced at her watch. She had an idea to implement and only a short time left in which to do it, but first, she needed to talk to Nick. "Look, we're running out of time, but would you care to share those reasons with a new friend?"

He didn't smile, merely met her gaze. "You want it? You got it. As close as Vaughn and I are, I'm tired of following in his perfect footsteps. Don't get me wrong. I love the guy like a brother and I'm grateful he let me invest in the lodge at a time when I needed a distraction from losing my announcing gig. Honest to God it never bothered me that he ended up the Heisman and Superbowl hero. I had a decent career and solid advertising endorsements. I invested wisely and I'm fine."

"Then what's the problem?" Annabelle asked.

He began pacing the vinyl office flooring. "Sometimes you reach a point when enough is enough. And sloppy seconds are more than even I can stand."

His stunning admission took Annabelle off guard. She'd spent all this time trying to decide if there was any festering jealousy on Nick's part, and here he was admitting it. In such an honest, straightforward way, she really couldn't bring herself to believe that Nick would ever hurt Vaughn intentionally. In fact, the more Annabelle got to know Nick, the worse she felt about doubting his intentions.

But why would he bring this up now? "What does Mara have to do with you and Vaughn?"

Nick let out a loud laugh. "They used to be an item."

Annabelle blinked. "Vaughn and Mara?" she asked, stunned. When he'd insinuated as much before, Annabelle had chosen to ignore the obvious. For obvious reasons.

Nick slowly nodded.

Her stomach churned as she digested the information. "Good God, is there a woman in this town the man hasn't been with?"

Nick walked over, wrapped an arm around her shoulder and gave her his trademark grin. "You're probably it," he said, jokingly.

She forced a laugh. With Nick's insecurities between them, it probably wasn't the time to tell Nick she intended to rectify her status soon. "I had no idea about Mara and Vaughn. I mean they act completely professional."

Nick shrugged. "They are. Vaughn's a straight-shooter. Any woman who gets involved with him knows going in there's no ring in her future. They part on good terms." He shrugged as if that were that.

But his words served to reinforce Annabelle's determination to keep her emotions firmly locked up tight in her relationship with Vaughn.

Nick's situation was another story entirely. "Mara has nothing to do with Vaughn now. Surely you can see that."

"What I see is a guy who's always accepted second best. If I want to settle down, I want someone who wants *me* and doesn't jump into the game because they already lost their first choice."

"Then why live in this town and subject yourself to something you hate?" she asked the second man in as many days, her frustration with the male brain and its way of thinking completely overwhelming her. "Oh, I know. Because this is home."

He nodded. "It is."

"Then you need to get over it," she said, bluntly.

He stepped back and seated himself on the corner of the desk. "And maybe I would if everyone didn't jump to the same damn conclusion. That I never quite measured up to my best friend and that it still bothers me."

"Oh, come on. People don't think that." Annabelle waved a hand dismissively.

"You did."

She sucked in a startled breath. "That stinking rat," she muttered. "Vaughn told you that?"

Nick grinned, once again taking her off guard by laughing. "No, but when you asked who had a motive to prevent this place from opening, you glanced at me. And I've heard the jealousy factor so many times, I'm used to it. You just confirmed my hunch."

"Nick—"

He shook his head. "Forget it. You're doing your job, helping out Vaughn and the lodge, and I'm doing mine.

I understand where your head is." He pinned her with his steady gaze. "So it shouldn't be too big a leap for you to see why I don't want to date a woman who's already been dumped by Vaughn."

Annabelle saw, but on a logical level, it made little sense. "But she's interested in you."

"Only because Vaughn is out of reach." He shook his head. "End of discussion, okay?"

She frowned. "Okay." She agreed, yet she intended to talk to Mara and help the other woman overcome Nick's insecurities, which she feared she'd just helped contribute to.

With a sigh, she glanced at the clock on the wall, ticking too close to early afternoon.

"What's our next step now that Vaughn's disappeared on us?" Nick asked, changing the subject back to business.

Annabelle smiled, grateful he didn't hold her thoughts against her. "Would you keep the reporter busy? Give him a tour and avoid the problem areas, okay?"

He nodded. "My pleasure."

"Meanwhile can I borrow your car?"

He narrowed his gaze. "Where are you going?"

"Just out to do a few errands." Following her gut, she had a few people from Vaughn's past she wanted to talk to before speaking with the reporter and giving their spin on things.

"Can you drive a stick?" Nick asked.

She nodded.

He reached into his pocket and tossed her his keys. "Don't hit anything, will you?"

"If I promise to take care of your car do you promise to think about giving Mara a chance?"

He rolled his eyes. "Yeah, yeah. I'll do anything for my Corvette."

She laughed. "Typical man." With a wave, she headed off to speak to one of Vaughn's old teachers. They were her only hope of finding out enough about the man to put his reasons for creating the camp in a positive light.

CHAPTER EIGHT

As a celebrity of sorts, Vaughn was used to the spotlight. He was used to stares, glares and whispers behind his back as well as blatantly in front of his face. So when he walked into his parents' home and conversation stopped, he had his first inkling there'd be trouble tonight. And he didn't think the gorgeous babe on his arm had caused the stunned silence—although she'd rendered him mute when they'd met in the front hallway of his house twenty minutes earlier.

Who'd have thought an appropriate-looking, basic black dress could appear so sexy, seductive and sultry? Of course it had something to do with the blonde filling out the material and even more to do with Vaughn and Annabelle's early-morning meeting in his bed. Because now, not only had he seen her body, but he'd held those firmly rounded breasts in his hands. He no longer had to rely on imagination, and the reality had taken up permanent residence in his mind.

Annabelle tugged on his arm, breaking him out of his daydream. "Are we going inside or are we going to stand in the entryway all night?" she asked, attempting to redirect his attention to where it belonged.

He wiped the sweat off his brow and focused on the company in the room. Their entry complete, the guests of his parents and the important trustees of the university had begun to talk among themselves again. And just his luck, his mother began to make a direct line toward them.

"We're going to mingle," he assured Annabelle, grasping her hand and heading in the opposite direction from Estelle.

Unfortunately she was a woman on a mission. "Oh, Brandon!" She waved, giving him no choice but to wait for her to accost them.

Only when she'd come close, so no one could hear, did she begin her tantrum. "You knew you were coming to this party, so how could you allow such a personal interview to come out today?" Her direct glare was more on Annabelle than on him.

Still, he wasn't about to turn an obvious family issue into Annabelle's problem. "Good evening to you, too, mother," he said, smiling for the benefit of the people around them.

"Hello, Mrs. Vaughn." Annabelle extended her hand but Estelle didn't take it. Instead she motioned with a regal tilt of her head. "In the study. Now, please."

Vaughn raised an eyebrow and shrugged. "Let's see what's on her mind," he whispered to Annabelle. And maybe then he'd find out why everyone else had paused when they'd laid eyes on him this evening.

It was obvious the shit was about to fly.

They entered the study and Estelle clicked the door closed politely, but her squared shoulders and heavy breathing spoke another story completely.

She appraised him, her gaze raking the length of his European suit. “Just what is all over you?” she asked, brushing at his lapels with her hand.

He glanced down. “Hair,” he muttered.

“Cat hair,” Annabelle added with a cheery smile.

Her cat had decided she liked *his* room best. He’d laid his suit out on the bed and when he’d returned from his shower, she was curled into a ball on top of the dark jacket. He’d tried to brush it off with no luck. Just why the animal had decided to make him her best friend, he had no idea.

“Well you could have made sure you were lint free before coming out for the evening. We have important guests,” his mother reminded him.

As if he didn’t know. As if he really cared. Despite not being thrilled with the influx of animals in his home, he had to admit he didn’t mind riling his mother a bit more and he shot Annabelle an amused glance. His coconspirator grinned back.

At the same moment, Vaughn realized her black dress was lint free, yet she’d had the dog and the rabbit staying in her room. “How’d you manage to keep clean?”

“Scotch tape. But you were in such a rush to leave, I didn’t have a chance to share the trick with you.”

His rush had actually been to get into a room with a crowd so he wouldn’t rip off her dress and finish what they’d started this morning.

Estelle cleared her throat. “If you two wouldn’t mind paying attention?”

They both glanced her way. “What’s going on?” Vaughn asked his mother.

She folded her hands together. "You both lied to me. Annabelle Jordan isn't an old friend opening a hotel in New York. She's your *publicist.*" She spat the word as if it were poison.

Was that all? Vaughn shook his head laughing. He'd tried to keep Annabelle's profession a secret only because he didn't want to be perceived as manipulating the public for his own selfish purposes.

As far as he was concerned, his mother had no reason to question who or what Annabelle was to him. She only cared now because somehow, she perceived herself as an affected or wounded party.

"Mrs. Vaughn," Annabelle began, "I'm—"

"I'm handling this," he said, interrupting whatever Annabelle had been about to say. "I hired Annabelle to help with a few PR issues surrounding the lodge. What's wrong with that?"

Estelle straightened her linen suit jacket. "Did you also ask her to go digging into your past? To bring up bad memories? To humiliate your father when all the trustees would be around?"

Beside him, he felt Annabelle stiffen. Still unsure what was going on, his skin began to tingle uncomfortably, but he ignored his mother's accusations and addressed the one thing he did know for certain. "I don't make any decisions in my life based around what you or Theodore want."

On the other hand, he did know better than to publicize much about his past and the only memories his father would consider bad ones involved academics. "What's going on?" he asked.

"The evening news ran a feature on your lodge."

"It was planned—"

Again, he cut Annabelle off, this time with a wave of his hand and turned to his mother. "You already know the lodge is a done deal."

She sighed. "You know I hate it when you're deliberately obtuse." She leaned over and picked the television and VCR remotes off the table. A few seconds later, she had a tape running of the local cable news.

The reporter began with the morning's vandalism and some of the other difficulties plaguing the lodge and then segued into an actual plea to people with reservations to hang on and trust in football legend Brandon Vaughn, "a man invested in the next generation."

He shot a glance at Annabelle, who was accepting being shut up too easily. She merely batted her lashes and shrugged, but the proud smile on her lips told him that she'd come up with that particular theme for the lodge. Her satisfaction was obvious from the glow in her cheeks and damned if a part of him didn't share her pride.

He glanced at the television. So far the reporter hadn't come up with anything to upset his mother beyond the usual. "This is it," Estelle said and raised the volume a notch.

"Although unreachable for comment, we were able to interview Vaughn's publicist Annabelle Jordan, who said her client, quote *'remembers what it's like to be a kid'* unquote."

So far so good, and Vaughn folded his arms over his chest and waited, pushing aside the uneasy feeling creeping over him that warned him there had to be more.

"Following a suggestion from Ms. Jordan, we made contact with Mrs. Peabody, a longtime teacher at the Greenlawn High School for interpretation." As Vaughn gritted his teeth, the camera panned to the high school where his old white-haired teacher stood on the lawn, the American flag waving in the background.

"Brandon is our star, our shining star," she said proudly, taking Vaughn off guard. "But he struggled mightily while here and if you think my recollection's faulty, school records speak for themselves. He's probably determined to open his lodge so he can bring kids with similar issues to a fun environment where they can also supplement their learning. I admire him, I surely do."

Estelle flipped off the television and stood staring at both Vaughn and Annabelle. Her cheeks were flushed pink with the embarrassment he remembered only too well from every parent-teacher conference she'd ever attended.

His stomach churned at having disappointed her again, at coming up short in his parents' estimation, until he reminded himself he wasn't that failing kid. He was an accomplished adult and that news report had been a *positive* one.

One that, for more personal reasons, he'd preferred hadn't aired, and he glanced at the source. Annabelle stood beside him, tapping her foot, and he figured she was waiting for the fallout. But with the afternoon behind him and plenty of time to think, he'd already come to the conclusion he wasn't being fair to her. He understood that and would deal with her and the repercussions later tonight.

Right now he had another problem. "And what exactly is wrong with truthful reporting?" he asked Estelle.

Before she could answer, a knock sounded at the door and Vaughn's father walked inside. "The guests are beginning to ask if anything's amiss. Are you ready to return?" he asked his wife, ignoring both Vaughn and Annabelle.

"Hello, Dad."

Theodore inclined his head. "I hope you're prepared to address the issues you stirred up today." Polite niceties were obviously too much to ask when he'd been disappointed again.

Well if his parents couldn't be polite, Vaughn damn well could. "I'd like you to meet my publicist, Annabelle Jordan. Annabelle, this is Theodore Vaughn."

"Professor Theodore Vaughn," his father said as he extended his hand toward Annabelle.

"A pleasure, Professor." Smiling, she shook his hand. "I'd be happy to answer any questions about the news piece, though frankly I thought they did a spectacular job portraying Vaughn as both a star and a compassionate human being doing his best to help others. I'm certain this will be picked up by the other networks and help sustain reservations."

"Other networks?" Theodore said, his jaw sagging.

"That's...that's— You don't say." Obviously unhappy, he turned as pale as his beige shirt.

For the first time in recent memory, Vaughn's father was speechless and he had Annabelle to thank.

"Well now you know how we feel, not that it will make any difference to you. It never does." Estelle shook her head and walked over to her husband, sighing as she crossed the room.

They turned to leave, but Theodore glanced back over his shoulder. "Brandon, please try to steer the conversation away from the interview. I'm certain the board members will overlook your academic background in favor of your *other* skills."

As usual, *other,* meaning his athletic ability, was not meant in a positive sense. Still Vaughn didn't miss the irony. His parents, who'd always disdained his sport, now begged him to take a coaching position because it would help *their* standing.

Well it was too damn bad. "I'm not taking the job," Vaughn said clearly.

But his parents were out the door, heads together, plotting which person deserved their attention next.

He shook his head and groaned. "Damn but they never change."

"What world do they live in?" Annabelle asked.

"Their own."

"How can they not see *you?* How can they not appreciate your talent? Your drive? Your altruism?"

As she extolled his virtues, something inside him softened toward her even more.

"Listen, about the interview—" she began.

He clasped her hand and cut her off midsentence. "You did a good job promoting the lodge." He swallowed hard. "Thank you for that."

She narrowed her gaze. "No yelling, no screaming?" She pressed the back of her hand against his forehead. "Are you feeling okay?"

He laughed. Shockingly he'd never felt better. "I'm fine. I'm also not stupid and I know what you were trying to do with that report."

Annabelle smiled. "I never said you were stupid. Now would you care to fill me in on why you haven't sided with your parents when it comes to the news report? I'm sure you hated it as much as they did."

And Annabelle had been steeling herself for the confrontation all day. She just hadn't expected it to happen at the party.

He headed for the couch, pulling her along with him until they were seated, thigh to thigh. "Let's get a few things straight."

She tried to concentrate, but his body temperature was too strong, her attraction too potent.

"For one thing, I never side with my parents."

"I can see why." Watching the family dynamics was painful in the extreme. "They really don't get you, do they?"

He shook his head. "And neither do you. At least not when it comes to gauging my reactions." But that wasn't her fault. He'd refused to let her in. "Do you know where I spent the afternoon?"

"Running around the lake at the lodge?"

"Hiring a new security firm and then adding extra

men so we don't lose much time. And all the while, I was thinking about how I could save the lodge. Which led me back to the fact that I'd hired you, then tied your hands with lack of information."

She blinked, startled into silence. "I really didn't expect you to realize that."

He reached his arm along the top of the couch and leaned back, laughing. "Well I may have taken a few hits to the head in my day, but eventually I can do the math. I need you to help me succeed and you need information out of me to do your job." He inclined his head. "You see? I get it."

She grinned. "So I can expect your cooperation from now on?"

He nodded.

Seeing opportunity, she snuggled closer. So close she smelled his delicious aftershave and her insides curled with warmth and desire.

She peered up at him and fluttered her lashes. "Your cooperation in *all* things?" she asked, deliberately coy.

"All things business," he said with a grin and a quick wink.

She laughed. "Well you can't blame a girl for trying." Meanwhile he'd given her his professional trust and she couldn't imagine a better gift. "Don't we have people to see?" She gestured to the study door.

He let out a groan. "That we do."

During the next excruciating few hours, time made more painful by the dominant overseeing of Vaughn's parents, Annabelle discovered a few more things. She learned not only did Vaughn consider this town home, but he had good reason.

The college board of trustees applauded the television interview. They felt Vaughn's devotion to children only bolstered their desire to hire him as a coach, and his old teacher's admission of academic difficulty made him more human to them. More real.

But not to his parents. They couldn't see beyond their own expectations and disappointments.

Annabelle saw everything.

Including the fact that he'd become the man he was today, not thanks to his parents but despite them. And that was a credit to Vaughn's strength of character. She admired him. Enough to know she intended to pick up where they'd left off earlier that morning.

And she'd do so tonight.

THEY'D DRIVEN HOME in comfortable silence, then parted at Annabelle's bedroom. Now she steeled her nerves, adjusted the straps of the only teddy she'd brought with her and knocked on Vaughn's door.

Her knees were shaking. For all the fun and teasing she subjected him to, she wasn't so brave now when her pride was at stake.

The door swung open wide and she stood facing Vaughn. Physically exposed, she felt emotionally stripped as well. But she hadn't come this far to turn back now.

She looked into his sexy gaze and drew a deep breath. "Hey there, Vaughn."

"Annie," he said in a gruff voice.

The sound of her nickname took her off guard. "I..." She glanced down, unsure of what she'd been about to say and discovered he was wearing a pair of black boxers and nothing more. Tanned skin, powerful muscles and a rock-hard body, she thought, trying to catch her breath.

Her gaze flew to his. "I thought you'd be a Jockey kind of guy," she said to break the tension.

"I'm dyslexic," he blurted out at the same time.

From arousal to understanding in seconds flat. Annabelle blinked and as Vaughn stepped back into the room, she followed him inside. Though she couldn't tear her eyes from his gorgeous body, she also knew what it cost him to admit his childhood weakness.

"Do your parents know?" she asked, settling herself on the edge of his bed.

He nodded. "And before you say anything, yes, you'd think a professor would understand. He doesn't," Vaughn said flatly. "All they know is that the educator's son couldn't hack school. I'm not their pride and joy, I'm their biggest embarrassment."

Annabelle winced. The insight was more than she'd expected and she wondered how he'd coped as a boy being misunderstood by his parents.

How sad. And how shocking that she wanted to make up for all he'd lacked. Though her parents had died, she'd had Uncle Yank to celebrate her successes along with Lola and her sisters to wipe her tears and help her through her frustrations.

"Well, I understand your family dynamics a lot better now." Not that she could comprehend how his parents could put their pride above their child.

"That's nice but don't think I'm looking for your sympathy," he said, folding his arms over his chest, erecting barriers in case she rejected him too.

Oh yes, she understood him so much better now. "Good." She cocked her head to one side. "Because I'm not offering any. So how'd you learn to compensate? I saw you going over contracts in the office and I know for sure you wouldn't have gotten to this point in your life if you were still struggling the same way."

He shrugged, still cavalier, still acting as if what she thought didn't matter. "I met someone who cared enough to point me in the right direction."

She rose and stood toe-to-toe with him. "You were fortunate."

"Yes, I was," Vaughn agreed. But he wasn't about to tell Annabelle it was her uncle who'd been his savior. He'd bared enough of his soul for today.

His body, however, he wouldn't mind stripping further. Hers either. He wanted her. Wanted to feel and stop all the damn talking, especially about him. And since she'd come here for just that reason, he knew she wouldn't resist.

He threaded his fingers beneath the flimsy silk strap. "I think this would break with one easy pull," he murmured.

Her gaze flew to his. "I take it you're finished talking?" she asked, a seductive grin tipping her lips.

"Personally I can think of better things to do." His voice grew rough with desire and he grazed her skin with his fingertips, deliberately caressing her silken flesh. He liked the feel of her, so soft and real.

She tipped her head back. "Do tell."

He grinned. "I'd rather show you."

Their gazes met and held. And when he couldn't take the teasing foreplay of words any longer, he lowered his head closer to hers.

Only he didn't kiss her on the lips. Instead he buried his face in her neck, suckling the sensitive area of flesh and inhaling the fragrant scent of fruity soap and shampoo he associated with Annabelle.

Her body trembled as did his.

"Mmm. You're good," she said on a low moan.

He nuzzled her neck and inhaled deeply. "You knew I would be."

"Arrogant man." She chuckled, the sound low and throaty and oh so sexy.

She broke free and strode over to the bed, shimmying her hips, making him sweat as he took in her lithe body covered only by the seductive garment she'd chosen to wear—for him. Lace caressed her firm bottom, teasing him, making him jealous of a piece of flimsy material.

As if she knew his every thought, she ever so slowly lowered first one sexy strap over her shoulder, then moved on to the next. When both straps fell temptingly around her arms, she shimmied them down further.

He watched, entranced, as she freed first one breast then the next until the teddy slipped completely down to her waist. Bare, she faced him, her rounded breasts and darkened erect nipples ripe and ready. For anything.

"Good Lord." He sucked in a breath, his mouth dry and parched.

"What are you waiting for?" she asked, crooking a seductive finger his way. "Come on, Vaughn. Don't back out on me now."

"Is that a challenge?" he asked.

She nodded, her tousled hair falling over her shoulders. Damn, he wanted to run his fingers through the strands, and then let her sweep that mane over his body, tantalizingly slowly. "Absolutely." She flashed him a knowing smile. "Because if you can't resist anything else, as an athlete I know you can't resist a challenge."

He raised an eyebrow. She knew a lot about him, but she didn't know everything. He intended to enlighten her.

"What I can't resist is you." He grasped her around the waist, his hands partly on the bunched teddy and partially on her bare skin, then moved her to the center of the bed.

Her eyes opened wide, pleasure and anticipation flooding her flushed cheeks. Never breaking eye contact, he joined her on the large mattress, lowered her to her back and kissed her full on the lips.

Vaughn immediately realized Annabelle wasn't about to be a passive participant. She grabbed his waist and slipped her hands into the band of his boxers. She cupped his buttocks in her palms and pulled him toward her with a sure and determined grip, a tempting smile on her lips. With difficulty, he managed to focus on her luscious mouth and devour her, completely lost in the moment.

In her.

He was in a heated sweat, his desire building with

each thrust of his tongue into her mouth, with every rotation of her hips that ground her feminine mound into his. Through her silk covering, through his boxers, he felt her, hot and ready. He wanted to bury himself in all that dewy heat and the knowledge that there was nothing stopping him drove his desire.

Slowly but surely, he slipped his hand downward, *there.* Needing proof, he edged his finger beneath the lace. At the first touch, her hips bucked and moisture trickled onto his fingertip.

"Annie," he said on a husky, shaking groan.

"I want you, Vaughn," she replied, proving to him that she was an equal partner in this seduction, giving of herself and taking in return.

He'd wanted to stop talking. He'd wanted to feel. Well right now his body was rock-hard and ready to explode. Oh, yeah, he was definitely *feeling* now.

Problem was, he was probably feeling too much—about her, and for her. He ought to run for cover, but he wouldn't.

And once he lost himself in her warm, damp body, he knew he'd be way past caring.

CHAPTER NINE

ANNABELLE TINGLED. She shook all over. And she was *this* close to making love with Brandon Vaughn. Oh, she could get used to this. So very easily. Too easily considering her past had taught her to know better. So for now, she just wanted to make sure she savored every moment of this experience. Just in case it never happened again.

He eased his finger beneath the teddy and began to torment her with exquisite friction. He ran his finger back and forth, his roughened skin arousing her already sensitized flesh. She grew hotter and wetter, cresting waves building inside her. Her hips pivoted in time to his rhythm and she arched her back, seeking harder, deeper contact.

"Slow down, baby." He slipped one finger deep inside her body. "I have every intention of giving you what you want. I just plan to prolong the pleasure first." As he spoke, his cheek snuggled against hers, his breath warm as it fanned the side of her face.

Pleasure or torture? she wondered. Then, deciding he needed to *suffer,* too, she reached between them and slipped her hand beneath the waistband of his boxers so she could grasp his long, hard length in her hand.

His groan of agony told her she'd accomplished her goal. "Still want to go slow?" she teased, gliding her palm up and down his shaft while her thumb caressed his moist tip. She ached for him to fill her completely, longed to feel every silken ridge as he thrust deep inside.

"Do you know what happens to bad girls who play with fire?" he asked as he rose and peeled off his shorts. A smile on her lips, she helped him until he stood before her, completely nude.

If Brandon Vaughn fully dressed was a sight to behold, *this* sight literally sucked the air out of her lungs. Her heart beat out a rapid rhythm as she took in the sight of the swollen, thick arousal she'd caused.

Turning her attention to the teddy she didn't want on her body one moment longer, she eased the flimsy silk down over her hips, revealing herself to this man in the most intimate way.

His stare never wavered. He watched, eyes dilated with hunger and need. Every last vestige of uncertainty and embarrassment was swept away in the heat of his appreciative gaze.

"What happens to bad girls?" she asked coyly, tossing the garment over the side of the bed.

"They get burned," he said and with the smooth grace of an athlete, he tackled her, tumbling her flat on the mattress, his body entangled with hers.

She shut her eyes and savored the feel of his hard body covering hers and she spread her legs, letting him settle in between. Needing more, she clenched her thighs around him tightly.

Vaughn gritted his teeth but a low growl escaped anyway. He couldn't wait another minute and from the way she writhed beneath him, neither could she.

She raised her arms above her head, which had her arching her back and pushing her chest toward him. Unable to resist, he lowered his head and captured one taut nipple in his mouth. He teased her with his tongue, nipped and grazed with his teeth. All the while she rolled her hips beneath him, damp, moist, and silently begging him to take her.

And he planned to. He reached into his nightstand drawer for protection.

"Always prepared," she said, her gaze following his movements. "I'd never have pegged you for a Boy Scout."

Her voice was light and teasing, but for a split second he thought he caught a hint of something more in her gaze. Something akin to wondering if she was one of many. Normally he didn't bring women home with him, an unwritten rule that went along with his distrust of females.

Yet he'd done both with Annabelle and for that reason he wanted to answer her unasked question now. "I bought these after you came to stay."

Her gaze softened. "I don't know whether to be flattered or mortified you think I'm easy."

He chuckled. "Baby, there's nothing easy about you." He sheathed himself with unsteady hands and as her gaze held his, he spread her thighs and drove himself hard and deep inside.

He'd expected it to be good. Hell, he'd even anticipated fantastic. But what he felt now was unbelievable.

She was soft and moist, warm and wet and as she drew her legs upward, pulling him impossibly further into her body, spiraling sensations of ecstasy swamped him from every angle.

He slid out, then in, picking up a rhythm that brought him faster and faster to the brink. She moaned and met his even thrusts with a rotating of her hips that ground her mound against him.

Her pelvic muscles contracted, tighter and tighter as her breath against his neck came faster. He drew a deep breath and thrust in more rapid succession.

"Vaughn." She cried out his name at the same time she came, her body milking his as the spasms hit and continued, triggering a shattering climax of his own.

"Don't stop," she urged, the rapid clenching and rotation of her hips continuing as she dug her nails into his back and her climax slowly subsided.

His own had been so powerful, he collapsed against her, cheek to cheek, her breasts crushed against his chest and her heart beating rapidly in time with his own.

ANNABELLE AWOKE after a full night's sleep feeling more rested and secure than she could ever remember being. As awareness came to her, she realized she lay in Vaughn's bed, his arms wrapped around her holding her tight. That was a good realization.

She hadn't dreamed last night, not that she remembered, anyway, which marked a milestone because she always dreamed. Always woke up in a heated sweat because in some form, she heard the social worker's words threatening to separate her from her sisters. No man she slept with had ever vanquished that nightmare, no friendships, no matter how strong, had ever replaced the bond with her sisters. A bond formed not because of family but because of a fear of loss.

Yet one night with Brandon Vaughn and she'd let those demons go, at least for this one time. And *that* wasn't a positive realization because Annabelle had promised she wouldn't invest any part of herself in this relationship. She refused to let her subconscious mind contradict her well-laid plans.

She turned her head to find Vaughn, eyes open, watching her. Her stomach did a flip at the sight of him, face stubbled, hair messed and utterly sexy.

"Morning," she mumbled, trying not to give thought to how awful *she* must look right now, the morning after they'd made love twice, each time more explosive and bonding than the last. The morning after he'd confided his deepest secret, trusted her to know about him what few people did.

Still she wasn't about to turn this into a fairy tale. Light and easy was the best course. "I can't believe I slept here."

He brushed a strand of hair off her cheek, the caress so gentle a lump formed in her throat.

"As I recall, I asked you to."

He had, when she'd gotten up to let the animals out for a quick walk, with thoughts of sneaking back into her own bed dogging her. But he'd told her to hurry back and when she had, Boris had followed her into the room and naturally so had the cat, which she'd named

Spike because of the short hairs standing up on her head. The dog now slept at the foot of the bed and the cat peered at her from the top of Vaughn's pillow.

"For the record, I'm glad I did." He confirmed his words with a long, deep, leisurely kiss that aroused her naked body all over again.

But Annabelle was determined to keep the morning light and carefree, to prove to herself and to Vaughn that last night was nothing more than a one-night stand. Or in guy terms, an easy lay. She winced at the notion, but forced a smile. "What do you say I put something together for breakfast?" she asked, sliding out of his arms and missing his warmth immediately.

He leaned back, arms crossed behind his head. "Dinner the other night, breakfast this morning. Careful or you'll spoil me." He winked in a way that made her feel all woman and uniquely special.

"Don't let it go to your head. You're just lucky I'm willing to include you in whatever I make." Ignoring her state of undress wasn't easy, but she stood and reached for the teddy she'd left on the floor. It'd seemed like a good idea last night but this morning she wished she had one of her jerseys to pull over her head.

As if reading her mind, he pointed to the dresser behind her. "You can grab a jersey from the middle drawer."

She shot him a grateful smile and seconds later, fully covered, she felt much better. Less exposed. "I'm going to let the animals out first and I'll call you when breakfast is on the table."

"Sounds like a plan."

"Can I ask you something first?"

He nodded warily.

"Did you call Laura back?"

He drew a deep breath, then exhaled. "Not yet."

"Well maybe you should." She hated advocating he establish contact with his ex-wife, but Annabelle knew his reluctance to get close to her emotionally was tied up with his ex. Resolution there could only help her. Though she wasn't so foolish as to harbor hope for more than this brief affair with him.

She turned to go.

"Annabelle."

She pivoted, her heart pounding in her chest. "Yes?"

His gaze, velvety soft, met hers. Then he shook his head. "Nothing."

She sensed he'd been as affected by last night as she'd been, but couldn't find the words to explain. Or maybe he was afraid to because, as she thought, he needed closure. In many areas of his life.

Without it, a quickie relationship was all she could expect from him. But that didn't mean she wouldn't enjoy every second of her time here. And last night was just the beginning of their adventure.

VAUGHN WATCHED Annabelle leave. His name on the jersey she wore stared boldly at him as she took her leave, the animals trailing after her. He'd experienced a surreal night in many ways, from the mind-blowing sex they'd shared, to the trust he'd allowed her by confiding his deepest secret and fear, to the connection he'd felt while buried deep inside her.

Sex was nothing new to Vaughn, though he'd become more discriminating and careful with age. *Feeling* while doing it was something else. And man, he'd felt last night with Annabelle.

But he refused to let himself be suckered by emotion. If he needed any proof as to why, he had only to look to Laura. Which was why he'd stopped himself just now, before he'd said something stupid to Annabelle. Something mushy. Something that indicated last night had been about more than a mutually satisfying lay.

He reached over and picked up the phone, then punched in the numbers on the paper on his nightstand.

The phone rang twice before Laura answered. "Hello?"

Her voice irritated him and he clenched his jaw. "I got a message that you called."

"Brandon, how are you? It's been too long."

He folded his arm behind his head and stared at the ceiling. "Actually it hasn't been long enough. What do you want?"

"Can't I just call to say hello?"

He exhaled hard. "Do me a favor. Tell me what you want or I'm hanging up now."

"Money," she said quickly. "I need money."

He narrowed his gaze. "You got plenty in the settlement agreement and the bars should be throwing off enough to satisfy even you."

Silence followed for a while before she spoke again. "It's not easy to admit this but I've run up some pretty high credit card balances. I need help or I wouldn't be asking. I mean do you think it's easy for me to come to you?"

"No, I'm sure it isn't. I need to think about it, okay?" As much as he resented Laura and everything she stood for, he couldn't help but think how desperate she sounded.

"You're such a doll, Brandon."

"Not exactly the words you used last time we spoke," he reminded her.

She laughed. "Things said in the heat of the moment, you know what I mean? Listen, I'm glad we can put the past where it belongs."

Had he said he'd forgive and forget? As usual, she heard what she wanted to.

"I really do have to go. Don't forget to call and let me know. I'll be forever in your debt, Brandon. I really will."

She hung up before he could reply, which was a good thing since he really didn't want her owing him a damn thing.

From his quiet room, he heard the sounds of Annabelle puttering around, making herself at home in his kitchen. After tossing off the covers, he rose from the bed and pulled on his jeans. He told himself he was going for breakfast and then heading to work, a day no different than any other.

Except he'd be coming home tonight knowing he could make love with Annabelle again, and again if he wanted to. Not even talking with Laura could dim the thrill that thought caused.

So by the time he'd taken a quick shower and headed to the kitchen, he had a dumbass grin on his face and looked forward to the day in a way he hadn't in a long while.

Not even the persistent ringing of the telephone, the caller ID showing his parents' number, could change his good mood. Especially since he'd made the decision to ignore anything having to do with his mother or father, determined to put them and their persistent negativity out of his mind.

He strode into the room and settled himself in a chair beside Annabelle. He glanced at her breakfast choice, surprised. "Cold cereal?" he asked.

Annabelle raised an eyebrow. "What? You were expecting pancakes? Eggs? Waffles maybe?" She shook her head, laughing. "This is as good as it gets in the morning so you'd better get used to it." Her eyes opened wide as she caught her words. "I mean, this is as good as it gets. Period."

"Hey, cereal and milk is fine with me." He ignored the slip-up because everything from her actions to her relaxed smile told him she was comfortable with what had happened between them, and that she didn't expect anything more than this. They were on the same wavelength, and things couldn't get any better, he thought.

"Are things quiet at the lodge?" she asked.

He nodded. "I'm paying the crews overtime to work weekends, but if it helps us fix the problems and open on time, it's fine with me."

She stirred her soggy Lucky Charms with her spoon. "Look, I've been thinking about the PR and the summer camp you have planned. I understand you're a private person, but there are subtle ways you can help kids with dyslexia to work with their problems all year round." She raised her gaze slowly, obviously unsure if she'd touched a nerve by bringing up the subject.

He drew a deep breath and exhaled slowly. He'd promised himself he'd give her the tools to do her job and not get angry or defensive, but he had to admit, defensive was still his gut instinct, especially after just talking with Laura.

"You had time between last night and this morning to think things through? I must not have kept you busy enough," he said, half joking, half filled with hope she'd halt the discussion.

"Guess you'll just have to try harder." She shrugged and his jersey slipped off one shoulder, revealing bare skin. Whether the move was intentional or not, his body temperature spiked another notch. A smile pulled at her lips. "Now stop trying to get me to change the subject."

He groaned. "Okay, what'd you have in mind?" he forced himself to ask.

"You're a successful businessman and a famous athlete, much as I hate to admit that and boost your already huge ego. But think what the revelation would mean to struggling kids who already look up to you."

"No. I am not doing some exposé on my life." He slashed a hand through the air to emphasize his point.

She pursed her lips in a pout, probably one she hoped he couldn't deny. "Just think about the kids who are too ashamed to admit they have problems and fall through the cracks because of it." Her cereal forgotten, her voice held a pleading edge.

"What I think about are the repercussions at home when you admit you can't learn like everyone else."

"Better to struggle?" she asked, frustration in her voice.

"Better to pretend you just don't like school than to be laughed at for being stupid."

"Then why offer the camp? Why give kids a place to come if you think it's going to stigmatize them?"

He leaned forward on his elbows. "The camp will give *any* struggling child, dyslexic or otherwise, an opportunity to even the odds of succeeding."

"An equal opportunity camp for delinquents and kids with disabilities alike, huh?" She shook her head. "I don't buy your theory. You're assuming your experience with your parents is the way all families will react to dyslexia or other disabilities. Are you suggesting kids shouldn't be diagnosed at all?"

"I'm suggesting that I don't force the issue. I'd rather give kids a place to come where they can experience the freedom of learning in a nonjudgmental environment, no matter what their problems or issues are."

She pushed her cereal away and rolled her eyes. "Sounds so good, you're definitely full of it. In fact, it sounds like you're running and not just from your parents' reaction." She rose and stood in front of him, her face inches from his. "Who else hurt you, Vaughn? Was it your ex-wife? Is that why you haven't called her back?"

He narrowed his gaze, unable to believe she was this feisty, this frustrating, this gutsy. That she would push him so far angered him beyond belief. But damned if it didn't turn him on, too. "As a matter of fact, I just did call her back."

"Oh."

"She wanted to borrow money."

Annabelle blinked. "I see. So was it her?" she asked softly. "Was Laura the one who hurt you and made you close yourself off?"

"You don't know what you're talking about," he said, though he was afraid she did. Afraid that once again, she'd dug into his psyche and understood him too well.

The truth was that as much as he wanted to help kids like him, he really was afraid to put himself out there for public scrutiny because then he'd risk rejection. Vaughn might have gotten help with reading but it was the psychological scars that remained.

"Okay I'll stop pushing. Just think about it," Annabelle said into the silence, her lips so close he could almost taste her.

Last time he'd agreed to *think,* he'd opened up and admitted his dyslexia. He feared with Annabelle here, he'd end up doing the same thing again and suffer public humiliation as a result. So instead of answering, he merely inclined his head slightly.

She grinned. "I'll take that as a yes. Now kiss me."

He blinked, surprised but definitely not opposed to her directive. "That won't solve our differences," he reminded her.

"Maybe not, but it'll sure feel good."

He laughed, breaking the tension. She had a way of doing that, easing his mind, making him feel good.

But just when he was about to kiss her, the damn doorbell rang.

"What is it with this place?" she asked. "Phone calls, door bells, interruptions galore. It's like Grand Central Station." She tucked her hair behind her ear and inclined her head toward the entry.

He hit the intercom button on the phone near the wall. "Who is it?"

"I should have known you'd be too damn lazy to answer the door yourself. No wonder you're getting old and flabby. Get the hell out here and let me inside," Yank Morgan ordered with the ferocity of a drill sergeant and a man used to getting his way.

At the sound of the older man's voice, Vaughn's stomach plummeted. "Were you expecting him?" he asked Annabelle.

Eyes wide, she shook her head. "No, but I'm going to get dressed while you let him in."

"Good idea." The last thing Vaughn wanted was to have Yank Morgan stroll in and realize it was the morning after Vaughn had had sex with his niece.

Yank's nieces were his pride and joy. If the man found out Vaughn had slept with Annabelle, no commitment involved, he'd have Vaughn's hide. Bottom line, he'd cut him out of his life again. And that was the *last* thing Vaughn wanted. He ran a hand through his hair, unable to believe he'd forgotten the main reason to steer clear of Annabelle.

Resigned, he headed to the front door to let his guest inside. Yank appeared scruffier than usual and more tired than Vaughn remembered seeing him in the city.

Added to that, this visit wasn't planned and Vaughn grew concerned. "To what do I owe the pleasure?" he asked, gesturing for Yank to come inside.

"Can't a man visit his niece without you asking one hundred questions?"

He narrowed his gaze. Was it his imagination or did Yank seem crankier than usual? "At last count, I asked you one question only and not an unreasonable one considering how far you drove to show up on my doorstep." He placed a hand on the older man's back and guided him to the large living area he used for his infrequent company. "So what gives?"

Yank settled himself on the sofa and motioned for Vaughn to do the same. Then he leaned close. "If I tell you, you can't tell Annie."

So something was wrong. His stomach cramped but he forced a casual shrug. He'd just resolved to steer clear of the woman. How hard would it be to keep Yank's secret? "Since when do I share things with anyone?"

Since Annabelle came the silent answer. But whatever Yank told him would remain between them. He had no choice. "You have my word."

Yank cracked his knuckles as he admitted, "The doctor says my eyesight's going."

Forget his stomach, now Vaughn's head began pounding, too. "Going as in..."

Yank slapped his hand over Vaughn's eyes like a blindfold. "As in can't see a damn thing."

He dropped his hand and Vaughn blinked to refocus. For a split second, Yank's face showed all the fear he'd been hiding, before he covered his emotions with an expressionless mask once more.

Vaughn had been in a similar position to Yank, faced with a huge loss when he'd shattered his knee. So he knew better than to offer pity or condolences. He also knew what it cost the older man to open up, and it showed that no matter how many years had passed since they'd been close, the bond remained. It would strengthen as Vaughn helped Yank through this tough time. But if Yank found out about his one-night stand with Annabelle, both men stood to lose.

Vaughn swallowed hard and focused on not pitying Yank now. "Dare I ask how you plan to keep this secret once you start walking into walls?"

Yank let out a gruff laugh. "Well, that may take a while. Macular degeneration doesn't always progress quickly. Time'll tell. In the meantime, I had to get away from Lola before she drove me insane."

"She knows?"

Yank rubbed a hand over his full beard. "She knew before I did, or at least she sensed it. First she dragged me to the dang doctor, then she read all the literature. Next thing I know she's buying little items *just in case.*"

"Such as?"

Yank placed his hand on his wristwatch and pressed a button. "It's 11:15 a.m.," a digital voice announced.

Vaughn stifled a laugh.

"She's made all kinds of crazy changes so I can get used to things before my sight goes," Yank continued, in a poor imitation of his assistant.

Vaughn inclined his head and tried not to grin. "I take it you think she's overreacting?"

"Is she a female?" Yank asked wryly. "You wouldn't believe what she's been up to."

"I can only imagine." Vaughn wondered what Lola was doing to take care of this stubborn man.

"Imagine what?" Annabelle asked, joining them in the family room.

Vaughn glanced up. She'd changed into a pair of plaid boxers and a solid red, body hugging T-shirt. Simple and sexy enough to have him drooling. To have him dreaming of repeating last night over and over and over again.

He shook his head hard. "Yank was just explaining his newest challenge," Vaughn said.

The older man nodded. "It's Lola. She's gone over the edge."

"How so?" Annabelle settled in beside her uncle, curling her legs beneath her and propping her chin in her hands. The love beaming from her eyes spoke volumes.

She'd want to know about her uncle's condition, Vaughn thought. Heck, she deserved to know. But it wasn't his place to spill that truth, nor would he break a promise. Still, the warmth in her eyes had Vaughn wishing for things he'd never have. Things like unconditional love and acceptance.

"Damn woman's become loose. Wearing tight-fitting pants, high heels, low-cut tops." His cheeks flamed at his description. "Lola, of all people."

Annabelle's eyes opened wide. "And this bothers you?"

"Hell yes, it bothers me!"

"Pardon me, but I don't understand the problem. The ultimate bachelor is having issues because his beautiful secretary is coming on to him?"

Vaughn could see Annabelle struggle not to let loose with laughter.

"Bite your tongue, Annabelle Jordan. I didn't say anything about her coming on to me. But she's been dressing and acting different." He narrowed his gaze. "And you automatically figured she's making moves on me. That tells me you must've instigated the change."

Annabelle rolled her eyes. "I did not! Though I have to admit I applaud Lola's determination."

"You see, Vaughn? The women are ganging up on me."

Annabelle's amused gaze shot to him and he forced a shrug. Since he'd vocally advocated Lola flaunting her assets, he opted to shut his mouth now. Besides he liked seeing the older man squirm and if Lola finally decided to give him a run for his money, and at a time when he needed a distraction, Vaughn was all for it.

"I think you can handle whatever life throws your way, Yank," Vaughn said with a deliberate dual meaning that the other man acknowledged with a grateful nod.

"Yank can handle anything except maybe a determined woman, right Vaughn?" Annabelle laughed and no doubt expected him to laugh, too.

After all, she knew of what she spoke. Her determination had landed them in the sack and he'd gone all too willingly.

He straightened his shoulders. "Yank knows better

than to let any woman lead him around like a dog on a leash," he muttered, hoping Annabelle picked up the fact that he was talking about himself as well.

"Damn straight, which is why I'm staying while Annie's working here. Get away from the floozy for a while."

"You're *staying?*" Annabelle asked, obviously as surprised as Vaughn. "Here?"

Yank nodded, unknowingly giving Vaughn a plausible reason to back off. A valid one that didn't need explanation since surely a bright woman like Annabelle would conclude there'd be no hank-panky with her uncle staying under the same roof.

CHAPTER TEN

ANNABELLE AND MARA were talking alone in the business office of the lodge later that day. Nick was off inspecting the damage with the electrical engineer and getting a time frame on fixing the problems, and Vaughn was tied up in meetings. Annabelle decided to use the time to implement some PR ideas with Mara's help.

Unfortunately the other woman had other things she wanted to talk about first. "So I hear you have unexpected company?"

Annabelle nodded. "My uncle. It seems he needs to get out of the city for a while." Though why her uncle had to show up now, when she'd just put the moves on Vaughn, and successfully, she might add, boggled her mind.

Mara leaned back in her chair and studied Annabelle, a smile creeping onto her face. "Having family around must cramp your style, hmm?"

Startled, Annabelle merely blinked. "I don't know what you mean." Could Mara know about her and Vaughn? She shook her head. Impossible. After all, they'd only just been together last night and had shown no public displays of affection at all.

"Oh, come on! Indulge me in some girl talk here. I know you have a thing for him. And I can't help but notice he stares at you constantly with those baby blues."

Annabelle was mortified. "I do not! And he does not! Stare or have a thing, I mean."

"And I think the lady protests too much," Mara said laughing. "Joanne at the coffee shop said you were asking lots of questions about Vaughn when you first got to town."

Annabelle cringed. "Would you believe I was gauging the lay of the land in PR terms?"

Mara shook her head, laughing.

"There are no secrets, are there?" Annabelle asked on a sigh, already resigned to divulging her feelings.

"No secrets in this town," Mara agreed. "So can I take that as an admission?"

Annabelle glanced over her shoulder, making certain the office door was closed. "Okay, I admit Vaughn and I are temporarily involved."

Mara nodded slowly. "It's good you aren't expecting anything long-term. The man just doesn't know how to open up. Nick's the same way."

Annabelle decided not to discuss Vaughn's inability to bond emotionally, especially since she felt she'd made progress. She would rather talk about Nick instead. She leaned forward in her seat. "Actually Nick's pretty transparent if you know what to look for."

The other woman's eyes shone bright with anticipation. "Go on."

"Not until I know you're serious about him." Annabelle had come to like Nick and sympathize with his issues. After all, she thought wryly, everyone had insecurities whether they admitted them or not. She ought to know.

Mara grew thoughtful for a moment. “I’m in love with Nick. Head over heels in love with the man and he won’t give me the time of day.”

Relieved, Annabelle felt more comfortable discussing Nick. “He has his reasons for backing off and they really aren’t personal to you. So I suggest you take the initiative. Go all out in your campaign and show him he’s worth the risk.”

Mara swiveled back and forth in her chair and smiled. “I never would have pegged you as an advocate of women making the first move.”

Annabelle thought back to her silk teddy and bold knock on Vaughn’s door last night and grinned. “You’d be surprised,” she murmured.

“Now you’ve got me confused.” Mara crinkled her nose in thought. “Don’t most men want to be the aggressor?”

Annabelle had no desire to give away Nick’s secrets and merely said, “Let’s just say that in this case, Nick would appreciate knowing you want only him.”

Mara narrowed her gaze and groaned. “This is about Vaughn, isn’t it?”

“What makes you say that?”

“In this town, all paths lead back to Brandon Vaughn. Besides Nick’s made comments that lead me to believe he thinks I’m still interested in Brandon. Of all the stupid things. I dumped him and trust me, I have no regrets.”

"Why?" Annabelle asked, not just interested but curious why any woman would give Brandon Vaughn the boot.

She shrugged. "No chemistry. Now Nick—" She swiped her hand over her brow in an exaggerated gesture. "He really does it for me."

Annabelle laughed. "Then make sure he knows that."

Anticipation sparkled in Mara's gaze. "I will."

"Now can we get back to business?" Annabelle asked.

Mara swiveled around in her seat so she was facing her computer screen and keyboard. "What do you need? Because anyone who gives me the advice you just did deserves my help."

"Not to mention your boss is paying us to work?" Annabelle asked wryly.

Mara chuckled. "That, too."

"Okay, here's the thing. I was thinking that we need to use Brandon Vaughn's generosity to counter the bad publicity caused by the sabotage."

"How?"

"By sending letters to all registered guests informing them that in exchange for not canceling their reservations during this time, they are receiving one free night's stay as thanks."

Mara nodded and began typing. "On letterhead, right?"

"Yes. And maybe we can include a brochure with a reminder that it's never too soon to book spring break?"

Mara jotted a note on a pad next to her mouse. "Got it."

"Okay then." Annabelle gathered her papers and stuffed them back into her briefcase, then swung her purse over her shoulder. "I have family back at Vaughn's that I have to deal with."

"I'll handle this and, sometime today, I'll deal with Nick."

Annabelle rolled her eyes and headed for the door, her thoughts on her obstinate uncle. "At this point, I'm not sure whose job I envy more right now."

ANNABELLE JUGGLED her cell phone against her ear as she searched for money to pay the taxi she'd taken to Vaughn's house. She slipped the bills to the driver and headed up the front walk.

"So I was thinking that if I tell Uncle Yank that Lola's coming on to Spence Atkins, he'll hightail it back to the city," Annabelle said to Sophie, explaining the plan she'd concocted to send her uncle home where he belonged. As much as she loved him, she had a limited time with Vaughn and she didn't want to lose any of it.

"I'm sorry but I don't see that happening, Annie. You see—"

"Hang on," Annabelle interrupted her sister and dug for Vaughn's spare house key she'd dropped into her too-big bag. Key found, she let herself inside.

"Don't be so analytical," she told Sophie. "It doesn't have to be true. I just need a gut reaction from Uncle Yank when it comes to—Lola!" Annabelle stopped short upon seeing the other woman standing in Vaughn's front hall.

"Not analytical, just factual." Sophie's voice carried through the phone line. "I assume you just ran into Lola? I would have warned you if you weren't always in such a rush." Sophie sounded truly amused.

"You'll pay," Annabelle promised her.

"I already am. I'm working with Randy, the jerk," her sister reminded her. "Say hello to Uncle Yank and Lola for me." And with a sudden click, Sophie was gone.

Leaving Annabelle alone to deal with her uncle. And Lola. Who looked beautiful, ten years younger and like a handful of woman for her uncle to handle.

"So you're both here," Annabelle said into the silence.

"Your uncle needs me," Lola explained. "And I missed you." She gave Annabelle a big hug.

Annabelle hugged her back. As she inhaled, she took in an old, familiar scent. "Love's Baby Soft?" she asked, quietly.

Lola smiled. "I want him to remember the old days."

Annabelle's mouth opened wide at Lola's admission. So she *was* trying to seduce her uncle. But couldn't she do it in the city so Annabelle could get back to seducing Vaughn?

"Did you come to take Uncle Yank home?" she asked hopefully.

"I can hear you," Uncle Yank called out from his seat on the couch where Boris lay on his lap and Spike curled on the sofa cushion near his head. "So don't be talking about me like I'm not in the room."

Lola shook her head. "Then stop acting like you're deaf, dumb and—"

"Don't say it," he growled. "And I thought I left you home to handle things for me." He glanced at Annabelle, a smug look on his face as he said, "She always does what I ask."

"Maybe she used to but that was the old Lola," the woman who'd raised Annabelle said. "This is the new and improved version."

The other woman was right. Annabelle didn't recognize her. Her usual long black skirt had been replaced by an above-the-knee number, her sensible flats were now stilettos that Annabelle would be proud to own, in red no less. And her prim, buttoned-to-the-collar blouse was now a form-fitting, boat-necked sleeveless black shirt. With stainless-steel studs along the neckline.

Before Annabelle could reply, Vaughn strode in and let out a whistle of appreciation. *Now* the gathering was complete, Annabelle thought.

"Thanks, Brandon," Lola said blushing.

He inclined his head. "The pleasure's all mine." He lifted his dark sunglasses off his nose and hooked them into his shirt.

Oh, he was good, Annabelle thought. The attitude perfectly matched the sexy body in tight jeans and a Polo collarless tee. Her temperature spiked just looking at the man.

Vaughn glanced from Lola to Yank. "She doesn't look loose to me."

Annabelle nearly choked.

"Loose?" Lola strode over to Yank and slapped him on the side of the head. "Maybe I will accept Spencer Atkins's invitation to dinner when I get back to town."

Annabelle stifled a laugh. Lola was doing what Annabelle herself had already contemplated. Using Spencer to make her uncle jealous. Judging by the red flush on his face, it had worked.

"The hell you will," her uncle bellowed. "He only asked you out because he thinks you've suddenly become easy."

Lola straightened her shoulders and held her head high. "At least he asked me out, unlike one stubborn old man I know."

"Old? Who are you calling old?"

"Oh my God, what's wrong with them?" Annabelle asked Vaughn in a low tone.

He cocked an eyebrow. "You really have to ask? It's unrelieved sexual frustration," he muttered.

"Oh Lord," she said, shooting a startled look the bickering couple's way. The two interlopers didn't seem to notice. "Think we ought to leave them alone?"

He nodded. "Might as well. It's not like we can do anything to help them. Any chance this'll blow over soon?" he asked her.

Annabelle shrugged. "I've never seen them like this. Uncle Yank's always been dense, but Lola's the unknown here. She's completely different. It's like she's set her sights on a goal and *he's* it."

In fact, Annabelle thought, as Vaughn headed to the kitchen and she went to walk the dog, Lola and her uncle reminded Annabelle a bit of herself and Vaughn.

She only hoped Yank's complete refusal to have anything to do with Lola wasn't a bad omen for all of their futures.

VAUGHN WONDERED how his life had gotten so out of control. At work he had someone looking to undermine his lodge and at home he had the invasion of the relatives. Except they weren't his relatives and he wasn't used to so much company and noise around him. Strangely enough, he enjoyed the tumult. He was even beginning to like having the animals underfoot, not that he'd admit as much to Annabelle.

He would prefer a big dog to the Q-Tip, but since it was only temporary, he could handle the fairy mutt. He snagged a piece of white meat chicken from his plate and snuck it to the pooch hopping at his feet under the dinner table.

"Stop feeding the dog. You'll spoil him," Annabelle said, catching him in the act.

He shot her an amused glare. "And sleeping in your bed isn't doing the same thing?"

She shrugged. "I like the company."

He figured as much. The animals obviously filled a void in her life, but with such a rambunctious family, he wondered why she felt the emptiness in the first place. He, on the other hand, had his parents alive, well and disapproving as ever. They lived in the same town and he might as well be alone. No wonder he'd sought out Yank Morgan again.

He glanced at Lola and Yank who were eating in unusual silence. "So everyone enjoying the meal?" Vaughn asked. He'd driven into town where a new Boston Market had opened up and brought home a full dinner of chicken, mashed potatoes, vegetables and dinner rolls.

Everyone glanced at each other and remained silent.

"Boris likes it," Annabelle finally said.

"It was delicious, Brandon. And I'm grateful for your hospitality." Lola carried her plate to the sink, despite his protests, rinsed and placed it in the dishwasher. Then she returned for Yank's, pulling the dish out from under him.

"Hey I wasn't finished yet," he grumbled.

"Would you rather clean up yourself? Because I'm exhausted from the drive and I'm turning in early."

Vaughn thought it best not to offer to clean for Yank and piss Lola off, and a smirking but quiet Annabelle obviously agreed.

"Fine, clear my plate," Yank muttered.

"You could stand to lose a few pounds anyway." Lola finished with his place setting.

"I'll take care of the rest, Lola. Why don't you go get some rest?" Annabelle said.

"Thanks, I think I will. Night all." Her gaze encompassed both Vaughn and Annabelle, deliberately excluding Yank.

"Night, Lola," they both murmured.

She headed for her guest room upstairs.

Vaughn had had his cleaning woman open up two of the upstairs rooms, dust and clean them out to give both Yank and Lola their privacy. From speaking with Lola, he knew Yank's eyesight wasn't a real issue yet and walking stairs posed no problem. Since Yank had wanted to feel like he'd gotten away from the world, Vaughn provided him an upstairs haven. The only drawback was that he had Lola close by, Vaughn thought wryly.

"Would you like dessert?" Annabelle asked her uncle once Lola had gone.

"Why not? Might as well give the dragon lady something else to yell at me about," he said, referring to Lola's behavior.

"Something tells me it's time for you to turn in, too," Annabelle suggested sweetly.

He frowned. "I thought Vaughn and I could talk some first."

Annabelle waved a hand. "I'll clean up in here. Maybe in the meantime, Vaughn can talk some sense into you as far as Lola's concerned. And as far as your staying here, don't you have a business that needs you in the city?"

Vaughn saw his cue and grabbed at it. "Yank's welcome to stay here as long as he wants." As a buffer between himself and Yank's niece, a woman whose every facet he liked more and more.

Annabelle narrowed her gaze. "You surprise me."

"Why? You thought I'd be an inhospitable pig?" he asked with a friendly grin on his face.

She shook her head. "I just thought you liked your privacy and needed your space." And with that, she began stacking the remainder of the dishes and cleaning the table.

He mouthed a silent thank-you her way before turning to her uncle. "Yank, want to go have a drink in the family room?"

A long drink. Long enough for the women in the house to go to sleep and let the men be in peace.

ANNABELLE FOCUSED on the night ahead. While Uncle Yank and Vaughn shared a drink and talked, she took

Boris for his last walk and cleaned Natasha's cage. Spike, she assumed, was perched on either Vaughn's or Yank's lap. She was female, after all.

Alone in her room, Annabelle washed up and undressed for the evening. Since Uncle Yank or Lola could walk in or catch her in the hall sneaking to Vaughn's room, the silk teddy was out. That left her with the jerseys she felt most comfortable in anyway. Once she was finished washing up and changing, she glanced over at her empty bed.

Loneliness seemed to emanate from the double mattress. She shook her head in frustration. Every night at home she slept alone, yet because she'd spent one night with Brandon Vaughn, one *spectacular* night, she craved his company. Not only had she gotten a tempting taste of sharing, and wanted more, but she knew her time with Vaughn was limited to this business trip. She'd be darned if she'd let an unexpected family visit ruin it for her.

At the reminder of family, Annabelle's concern for her uncle rose. Something was up with him, she had no doubt. He wouldn't travel all this way to Vaughn's just to escape from Lola. Annabelle pursed her lips and thought hard, but came up blank. She obviously wouldn't be finding out what Uncle Yank's real problem was, at least not yet. So she turned her focus to her own issues.

Vaughn was shutting down. He was using her uncle's visit as a means of putting up a wall between them. No shared meals, no joint cleanup, no long talks over dinner. Nothing. Annabelle had had every intention of correcting the situation. Though she was by no means certain she'd be welcome, as soon as she heard the door to Vaughn's room close, Annabelle drew a deep breath for courage and headed down the hall.

Like last night she knocked on his door. Seconds passed that felt like forever. Finally the door opened wide and Vaughn stood before her.

"Annabelle," he said gruffly, his voice filled with longing and desire. But he didn't invite her inside.

"Can we talk?" She swallowed hard.

He nodded, his big body blocking the doorway.

"Inside," she prodded. "So we don't have an audience."

With a groan, he stepped aside and gestured for her to come in. "This is crazy," he said as he shut the door behind them. "Your uncle's upstairs."

"I'm over twenty-one," she reminded him. "Uncle Yank has no say. I respect him, but I won't let you use that as an excuse to avoid me."

"It's not an excuse. I need to earn back your uncle's respect," Vaughn said.

She reached a hand out and stroked his cheek. "I'll sneak out in the morning."

His blue eyes dilated and darkened in hue but his next words smothered her hope. "I'm not sleeping with you while your uncle's under the same roof."

She admired his chivalry and old-fashioned values. "All I want to do is share your bed." She didn't want to disrespect her family any more than he did, but she wanted to be with Vaughn. Just lying next to him would be enough.

Uh-oh.

Obviously despite her self-made promises not to get attached, there was a definite emotional component to her need.

"You can stay," he said, understanding in his expression.

She'd thought his mere presence would be enough yet as she joined him in bed and Vaughn shut the light and rolled over to go to sleep, she realized it was definitely possible to be with someone and still feel alone.

CHAPTER ELEVEN

VAUGHN AWOKE to the unfamiliar sounds of someone tossing and turning. It took only a second for things to register and for him to realize it was Annabelle, murmuring fitfully in her sleep while her body jerked against his.

He might have successfully fought temptation last night, but only because he hadn't touched her. Hadn't allowed himself to connect emotionally. That was then. With her this upset even in sleep, he had no choice but to break his vow to keep his distance.

Unless he wanted to watch her suffer. He didn't.

"Annie." He reached over and pulled her tight against him, shaking her gently. "Wake up, sweetheart. You're having a bad dream."

Her head turned from side to side. "We'll be good, I promise. Don't separate us," she pleaded, then suddenly jumped up and looked around with unseeing eyes.

"Annabelle," he said softly.

She turned and focused on him.

He saw in her face the exact moment she realized where she was.

"I'm sorry," she murmured, ducking her head and not meeting his gaze. "I should go." She tried to pull away, but he wouldn't let her leave.

"Tell me about the dream." He brushed her hair with his hand.

She eased back into his arms and her muscles seemed to relax a little. "I've had these nightmares for as long as I can remember."

Holding her tight, her lithe body molded to his, he inhaled the fragrant scent of her hair and fought his body's response and the desire building. A desire to ease her pain the only way he knew how, to bury himself deep inside her body and make her think of nothing except him.

But even he knew better than to think sex was the answer to anyone's problems. "The dreams started when your parents died?" he asked.

"Yes. I told you I wasn't even sure Uncle Yank would take us in."

He swallowed hard. "I thought you just meant you were frightened and made that assumption."

"It was more than that. I heard the social worker tell him that if he didn't take all three of us, we'd go to foster care. Separate homes."

She swallowed a sob and he thought his heart would crack at the admission. "But your uncle kept all of you."

"And I kept an eye on my sisters. I made sure they behaved, or I tried to. I figured if we were good girls, he wouldn't send us away."

He massaged her shoulder with one hand, trying to

ease a pain too ingrained for mere reassurance to touch. "Yank would never have let you be separated."

She tried to laugh, but choked instead. "I was twelve and I had no way of knowing that," she said, her voice trembling.

"Good point. And these dreams?" he asked, pushing when he should let things go.

She sighed. "They come almost nightly."

His gut told him he'd regret what he was about to say next. "But you didn't have any the first night we were together. At least not that I heard."

"You didn't reject me that night." She drew a deep breath and rolled over to meet his gaze. "Look, I'm not trying to give you a guilt trip, it's just fact," she said, her tone earnest. "But last night you let me stay because I begged. You didn't want me here and I'm sure the dream came back because in my heart, I knew that."

He winced, his gut churning, his emotions too wrapped up with this woman. "I want you here. It's just that it's complicated."

A soft smile curved her lips. "Welcome to my world."

He couldn't help but laugh and at that moment, the alarm clock Annabelle had set the night before went off, signaling it was time for her to leave before her uncle or Lola woke up, ventured downstairs and found them together.

"Saved by the bell," Annabelle murmured and once again tried to roll away, this time to rise for the day.

Though he should have let her go, he allowed his heart to overrule his head. "Annabelle?" he said, pulling her back.

"Yes?"

He sucked in a deep breath. "Don't ever doubt I want you. Here. In bed with me."

She deserved to know that truth and not have old insecurities resurrected because he had his own anxieties, he thought. He laughed, shaking his head.

"What's so funny?"

He groaned. "I am. Or should I say, life is. So, same time, same place tonight?" He extended the invitation despite himself.

She answered with a huge smile and a kiss. Her lips came down on his and parted immediately, her tongue slipping deep inside his mouth. The kiss spoke of suppressed need and longing, of an emotional yearning.

And damned if he didn't respond to that. All rational thought fled and he rolled her over until his body covered hers and then he took control of the inferno between them. Or so he thought until her hand slipped into the waistband of his boxers and unerringly found him, hard, erect and wanting her.

He eased to his side, giving her better access and she curled her hand around him and began the perfect up and down gliding motion, imitating the act of him pumping into her body as they made love. He let out a strangled groan, feeling his climax building fast. His eyes shut tight and he lost track of his surroundings. All he was aware of was the incredible friction she created and the warm, rhythmic contractions pummeling his body relentlessly until he came in a scalding hot climax that left him spent and shaken.

And when he opened his eyes to deal with what had

just transpired between them, he saw Annabelle leaving, the door to his room closing silently behind her.

SHOWERED AND DRESSED for the day, Annabelle made her way to the kitchen, both Boris and Spike trailing at her feet. She refused to think about her talk with Vaughn or what his face had looked like in the throes of climax, or to even analyze things too deeply. Including how she'd taken control and perhaps even advantage of him, despite knowing he was conflicted and had labeled her in his mind as complicated. What in life wasn't?

Her stomach grumbled. Cereal and milk was something she could make for breakfast without much effort. Expecting to be alone, she stopped short upon seeing her uncle sitting at the kitchen table. He held the newspaper up in front of him, first moving it to arm's length, then directly in front of his eyes, before growling in frustration and tossing the paper across the table.

"What's wrong?" Annabelle asked, joining him. "Did your favorite horse lose an important race?"

"I'm losing something," he muttered cryptically.

She narrowed her gaze. "What's going on with you?" She placed a hand on his shoulder. "What's wrong?"

"What makes you think something's wrong?"

"You're crankier than usual for one thing."

He snorted. "And Lola's not?"

"We aren't talking about Lola, and it's not Lola I'm worried about. It's you."

"I'm fine." He leaned back and folded his arms across his chest, defiant and angry.

"Bull," she said, walking over to his chair and staring him in the eye. "You're keeping something from me. That I can handle. I'll figure it out soon enough. But you're being mean and nasty to Lola and I'm not going to stand for it."

"Damn women. You always stick together."

She pursed her lips tight. "This isn't a gender thing. By siding with Lola, I'm siding with you. She's good for you and I don't want to see you drive her away. You need her."

"I don't—"

Annabelle waved away his final words with a sweep of her hand. "Be careful what you wish for or you'll end up alone," she said, voicing her biggest fear.

Except in this case she wasn't projecting. Uncle Yank's bad behavior threatened the one person who'd kept him sane all these years. She didn't want him to suffer.

But he remained stubbornly silent. "Okay, if you don't want to talk about it, we won't." She pulled a bowl from the cabinet, Special K from the pantry, and skim milk from the refrigerator and proceeded to make herself breakfast. "Want some?" she asked him.

He shook his head. "I had coffee."

She glanced at the full mug in his hand and the empty canister on the table with the word Salt inscribed on it. She bit down on the inside of her cheek, wondering whether to mention his error or not.

Finally she said, "Did you pour salt in by mistake?"

"It's not my fault the damn stuff is side by side on

the counter," he said defensively and glanced away not meeting her gaze.

She frowned and without further discussion, made him a fresh cup of coffee without being asked. Then she settled in to eat her now soggy cereal.

The two of them ate in silence. Neither Vaughn nor Lola showed up for breakfast. Annabelle didn't take Vaughn's absence personally since she'd snuck out on him. She refrained from touching her lips, which she imagined still tingled from his kiss. He was such a mix of contradictions. He wouldn't touch her with her uncle under the same roof, but he let her stay in his bed, in her mind, a more intimate act than something purely physical. Yet with desire flooding her body from being near him, she hadn't been able to help but test him with the kiss, which had led to so much more.

Even now her body vibrated with unslaked need, but she didn't mind. Just knowing she could affect the great Brandon Vaughn on any level gave her immense satisfaction, she thought, curling her hand around her coffee cup, and revisiting their morning in bed in her mind.

An hour later, Uncle Yank had volunteered to take Boris for a walk and Annabelle used the opportunity to call her sisters from the privacy of her room. She caught Sophie on her cell phone as she was getting out of a taxi on her way to a breakfast meeting. Sophie said she hadn't noticed anything unusual about Uncle Yank, but then she'd been so busy she hadn't been focused on anything but business, she'd admitted with a touch of guilt in her voice. Same answer when Annabelle had spoken with Micki.

But causing guilt hadn't been Annabelle's intention. She was equally busy, equally absorbed with business and Vaughn. She didn't blame her sisters for their distraction. But between this unexpected visit and Lola's drastic change in appearance, Annabelle just wanted to understand what was going on with the man who'd raised them. So she and her sisters had agreed to sit Uncle Yank down at the upcoming family party and find out once and for all.

VAUGHN HEADED to his gym downstairs, the one place in his home where he was guaranteed to be alone. No phone calls from parents trying to reach him, no animals begging for attention, no Annabelle guaranteed to distract him, and no bickering Yank and Lola needing him to referee. Or so he thought.

He walked into the partially mirrored room and caught sight of Yank in the reflection. He turned in the other man's direction. "What're you doing here?"

Yank shrugged. "Same as you, I suspect. Want to get away from animals and women. Not necessarily in that order."

Vaughn chuckled. "Okay, I admit to thinking something along those lines. Is Lola making you insane?"

He snorted. "Does a bear—"

"Don't even say it," Vaughn muttered. He sat down on the padded seat of the bench press and resigned himself to working his jaw not his muscles. "I'm going to pry," he said, warning the other man.

"Figures."

"Why aren't you interested in Lola? Not only is she beautiful, but she's as loyal to you and your nieces as they come. She's stuck with your obnoxious personality all these years, and she obviously loves you. Enough to completely alter her appearance to get your attention. So either there's just no attraction, which frankly I don't buy, or you're scared to death after all these years as a single man. The latter gets my vote." Vaughn shot Yank a pointed stare and waited for the older man to tell him to mind his own goddamn business.

"Hell, you think I don't know how she feels? And I'd be blind not to appreciate how she looked before and after this dumbass transformation." Yank burst out in what could only be described as a guffaw of laughter. "I'd have to be blind, get it?"

Vaughn shook his head. At least Yank still had his sense of humor. "Well you're not blind yet, so what gives?"

Yank kicked at an old ball Vaughn kept in the room. It hit the far wall and rolled back. He repeated the distracting motion while he talked. "Did you know Lola and I had an affair once?"

Vaughn's eyes opened wide in shock. He knew this because his head jerked up at the same time and he caught his stunned expression in the mirrored wall. "You and Lola?" he asked, completely taken off guard.

He laughed. "Yeah. Right before the girls' parents died and they came to live with me. Man, we were hot for each other."

Vaughn groaned. "That was probably more information than I wanted to know," he muttered.

Yank scowled at him. "My point is, of course I appreciate who and what she is."

Vaughn doubted any of the nieces knew about the couple's past and wondered how they'd feel if they learned the truth. They'd probably applaud.

"So what happened?" Vaughn asked. "My first guess would be that she came to her senses, but if that were the case she wouldn't have stuck by you all these years and wouldn't be flaunting her, uh—assets, at you now."

Yank rolled his eyes as if Vaughn were an idiot. "The girls happened and I couldn't split my focus."

This time it was Vaughn's turn to laugh. "Give me a break. You were the legendary womanizer in your day. The girls may have limited *where* you could do things, but I doubt they slowed you down," he said chuckling.

"Yeah well, I'd never felt about anyone the way I felt about Lola."

Vaughn nodded, understanding completely. "And it scared you," he guessed, mainly because he was in that same sorry state himself.

"Hell yes. Lola was a bright, beautiful woman who deserved a hell of a lot better than a man like me."

"Don't you think that was her decision to make?" Vaughn asked of Lola.

Ball forgotten, Yank leaned back against the wall. "Well, this is all hindsight, you know? All I knew then was, I was suddenly a guardian of three girls who wore panties with bows on their butts and had big, sad eyes. That scared me spitless. Add a woman ready to make us a family—" He shook his head. "I couldn't handle it back then."

"And now?"

"I'm not about to saddle her with an old man whose going to lose his eyesight," he muttered, then rose from his chair.

"Isn't that her choice?" he asked again.

"This discussion is over. We can move on to my niece."

Vaughn stiffened in his seat. For all his careful planning, he'd blown it now but good. "Look, Yank—"

"My Annabelle's got a tendency to pick losers." As Yank paced the floor and muttered, Vaughn furrowed his brows and shut his mouth. He was clueless as to where this discussion was going, so he might as well find out before he created trouble he might not be in.

"Annabelle needs a good man," Yank continued. "All three of my girls need a good man."

Vaughn swiveled around fast.

"Can't argue that point, can you?" Yank asked Vaughn.

"Uh, no I can't." He had no doubt what Yank's point was. His niece deserved the best and Vaughn, with his sorry excuse for a family, dyslexic background and the way he'd betrayed Yank years ago, wasn't it.

Yank walked over and slapped Vaughn on the back. "Glad to hear it. I knew we'd understand each other."

"We do." Vaughn swallowed hard. He was damn glad he had Yank Morgan back in his life and he'd already known to steer clear of his niece. Now he had confirmation. He understood Yank's unspoken words.

After this business deal, when Annabelle left for New York, anything they shared while she was here was over.

BY MIDDAY, Vaughn arrived at the lodge. As Mara had informed him, Annabelle had called Nick for a ride and had gotten there first. He was way past being jealous of Nick. After all, he was the one who had Annabelle in his bed. He did a quick tour of the construction area before returning to the office where Mara sat at her desk stuffing and stamping envelopes.

"Hey there," he said, treating her to a wink.

"Hey yourself." She pushed a too-tall pile aside before it toppled over. "I think offering a free night to all your registrants is a great idea."

"At least it's a start. Finding out who wants this lodge not to succeed would be even more helpful."

She nodded. "What do the police say?"

"That they're following up leads, whatever that means."

"Hey, at least you know you've got the best working for you here," Mara said.

Vaughn rolled his eyes at the blatant pat on her own back. "I just gave you a raise when we started this project," he reminded her. Before the lodge's inception, Mara had been his personal assistant. Now she ran things here, too.

"Are all men this thick or is it just you?" Mara asked, laughing. "I'm talking about Annabelle, not me." She stuffed another envelope, licked, sealed, stamped and began another pile.

"Oh." She had a point. Annabelle *was* the best. "Where is she, anyway?"

"When she arrived, she asked to use the computer

and printer, worked for an hour and then headed to gather the employees."

"Uh-oh. What's she up to now? Anything I need to be forewarned about?"

"It's pretty basic. And nice, too. She's inviting all high-level employees, including construction foremen, to a big party her firm is throwing in Manhattan."

He raised an eyebrow. "That's a long drive from here."

Mara tried to lick an envelope, then grimaced. "I've got no spit left." She wrinkled her nose in disgust. "I doubt anybody minds the trip."

"And she's doing this..."

"For you, blockhead..." Mara rose and smacked him on the side of the head.

He rubbed the sore spot and laughed. "I haven't been called that since—"

"I broke up with you," she said, grinning.

"You're too pleased with yourself," he muttered.

She shrugged. "Yeah well it's not a distinction too many women share, so you'll have to forgive me for gloating."

"So how're things going with Nick?"

She frowned. "Not real well. He's frustratingly withdrawn."

"So when have you ever let that stop you?" He ribbed Mara. They had a close friendship that had withstood both a fling and a breakup. She'd take his jokes in the helpful spirit in which they were intended.

"You sound like Annabelle," Mara said.

"Do I? What's Annabelle been saying?" he asked, leaning closer.

"That I should let Nick know I'm interested in him, for one thing."

"And for another?"

Mara bit down on her lower lip, probably wondering whether or not to confide in him. Finally she said, "Annabelle suggested that I not approach Nick unless I'm seriously interested."

Considering her eyes lit up at the mere mention of Nick's name, Vaughn doubted lack of interest was an issue. How serious Mara was about his friend or how Nick would react, Vaughn didn't know.

He had no idea what Nick wanted out of life, he realized. Did his friend want an affair or something long-term with the right woman? Vaughn had given up thinking the perfect woman existed, or at least the perfect woman for him, and he'd shoved that view down his best friend's throat so many times Nick probably wouldn't bother expressing his feelings on the subject if they differed from Vaughn's own. And they might.

Look at Yank and Lola. Vaughn had encouraged Yank to give her a chance. Vaughn had gone as far as to insist the choice to opt in or out of a relationship with Yank ought to be Lola's to make. But he didn't think the same rules applied to Annabelle.

And when Yank had said Annabelle needed a *good* man, Vaughn knew the other man was politely insinuating Vaughn wasn't him. Because despite all he'd overcome in life, he was still the kid who couldn't succeed and the man Laura had left behind because he was lacking. In the years since they'd been close, Yank obviously had come to believe that, too. Vaughn might help Annabelle ease her insecurities at night because it was what she needed, but long-term he owed it to her to make the best decision for them both.

Nick, on the other hand, didn't have the same hang-ups or insecurities. He glanced at Mara who, used to his long silences, merely waited until he was ready to talk.

"I think Annabelle's right. You should go for it," he told Mara at last.

She jumped up and gave Vaughn a big kiss on the cheek, just as Nick walked in, catching them.

Vaughn shook his head in frustration and shot an apologetic look Mara's way. "I'm outta here, kids," he said to his partner and assistant.

Nick clenched and unclenched his fists, his expression hard and unyielding. Mara definitely had an uphill battle ahead of her, Vaughn thought.

Good thing she was woman enough for the job.

He strode out of the office and headed to find Annabelle. She had a heart of gold and knew how to reach people on a gut level. She was bringing to the job the same skills Vaughn lacked to help his lodge. If he wasn't trying so hard to convince himself otherwise, he'd say they made a great team.

NICK WATCHED AS VAUGHN left the room after being caught with his arms around Mara, then he exhaled slowly. How many times in his damn life would he have to come in second or back off from something he wanted because of Vaughn—a man he had the utmost respect for and considered closer to him than his own brother? It made it all that much harder.

"Nick."

He turned, his thoughts unexpectedly cut off by Mara. Every time he looked at her, he felt that kick to the gut signaling getting over this woman wouldn't be easy. He liked her outspoken manner and business sense, enjoyed her sense of humor and bold laugh.

And he loved how her brown hair framed her face in chunky layers, disobeying her fingers when she brushed her hair back from her cheeks. No, he thought, getting over her wasn't happening soon. But as he'd told Annabelle, he wanted a woman who was all his, not one who had lingering feelings for his best friend.

"What?" he barked at her.

She folded her arms across her chest and her chocolate-colored eyes locked with his. "You're an ass."

"So you've told me many times," he muttered. "What prompted it this time?"

Head held high, she stormed over to him and grasped his forearms with her much smaller hands. "High school was a long time ago, and Vaughn's just my employer and my friend."

He swallowed hard. "And I care because?"

"Of this." She leaned in and kissed him on the lips, taking him off guard.

He didn't know what the hell was going on here, but he wasn't stupid and understood interest when he felt it. Going on instinct alone, he lifted her by the waist and sat her down on the desk. Then he sucked her lower lip slowly and gently into his mouth, taking control of this situation. And of her. The kiss went on, dueling tongues and undeniable chemistry aflame between them. By the time they broke apart, Nick wasn't sure who'd started it any more than he could say who actually had control.

With the way his hands were shaking, he doubted it was him. He met her gaze. Her cheeks were flushed, her eyes dilated. Maybe it was a draw.

"What was that for?" he asked. He ran his tongue over his damp lips, tasting her.

"I'm not interested in Vaughn."

He raised an eyebrow, unsure of how to respond.

"So you can stop acting like an idiot—or should I say a typical man—and take me to Annabelle's party or you can forget this ever happened and find yourself another woman to scowl at every day." She exhaled hard. "Whew. So what have you got to say for yourself?" she asked.

He grinned. "You've got yourself a date."

CHAPTER TWELVE

WORKING IN PR, Annabelle was used to creative ideas that had to be implemented at the last minute. Inviting Vaughn's top employees to The Hot Zone's party wasn't a daunting feat and she was nearly finished handing out the invitations she'd created and printed that morning.

As she extended the last invitation, she looked up into a familiar face. "How are you, Roy?" she asked, politely taking a step back.

Something about the other man disturbed her, though she couldn't say what since the few times she'd seen him around the site, he'd been nothing but polite, perhaps even a bit distant.

"I'm good. Busier with the break-in and all," he said.

Annabelle nodded in understanding. "Well if you and your wife are interested in taking a night off, The Hot Zone always throws a good party." She passed him the final envelope.

He grasped the paper, taking the opportunity to brush her hand with his and hold on a few seconds too long. As she tried to shake free, she smelled Vaughn's unmistakable musky scent and felt his overpowering heat. Boy was she happy to see him and for once sexual attraction wasn't the reason.

"Vaughn!" She whirled away from Roy and toward her savior, gratitude and relief washing over her.

"What's going on here?" Vaughn's gaze darted to his foreman.

"Miss Jordan was just inviting me to her shindig in New York." Roy grinned showing too many teeth.

"Actually I called a meeting and invited *all* of the people important to this project." She wanted him to understand the facts, not Roy's distorted perspective. "I even invited their wives," she added.

An unexpected smile crossed Vaughn's face. "You're just full of surprises," he said and obviously catching on to Roy, he wrapped a casual arm around Annabelle's shoulder as if staking his claim.

Roy stood up straighter. "And you know what, boss? I know my wife'll want to go. She's always up for a party."

"Yeah, to keep an eye on you," Annabelle said under her breath.

Vaughn inclined his head toward the lodge. "Don't you have work to do?"

Roy nodded. "That I do." With a wave, he slunk back toward the main building and the work that needed repair.

A big shot when one on one with Annabelle, he shrunk when faced with the great Brandon Vaughn, she thought, not surprised.

"Thanks for saving me," she said.

"Something tells me you wouldn't take any crap from Roy." Vaughn had watched this strong, capable woman hold her own with the foreman.

"Probably not but it sure is nice to watch Roy be intimidated." Annabelle's eyes glittered beneath the midday sun as she amused herself at Roy's expense.

Vaughn laughed. "I hear you, but I can't fire a man for wanting to cheat on his wife."

"I understand." She placed a warm, soothing hand on his arm. The electrical jolt was instantaneous.

Unexpectedly he covered her hand with his, surprising even himself. "Besides Roy's got a wife and kid and I don't want to be responsible for laying him off."

"You're a nice man." She smiled, turning everything inside him to instant, unmanly mush. "If you did fire him, he probably wouldn't get another job," Annabelle said.

"Exactly." Once again he was struck not just by her beauty or incredible body, but by her intelligence and insight.

"The invites," he said, getting to the reason he'd sought her out.

"Walk with me," she said, starting toward a line of trees in the distance.

He sensed she'd talk eventually and decided to humor her. They strode across the lush green grass. The blue sky overhead held a few bright, fluffy clouds. He glanced over. A warm breeze blew her hair around her cheeks. Not a man to stop and smell the proverbial roses, he still marveled at the precious simplicity of the moment.

"I had a reason for inviting everyone, you know."

"I'm sure you did just as I'm sure it's brilliant."

She paused and tipped her head to one side. "Was that a compliment I just heard?" she asked, her tone teasing.

"Am I that hard on you?" he asked.

"Only when you're trying to be." She slid her hands into the back pockets of her skirt, which had the effect of thrusting her breasts tight against her lacy T.

He swallowed hard.

"So don't you want to know the methods behind my madness?"

"Goodwill toward the employees?"

She frowned. "Don't tell me Mara gave me away."

He laughed. "Not exactly. I figure you're hoping that if the person who's behind the tampering works for me, we'll see it in their attitude outside of work." Vaughn voiced the notion he'd been thinking about since he'd heard about Annabelle's invitations.

"Not bad," she said, obviously impressed.

"You sound surprised. You didn't think I could figure you out?"

She flashed him a flirtatious smile. "I'd like to see you try."

And man would he like to.

Without warning, she took off at a sprint, giggling as she went, and he followed, chasing her through the trees. He could catch her easily but what fun would that be?

He let her dodge around one tall tree and another. Only when she was winded, did he do an end run, ducking around the opposite way and meeting her head on, then tackling her to the ground.

Her cheeks were flushed pink and her smile wide and carefree. For a brief time she wasn't running from her demons and for now he was content to leave his behind as well.

He wrapped his arms around her waist and pulled her close. A bird chirped in the distance as his lips came down hard on hers. He kissed her hungrily, his lips devouring her mouth like he couldn't get enough. Which he couldn't and feared he never would.

She teased him back, running her tongue over the seam of his lips and daring him to part them and slip inside. How could he not when she ignited a flaming desire this overpowering? He thrust his tongue into her mouth in an imitation of the most intimate act itself and Annabelle moaned from deep in her chest. Vaughn shook in reaction to the erotic sexy sound.

As she slid her hands into his back jeans pockets and pulled his hips close, she arched her back and thrust upward at the same time. The teasing contact of body parts, made frustrating by the barrier of clothes, drove him insane. He twisted his lower body, grinding his hard erection into the vee of her legs and she bucked beneath him, seeking closer, impossible contact.

A sudden sound ripped through the silence around them and Mara's static-ridden voice carried through the walkie-talkie clasped on his right hip. The intrusion couldn't have been more unwelcome.

"Hey boss?" Mara called a second time.

Vaughn groaned and touched his forehead to Annabelle's, their breathing coming in rapid gulps. "I am not answering," he muttered.

Annabelle laughed. “I second that.”

“Vaughn, the police are here to see you,” Mara said this time, her tone more urgent. “Are you there?”

“You are definitely getting it,” Annabelle said, changing her mind and reaching for the gadget on his belt.

“Yeah I guess I am.” With more regret than he’d believed possible, he rolled off her, unhooked the walkie-talkie and pressed the talk button. “I’m here,” he said to Mara. “Tell them I’ll be there in five.”

“Will do, boss.”

“Well that was fun,” Annabelle said with a grin.

He shot her an apologetic glance.

“Hey, it’s no big deal.”

He stood and held a hand out for her to grab and then helped her to her feet. She brushed herself off and he did the same, the remnants of dirt and grass covering them no matter how hard they tried to clean up.

He picked a stray leaf from her hair and a twig from the back of her shirt and she merely chuckled. “You surprise me again,” he said.

“Why’s that?” she asked as she straightened her clothing.

His gaze roamed appreciatively over her. “I’d never have pegged you as an outdoor girl.”

She shrugged. “What can I say? I adapt to any surroundings.”

“Another thing to admire,” he said out loud before he could stop himself.

She reached out and brushed his rear end with the palm of her hand. Once, twice, then she lingered, her fingertips squeezing his buttocks.

His groin hardened all over again, forcing him to grab her wrist. "If you don't stop now I'll never get back to the office."

She grinned. "Then it's a good thing you know where to find me tonight, isn't it?" she said in a sultry voice.

He swallowed hard. "I'm heading back to the lodge. Why don't you just take my car home? I'll get a ride."

"You sure?"

In reply, he reached into his pocket and handed her his keys.

She smiled. "Thanks."

He nodded. At least he'd have the walk back to the building to get his body back under control. Nothing else that Annabelle was doing to him would be that easily managed until she was gone from his house and his life. Of that, Vaughn was now certain.

ANXIOUS TO HEAR what the police had to say, Vaughn strode into the lodge office. The detective in charge of the investigation waited for him, drinking coffee courtesy of Mara and obviously flirting with her, though by her stiff posture and dismissive expression, she was definitely putting out signals that said *don't mess with me*. It looked like her interest in Nick was the real thing, Vaughn thought.

He walked up to the detective and extended his hand. "I didn't mean to keep you waiting," Vaughn said.

Detective Ross rose from his seat and grasped Vaughn's hand for a quick shake. "Not a problem. Your lovely assistant was keeping me company."

From behind his back, Mara rolled her eyes and stuck out her tongue.

Vaughn bit back a laugh. "Mara, why don't you take a break?" he suggested.

She shot him a grateful glance. "See you later." Ignoring the detective, she swung her purse over her shoulder and strode out of the room.

Once they were alone, Vaughn turned to the officer. He stood scanning the pictures on the wall, which included some old newspaper clippings of Vaughn's playing days and photographs of him receiving various trophies.

"So what did you find out?" Vaughn asked, not in the mood for idle chitchat.

"We discovered that your parents don't approve of your successful career," Ross said, scratching his head.

Vaughn swallowed hard. "Tell me something I don't know."

"They're not too thrilled with this place, either." He gestured around the lodge office.

"And?" Vaughn asked, annoyance percolating in his veins. Was this cop going to spend all day listing his family problems?

"And we've ruled them out as suspects anyway because there's no motive. They want respectability and clean hands too badly to do anything stupid around here."

Vaughn inclined his head. "Again, tell me something I don't know."

"Your old restaurants are in the red," Ross said. "Did you know about that?"

Vaughn jerked his head up at the suggestion. "You're

kidding. Laura would have had to bend over backward to screw those up."

"Well, she managed. Your ex owes most of her landlords, all of her vendors and then some."

Vaughn was amazed.

"Are you in contact with her?" the detective asked.

"I haven't been. But she called me recently out of the blue." Coincidence? he wondered.

"What'd she want?"

"Money. She said she had some huge credit card bills."

Ross pulled out his pad and jotted down notes. "And you believed her?"

"I had no reason not to. I asked about the restaurants and she never mentioned business trouble." Vaughn looked out the window and tried to think, but when it came to Laura he was blank.

"Well, we're looking for motive and I can't imagine her wanting your star to rise again while hers is falling," the detective said.

"Laura's vain but she isn't destructive. Besides if she's behind the vandalism then why would she call me now and put herself back on my radar to begin with?" Vaughn asked.

"Do you play chess?"

Vaughn shook his head.

"It's called a Forked Attack. She calls you saying I want money but behind your back she's sabotaging you so the lodge won't have any success." Ross met his gaze. "In a sense she'd be coming at you from two fronts."

Vaughn shoved his hands into his back pockets and

paced the floor. "I won't deny anything's possible but this doesn't feel right in here." He jammed his fist over his chest. "Do you know what I mean?"

The other man took a few steps toward the door. "We'll take those feelings under advisement but we have to follow up on all possibilities, no matter how remote. And this doesn't feel all that remote to me."

"Well, I appreciate you keeping me updated," Vaughn said, walking the detective to the exit.

With Ross gone, Vaughn thought back on their conversation. Laura behind the problems here? He snorted. Not likely. Which brought him back to square one. He headed home, hoping Annabelle would have greater insight than the detective in charge of the case.

UPON RETURNING to Vaughn's, Annabelle walked in on a loud discussion and realized immediately she'd intruded on a private talk between Lola and Uncle Yank. Her uncle sat in the large living room area on the couch while Lola, dressed in her new high heels, flowing skirt and low-cut, sleeveless peasant blouse, paced across the hardwood floor and back again.

Though Annabelle gave a wave to them both and went toward her room, she paused in the hallway now and couldn't help but overhear their conversation. In all honesty she was too riveted to step inside, close the door and shut their voices out.

"We had something once," Lola was saying. "And even if it didn't continue in the same way once the girls arrived, it continued. We continued. For years."

Annabelle inched closer to the wall and leaned

against the cool Sheetrock. Lola and Uncle Yank? Well she supposed it made sense even if she hadn't known or wanted to think about it before. It'd be like her as a kid thinking about her parents having sex.

"I told you then and I'm telling you now, you deserve better than me," her uncle said, raising his voice.

"Same story, different reasons. Back then you really were afraid of commitment but now you're just afraid of yourself," Lola said, pushing him.

Annabelle couldn't decipher what Lola meant but she assumed it had something to do with the reasons her uncle had come for this visit now. He was running scared, but of what she couldn't imagine.

"I'm not afraid of a damn thing," Yank yelled back, but Annabelle thought the slight quiver in his voice told a different story.

"Neither am I," Lola informed him. "And I'll prove it. Come with me to the company party," she said in a complete subject change, shocking Annabelle.

She couldn't imagine her uncle's expression right now and she actually found herself holding her breath for Yank's answer.

"I'm always at the company parties," he said.

Typical male. Annabelle grinned. Bless Uncle Yank and his stubborn streak.

"Come with me as my date." This from Lola.

A very silent pause ensued before Lola continued. "If you don't at least give us an honest try, I'm gone, Yank. Gone from The Hot Zone and gone from your life."

Unbelievably Annabelle's eyes filled with tears and

her heart, already beating fast, squeezed tight in her chest. Though she was an adult, and though she knew she'd always have Lola in *her* life, standing here in the hallway now, she felt small and insignificant. The same way she'd felt as a child, as she'd listened to Uncle Yank, a virtual stranger, and the social worker deciding her and her sisters' fate.

Powerless and out of control, Annabelle thought and began to tremble. Without realizing when, she sank to the floor and stared at the wall barely registering anything else. By the time she pulled herself together, silence reigned in the living room and she realized she hadn't even heard her uncle's reply.

VAUGHN ARRIVED HOME later than planned because Roy cornered him with football questions so he could help Todd on his day off. The other man seemed more desperate than usual to be a part of his son's life and Vaughn felt for him. After all, he'd have given anything to have a parent interested in his life. But after a while, Vaughn had pleaded a combination of exhaustion and a headache in order to escape.

He walked into a too quiet house. He didn't see Lola or Yank and assumed they were in their respective rooms. How long they were staying was anybody's guess.

He rounded the corner to the hall and shut himself in his room. Boris attacked first, hopping up and down on his hind legs like a pogo stick, never quite reaching above Vaughn's bad knee.

"Down," Vaughn muttered.

Boris sat.

"Wrong action, Q-Tip."

He wagged his tail with way too much enthusiasm and his tongue hung out as he panted.

"Don't you realize I'm the wrong sex for you to get excited over?" he asked the dog.

Yet he found himself leaning over and picking him up, holding him against his chest, as he'd seen Annabelle do, and petting his fluffy fur. Hair. Whatever it was the dog had covering his body.

Speaking of animals, Vaughn hadn't seen the rabbit since Annabelle had arrived and as for the cat... He glanced over at his bed and saw the expected: the animal curled up in his favorite place on Vaughn's pillow.

Right above Annabelle's head.

That surprised him. He'd thought she was in her room. And seeing as how it was dinner and not bedtime, her presence in his room took him off guard.

He walked over quietly and lowered himself beside her, but the bend and shift of the mattress caused her to stir. She stretched her arms high above her head, pulling her T-shirt up high and exposing her flat, smooth stomach and her unusual outtie belly button.

He stared. He grinned. And his mouth watered at the sight, not to mention his lower body's reaction. He swallowed hard.

Annabelle opened her big blue eyes. "Hi there."

He smiled. "Hi yourself."

"I see you've got yourself some company." She reached out and scratched Q-Tip under his chin.

He laughed. "He seems to like me. Go figure."

She eased herself to a sitting position. “Yeah go figure,” she said, her solemn gaze meeting his.

“What’s with the afternoon nap?”

She shook her head. “It just seemed the lesser of two evils.” Her gaze darted toward the far wall, away from his.

“The other one being?”

“Thinking,” she said simply.

He sensed it was anything but simple. He’d come home expecting to share the police theory about his ex-wife with Annabelle, but instead he realized she had something deeper on her mind. “Thinking about what?” he asked, digging for answers.

When she remained silent, he tried another tact. “Why’d you come in here to rest?”

The dog wriggled out of his arms, jumped to the mattress and snuggled in beside Annabelle.

She absently stroked his head as she said, “I feel better in here.”

“Because you don’t feel alone.” He understood that in here she sensed his presence and it gave her comfort.

“That’s part of it,” she admitted.

The irony here was great. “You’re a successful businesswoman, someone your family turns to when they’re in need, yet you feel isolated.” He reached out and stroked her cheek.

She nodded, tears welling in her eyes. She wiped her damp eyes with the back of her hands.

“Here use this.” He handed her the corner of his comforter to use and she dabbed at the moisture.

“Thanks,” she said, chuckling. “I just wish the simplest things wouldn’t evoke déjà vu.”

"What happened?" he asked, his concern for her all encompassing. More important than figuring out if Laura could really be responsible for the problems around the lodge.

Vaughn wasn't used to caring so deeply for another person, especially a person he had to let go. And still he couldn't turn Annabelle away. He listened as she detailed a conversation she'd overhead between Lola and her uncle, one that had left her sobbing like a child and retreating to bed for comfort. To his bed.

In response, he gave her the one thing she needed more than mere words. He lay down beside her and held her in his arms, until her breathing became deep and even and she'd fallen back to sleep, knocked out from emotional overload.

Vaughn let out a long sigh. It was a good thing she hadn't been looking for any words of wisdom. He'd have had none to give. While he wished he could tell her that the unconditional love she sought existed on some level, he couldn't. Nobody could give her that kind of security or guarantee. Hell, he hadn't found it in his life, either, so who was he to give advice?

But he understood now that the animals did give her what the people in her life hadn't been able to do. And he hoped like hell he wouldn't be the next person to disappoint her.

HAVING SLEPT THROUGH dinner, Annabelle awoke to the delicious aroma of pizza. She was certain she was dreaming, conjuring up what her growling stomach desperately desired. But when she rolled over and opened her eyes, Vaughn stood by the bed with a pizza box in his hand.

"Dinner?" she said, her mouth watering at the thought.

"Not home cooked, but yeah." His cheeks flushed, obviously embarrassed by his good deed.

It wasn't his first nice act tonight, either. He'd catered to her insecurities and understood her feelings, all the while not flinching at finding her in his bed.

His thoughtfulness showed yet another dimension to his strong yet sensitive character. "Thank you, Vaughn. You probably don't know this but I love pizza." She rubbed her belly and curled her legs beneath her.

He grinned. "Most single people do."

She shot him a wry glance. "Let me get dressed and we'll go to the kitchen."

He shook his head. "I'd rather eat here."

"Avoiding the company?" she asked.

He didn't reply, but instead sat on the bed and placed the box on the comforter.

"You really can't mean to eat in your bed."

"Hey, I don't mind if you don't."

"I'm easy." She opened the box and handed him a slice.

While they chowed down on the most delicious pizza she'd tasted, she turned the conversation to him. "What did the police have to say?" She asked about the lodge. "Any leads yet?"

He reached for a tissue on the counter and wiped his mouth. "None that are plausible."

She took a final bite of her second slice and left the crust in the box. "Who'd they suggest?"

"Laura." He said the name with no emotion, and having finished his pizza, he shut the box and rose to place the garbage on the dresser.

"You're kidding?"

He nodded with a brief jerk of his head. "She's done some slimy things and she can play head games with the best of them," he acknowledged. "But I don't see her as being capable of physical destruction."

"How about hiring someone to do the job?"

"No. Plus she asked for money. Unless she's having me fund my own destruction, it doesn't make sense. I just don't buy Detective Ross's two-pronged attack theory."

Annabelle bit down on her lower lip. He was so adamant, she wanted to believe his instincts. Still, at least one of them couldn't afford to be in denial. "I think I'll reserve judgment since I don't know the woman at all."

"That's what the police said. They're going to keep digging."

"Good. But it sounds like you've decided to give her the money?"

He shrugged. "On the off chance the cops are right, why make her more desperate, angry or jealous by saying no?"

She mulled that one over. "So what was the story with you two?" she asked, curious despite herself.

He rejoined her on the bed and leaned back against the headboard, hands clasped behind his head. "It's boring and I really wouldn't want to put you back to sleep."

She rolled her head to the side and felt a silly smile tilt her lips. "Your past could never bore me and considering how much of mine I've dumped on you in the past few days, I think it's only fair I listen to yours."

"You mean you think it's only fair I share?"

She grinned. "Yes, Vaughn. I'm asking you to do the one thing men dread. Open up and spill your guts."

He glanced at the ceiling and exhaled, obviously resigned to talking. "Okay look, Laura and I hooked up because I thought she was real. Except looking back, my reasons for thinking she was a decent human being were about the dumbest I can imagine."

"We all want to see the best in people. What were your reasons?"

"I figured because she was a school teacher, she'd have a better understanding of all I'd been through—dealing with the dyslexia, struggling academically, turning to sports because it was the one thing I excelled at."

"You excel at many things," she assured him.

He shot her a heated look, then they both laughed.

"But seriously your thinking seems sound. What went wrong?"

"It didn't take long before my lifestyle became more attractive to her than me."

Annabelle reached out with one foot and entwined her leg with his. "Now that I find hard to believe."

"How else would you explain the fact that while I was lying in the hospital doped up on painkillers, thanks to a shattered knee and a concussion, my loving wife brokered a deal with Yank's competition?"

Annabelle cringed, but still tried to understand what was going on in their lives at the time. “Maybe she thought Spencer Atkins was in your best interest.”

Vaughn frowned. “She thought Spencer had better contacts in television, and since she realized my career was over long before I accepted it, she decided to plot my future—hence, ensure her status as the wife of someone important in the industry. God forbid the invitations to the important functions should stop coming in and she’d have to spend a night home with her idiot husband,” he muttered, his bitterness so obvious it hurt Annabelle’s heart.

She could not comprehend how a woman could claim to love and understand a man, then hurt him with such calculated words, not to mention blindside him at the lowest point in his life. “It’s obvious Laura was looking out for number one, but why do *you* have to be so hard on yourself?” she asked.

“What the hell are you talking about?”

She climbed onto Vaughn until she straddled his hips. She wanted to get in his face and force him to discuss his greatest weakness. “I want to know why you call yourself stupid and belittle yourself over something which you had no control,” she stated.

“Because I’m quoting Laura’s words, sweetheart,” Vaughn informed her. “And there’s no sugarcoating her version of me. When we agreed on a divorce settlement, she said she’d turn the restaurants into an even bigger success than I ever could since she could read the fine print.”

“Bitch,” Annabelle said, defending Vaughn. She

leaned down and planted a kiss on his mouth. “Laura’s the one who sounds like an idiot,” she murmured, nibbling on his lips.

“Mmm. I’ve come to realize that.” He wrapped his hands around her neck and held her head in place while he deepened the kiss.

His tongue lazily traced circles on her lips until she parted and let him inside, the kiss quickly turning hot and heated. She loved the feel of him beneath her, his body hard and aching as he took control of both the kiss and of her. Her body melted, molding to his, but she knew they weren’t finished talking yet. Until they’d wiped Laura’s painful words from his mind, he’d always block a part of himself from her in order to prevent himself from being hurt again.

“Why do the police think she’s a possible suspect?” Annabelle asked, pushing herself upward so she could talk and think rationally, something she couldn’t do when Vaughn was kissing her senseless.

He exhaled hard and forced his eyelids open. “It seems her businesses are failing.”

Annabelle clapped her hands together with glee. “Oh, that’s rich! I love it,” she said, laughing.

“Pardon me?”

“Don’t you see?”

Vaughn scowled. He didn’t see anything except a woman he desired more with each passing breath sitting on his straining groin and making him talk about his ex-wife. The one thing guaranteed to kill any erection. “Don’t I see what?”

“The woman who accused you of being stupid and

unable to read the fine print ran the business into the ground. Success or failure has nothing to do with reading ability, Vaughn. And you of all people should understand that. But in case you don't, Laura's just given you proof."

He shook his head, amazed at her insight. "Good point," he said, then gave her a suggestive smile. "Now I think we can let the police follow up, don't you?"

She nodded. "Which leaves us free to do...other things." A hopeful note rang in her voice.

"Sounds like a plan to me. Other things that don't involve talking."

"I like the sound of that."

Within seconds he had her flipped to her back, their positions switched. He glanced down. The jersey had hiked up her thighs revealing a hint of lace and expanse of skin that had him drooling.

Suddenly a saucy glint sparkled in her eyes and she stretched her arms above her head, deliberately, slowly, arching her back and pulling the hem of the jersey upward, inch by tantalizing inch.

"You're a tease," he said, his voice gruff with desire.

"So what are you going to do about it?"

Unable to resist her blatant dare, he slid downward, placing his hands on her thighs. Never breaking eye contact, he eased her legs apart and watched her tremble.

He took immense satisfaction from knowing he had this effect on her and it made him want more. He wanted to make her climax and watch her as she came. He had a hunch the vision would be enough to make him follow suit.

He bent over and, hands still holding her thighs open wide, he licked his way up first one inner thigh, then the next. Her muscles shook and her hands clenched the sheets at her side.

It wasn't enough. He eased her panties down her thighs, revealing a blond triangle of hair and dewy moisture. Moisture he'd caused. He inhaled her essence and inched closer.

"Vaughn—" She turned her head from side to side, yet she remained open for him, waiting for whatever he'd do next.

"Relax, baby." He exhaled, blowing on the swollen folds of her sex.

Her hips jerked off the bed and she let out a low moan. "You really don't play fair."

He chuckled, though the noise sounded strained with desire. "Since you're not really the opposing team, let's see what I can do to change that."

"Hurry," she said, drawing out the single word.

So he dipped his head and began to torture her with long, slow laps of his tongue. First up, then down, then up again, until he latched on to the full nub and teased gently with his teeth. Her body began to shake and tremble, the muscles in her thighs contracting around him.

"More, Vaughn." She thrust her hips upward, a silent plea backing up her spoken desire.

A desire he wanted to fulfill, but his own body was near to bursting. He held his breath, then tried counting backwards from one hundred to distract himself and his body begging for relief. It didn't work, the need to thrust his hips forward and bury himself deep inside her was overwhelming.

But so was the urge to watch her come, to know he could control her response as she enjoyed his ministrations. Lord knew it'd been forever since he'd cared about a woman's pleasure. Oh, he'd always wanted to make a woman come but that was ego. This was about Annabelle and how deeply and easily she responded to him. This was about making Annabelle *all his.*

He thrust his tongue deep inside her hot, wet body and when she moaned in sheer pleasure, he caressed her outer folds with his fingertip, then inserted his finger deep inside.

Her inner muscles clenched around him and his body couldn't take it anymore. And obviously neither could she. "I don't want to come unless you're inside me," Annabelle pleaded, her voice cracking, her body racked with tremors that felt good but didn't quite take her up and over.

To hell with wanting to watch. He needed to be an active participant. Vaughn had never shed his jeans and boxers so quickly. Shaking with desire, he came over her and looking into her eyes, he thrust deeply inside. In, out, and all the while she milked him, drawing out of him every last drop of passion, and emotion as well.

CHAPTER THIRTEEN

ANNABELLE TOOK BORIS for a walk around the lodge grounds, admiring the landscaping along with the expanse of land Vaughn owned. She paused by the tree where she'd had a picnic with Nick and settled in, releasing the leash and letting the dog run free and get enough exercise so, with any luck, he'd pass out later on.

Two days had passed since Lola's ultimatum to Yank and her subsequent departure. Her uncle had remained, sulking and finding excuses to call the office and Lola, though Annabelle knew Lola wasn't giving in on her ultimatum. But with her sisters both away on business, Annabelle had nobody to talk to back at the office to find out what was really going on. All of which left her to focus on her current job and her life here in Greenlawn.

Since Mara had followed up the promotional mailing with an e-mail offer, calls were coming in accepting the free night and confirming holiday reservations. True there'd been a fair share of cancellations from people not willing to risk not having a place to go for vacation, but according to Mara, most of the calls praised Vaughn and the summer program. They were all too willing to take a chance on Vaughn's lodge, and of course the free night incentive helped.

In addition, the electrical damage was nearly fixed, thanks to the crews working double shifts. All in all, things were looking up and Annabelle had just one more suggestion for Vaughn before she returned to New York. In fact, she could probably return home soon, but a desire to make the most of her time here stopped her from suggesting an early departure.

Closing her eyes, she too easily recalled the last few nights with Vaughn. He had obviously decided his hands-off policy wasn't working for either one of them, and the nights they'd shared had been spectacular. The stuff of fantasies, Annabelle thought.

Waking up safe and secure in his arms after a dreamless sleep was nothing short of pure bliss. Careful, she warned herself. Short-term was still the rule of the day. Falling for the lush, green landscape of the lodge or the big empty house that begged for a woman's touch wasn't part of the deal.

Time to focus on business. She whistled and Boris came running. She scooped him into her arms and headed back to the main building. She was about to walk into the office when she heard the laughing and hushed voices of Nick and Mara, and from the sound of things they weren't working.

Not wanting to interrupt, she turned away and bumped directly into Vaughn's solid chest.

"Whoa." He grabbed her forearms and steadied her, while Boris scrambled to escape confinement in her arms in exchange for licking Vaughn's face.

"Guess you'd better take him," Annabelle said, laughing.

She handed him the pooch and he grabbed him awkwardly, clutching Boris around his middle so his legs dangled and his head bobbed as he tried to get closer to Vaughn.

Annabelle shook her head. "I don't know which one of you is more pathetic. Here. You hold him like this." She adjusted Vaughn's large hands so he held Boris's bottom in one palm and supported him with the other.

"I've got his butt in my hand," he grumbled.

The dog squirmed up and licked his face in reply. Next thing Annabelle knew, Vaughn let Boris snuggle into his chest as he cradled him in his arms.

She grinned. "See? That wasn't so hard. Now, I wanted to talk to you."

He stepped around her. "Then let's go inside."

"No!" She cleared her throat. "I don't want to interrupt Nick and Mara," she explained. "I think they're... busy."

"Aaah." He nodded in understanding. "Then let's take a walk and talk?"

"I just came from doing that, but you can never get too much fresh air in the summertime." She tipped her head toward the exit. "Let's go."

They took a different route, this time toward the parking lot. Since Boris refused to go down, Vaughn was forced to hold him while they walked. Annabelle couldn't help but notice his discomfort with the dog, though he had come a long way since he'd yelled at her in front of her apartment building about bringing the animals.

"What did you want to talk about?" Vaughn asked.

"What's your real problem with pets?" Annabelle wondered aloud at the same time.

He stopped and leaned against a parked car. His dark gaze met hers. "What is it that you like about animals? Besides the unconditional love?"

She narrowed her gaze, unsure of where this was headed. "I don't know. I suppose I like taking care of them," she said. "I like that they need me," she slowly admitted.

Vaughn nodded. "Exactly. Remember the fish I told you about?"

"T.D." Annabelle said, surprising Vaughn.

"I'm shocked you remember his name."

She shrugged. "It seemed important to you. What about him?" she asked.

"A kid wins a fish at a carnival. He has to read the instructions to feed him properly, doesn't he?" Vaughn winced at the memory, the pain of discussing this episode harder than he'd ever imagined.

"Or he can ask an adult to read it for him..." Annabelle's voice trailed off.

No doubt she'd just recalled the grown-ups in Vaughn's childhood and drawn the obvious conclusions. "Right," he muttered. "And after I killed my first pet, I decided it wouldn't be a good idea to let anyone rely on me again."

She reached out a hand and caressed his cheek, offering him the kind of understanding and caring he'd never been given before. Not even, he knew now, by Laura. In his first wife, he'd mistaken education for understanding. The realization now helped him put some of his anger and resentment to rest. Something else for which he owed Annabelle.

"You need to trust yourself more," she said softly. "I trust you." She leaned close and brushed her lips lightly over his.

Boris barked madly, forcing them apart.

Annabelle jumped back fast. "He's jealous," she explained.

Vaughn scowled at the dog. "Are you sure you're male? Cause if you were, you'd know where I was coming from."

Annabelle chuckled, lightening the mood and he took the opportunity to change the subject. "Since I know you didn't come here to talk about my childhood pets, what did you want to discuss?" he asked.

"A charity to correspond with the lodge. I don't know your financial situation of course, but I thought if we booked an appearance or something big for you, we could donate the proceeds and create a scholarship for children suffering from dyslexia. We could discuss ages and requirements later, but I was wondering if the idea appealed to you at all?"

He paused in thought. He'd flatly refused to do any publicity on the summer camp, then Annabelle had taken charge and turned things around for him. She was making sure the lodge didn't suffer while they finished construction and the police investigated. Her instincts were strong. Yank had every right to exude pride in his nieces.

This niece in particular. "Yes, the idea appeals to me."

Annabelle let out a pleased and shocked whoop of glee. "Thank you!" She started toward him for a hug, then catching Boris's glare, she backed off, laughing. "I'll just save that for tonight." She winked at Vaughn, then ran off to do her job, just one of the things she did best.

Unfortunately she left him alone with Boris, who'd decided he loved Vaughn and wanted to express it with licks and kisses, every chance he could. Vaughn groaned, yet he ended up laughing. The dog made him laugh just like Annabelle made him smile.

All things he'd done too rarely before she'd come into his life.

AFTER AN AFTERNOON of making phone calls regarding advertising opportunities for Vaughn and catching up with her sisters by cell phone, Annabelle leaned back in her chair, exhausted.

She raised her arms over her head and stretched backwards, feeling the pull on her cramped muscles. "Boy it's been a long one."

"I agree. What do you say we call it a day and have some fun?" Mara asked from her seat at her desk across the room.

Annabelle tipped her head. "Do you have anything particular in mind?"

Drumming her fingers against the desk, Mara grinned and said, "I might."

Half an hour later, Annabelle and Mara were climbing the bleachers behind the high school, a brown bag of wine coolers in hand. "I know where we are," Annabelle said. "But I'd like to know why we're here."

Mara pulled two coolers out of the bag and after opening the first one, she handed the bottle to Annabelle. "We're going to guy watch."

Annabelle raised an eyebrow. "You're kidding."

"Nope." Mara tipped the bottle and took in a good amount of alcohol. "You should have some. It goes well with what we're about to see." She gestured across the field to where a bunch of young men in shorts and T-shirts had stormed the field and begun doing laps.

"I'm sure we're not here to fish for jail bait," Annabelle muttered and just in case, took a hefty sip of the fruity wine cooler herself.

"No, we're here to watch the coaches." With that, Mara let her gaze drift to the two men striding out from behind the school. Nick wore a dark green T-shirt and shorts and Vaughn sported a similar look in light gray.

At the sight of him, Annabelle's heart did a flip reminiscent of her teenage years and suddenly she understood what Mara meant by guy-watching. "You're taking me back in time." Annabelle laughed.

"Except things only get better with age and I'm not just talking about the men. When we were younger, we'd watch and hope the guys would notice us, right?"

Annabelle nodded.

"Well at our age we're well past hoping." She whistled loudly and both men's heads whipped toward her. Mara waved.

Forced to acknowledge Vaughn and Nick, Annabelle did the same.

Mara lowered herself to a sitting position. "Well

they know we're here for one reason only. To see them, which pretty much guarantees they'll be flattered, which pretty much guarantees a successful evening." Mara held out her bottle and clinked it against Annabelle's. "Cheers," she said.

"I thought you and Nick weren't going on a date until the party."

"We're not." Mara placed her now empty bottle on the bleacher beside her. "Do you see two people on a date? I don't see anyone on a date."

Annabelle, feeling light-headed from the combination of the wine cooler and the sun, sat down beside Mara. "I see a woman who changed from her work clothes into tight shorts and a skimpy top all in an effort to drive a man insane with lust." And Mara had encouraged her to get casual as well, so she'd changed into an old Gap miniskirt and a *Flashdance*-style top.

"Can't put anything past you." Mara grinned, then waved at Nick again.

Annabelle figured that by now the man was in a sweat that had nothing to do with the weather. Then there was Vaughn.

She had no idea he'd extended his coaching obligations into the summer, besides helping Todd on occasion, but of course every surprise she learned about him was a positive one. She couldn't read his thoughts now but if they mirrored her own, he couldn't wait to get her alone.

"Hello..." Mara snapped a finger in front of Annabelle's face. "I asked if you planned to take advantage of being older and wiser, too."

"Hmm." Annabelle tipped her head to one side and let her gaze devour Vaughn. "Interesting way of putting it," she murmured.

Annabelle took a long sip of her drink. Since she was here watching Vaughn, she might as well enjoy the sight. As he urged the kids to work out, he kept pace along with them. And every so often he'd pause and glance up. At her. Though she couldn't see his eyes beneath the dark shades, she sensed his heated stare and couldn't mistake the yearning in his expression.

Desire was equally at work inside her. He was so sexy in his cut off T-shirt and shorts, his hair mussed from sweat and hard work, she could barely catch her breath.

He kept up with the guys but it was obvious he and Todd had a bond. He worked the kid extra hard and rewarded him with encouraging words and back slapping for a job well done. Vaughn obviously felt a kinship with the kids. If he could feel this kind of affection for other people's children, Annabelle realized what a fantastic father he'd make for his own child. She trembled at the thought.

The sound of Vaughn's whistle startled her and brought her out of her musings. The guys gathered around Vaughn. Annabelle glanced at her watch, surprised to see that a full hour had passed.

Beside her, Mara stood and collected her things.

"Where are you off to?" Annabelle asked.

"Just to say goodbye to Nick and see if he takes the bait."

Annabelle nodded. "Sounds like a plan."

"You?"

"I thought I'd go back to Vaughn's, check my messages, see if anyone called me back for bookings. I'd really like to get Vaughn's face out in front of the general public again."

Mara rolled her eyes. "Are you telling me I just plied you with alcohol, let you watch two gorgeous sweaty guys, and all you can think of is work?" She nudged Annabelle in the ribs with her elbow. "Surely you can think of something more exciting to do with your evening."

Annabelle closed her eyes and let her imagination flow. What would she want to do if nothing stood in her way? she asked herself. *Spend the night alone with Vaughn.* Under the stars in a place where no one would bother them. Not his parents, not her uncle, her sisters or even her pets.

She opened her eyes and began digging into her purse.

"Now what are you doing?"

Annabelle scribbled a note onto a sheet of paper, then folded it in half. "Do you think you could give me a ride back to the lodge?" she asked. The rest she could handle from there.

Mara sighed. "Okay, okay. So you learned nothing during our hour together. You're still determined to work."

Annabelle folded the paper in half yet again. "One thing about me, Mara. I'm a quick study." She glanced at the other woman. "Watch and learn."

She rose and adjusted her clothing, pulling the waistband of her skirt up a notch, which had the desired effect of raising the hem. Next she shrugged until the left side of her wide-necked top fell casually off one shoulder. She ran a hand through her tousled hair, popped a mint from her purse into her mouth and walked down the bleachers toward her unsuspecting target.

VAUGHN AND NICK dismissed the guys from the huddle. They were a select group of talented high schoolers who'd asked them to coach them throughout the summer and give them pointers before the season started again in the fall. Like Vaughn, Nick always enjoyed a chance to hone a kid's skills and so they'd agreed. But even while busting the guys for being too damn lazy, Vaughn's focus had been diverted more than once by the beautiful blonde hanging out on the bleachers.

He was sure the visit had been Mara's idea but if Nick had been as distracted as Vaughn, he hadn't let it show. And Vaughn was determined to have the same restraint and focus on the players, not the women, until his work here was finished.

"Hey, Todd."

The kid ran over. "Yeah, Coach?"

"Good practice today."

"Thanks." He glanced down and kicked his feet at the dirt.

"How's the summer going?" Vaughn asked him.

He shrugged. "Not bad considering I have to mow lawns and work with a tutor instead of hanging out with the guys."

Vaughn laughed. "I'm sure you're finding time for your friends too."

Todd grinned. "Yeah, yeah."

"Whenever you get frustrated, just remember the goal. You need an education as a fail safe. Just look at me. If I'd blown out this knee in my first season, I'd be out of luck because I didn't have the help you did to work on the problem."

Todd glanced up at him, trust and idol worship in the kid's gaze. Vaughn wasn't comfortable with either but hell, if he kept the kid motivated, who cared if he thought Vaughn was a saint?

"I hear ya, Coach."

On impulse, Vaughn reached out and ruffled the boy's hair, then shoved his hand back into his pocket.

"Hey, Todd, you coming?" one of his friends called.

Vaughn inclined his head. "Better get going."

"Yeah. Uh, Coach?"

Vaughn raised an eyebrow. "What's up?"

"Thanks," Todd said, then turned and ran to catch up with the other guys.

Vaughn turned back to Nick. "Man does that kid have talent."

Nick nodded. "And he's a damn hard worker. The only drawback to the kid getting ahead is his—"

"Hey now!" A loud voice interrupted them. "I heard today was practice day and I thought I'd stop by and see how my boy's doing." Roy strode up to both men.

"Speak of the devil," Nick said, laughing. "The kids just left." Nick pointed to the parking lot.

Roy shuffled from foot to foot. "I saw 'em go. I didn't want Todd to know I'm here asking about him. It embarrasses him in front of his friends."

Vaughn shoved his hands into his front pockets.

Then why bother him? Vaughn wondered. Although he had always wished his father had shown interest in his games and his athletic ability, Roy's smothering would end up driving his son away if he wasn't careful.

"Todd's a real talent and you should be proud," he informed his foreman.

Roy's shoulders straightened and his head lifted a little higher. "He's the best thing in *my* life." In the split second that Roy emphasized his relationship to Todd, a flicker of what looked like jealousy crossed the other man's features. For all Roy's talk, did he resent the time Vaughn spent with his son?

Nick slapped a hand on the man's shoulder. "I'm sure Todd knows it, too."

"Todd needs your help," Roy said, meeting Vaughn's gaze with a pleading one of his own and making Vaughn think he'd imagined the envy.

"And he's got help from both myself and Nick."

Roy kicked at the dirt. "Part-time help. Imagine how far he could go if you'd take the coaching job at the university."

Vaughn caught Nick's look which seemed to say *I feel for you, man.*

Vaughn clenched his teeth. For as much as Roy loved his kid, it wasn't Vaughn's job to see to it Todd succeeded. He had his own life and problems to deal with.

"Listen, Roy. I love the kids and I'll always be here for them in one way or another, but my focus is on the lodge now," Vaughn said, trying like hell to ignore the disappointed look in the man's eyes.

"Why don't you lay off Vaughn and go see if your

boy wants to throw a few balls with you in the yard?" Nick suggested. "That's always good for both of you."

Roy frowned. "He's busy with his friends."

"Then give him his freedom," Vaughn said. "Boys his age need that, especially with all the demands on Todd this summer. He knows you'll be there for him."

"I guess. Well I'm gonna go back to work. I'm determined to get you back to your normal schedule despite the problems."

As he stomped off toward the parking lot, Vaughn and Nick exchanged glances. "He's got nothing else in his life," Nick said. "So he drinks and cheats on his wife and puts all his hopes and dreams on Todd. Don't make it your headache."

"I hear you." It was just the stupid pain in his chest he got when he thought about both the similarities and differences between himself and Todd. "I'm going to hit the road," he said to Nick.

"You're going to deal with Ms. Jordan first." Nick grinned, looking across the field.

Vaughn drew a deep breath as Annabelle approached, those too high heels and impossibly long legs drawing his attention with each step.

Mara was right behind her, calling, "Nick, I was hoping to have a word with you."

Vaughn chuckled. "You're not out of the woods, either, my friend."

Annabelle sauntered up to him, a sassy sway to her hips. "I knew you coached during the school year but I didn't realize you did it during the summer, too."

He shrugged. "You didn't ask."

"I told you I could use everything about you to work the PR angle, yet you continue to withhold information." She sashayed closer. "I'm not into secrets." She bunched his T-shirt in her hands and rose to her tiptoes so they were eye to eye, though it was her lips he couldn't take *his* eyes off of.

"You know I prefer to get things out into the open," she said and, continuing to tease him, she brushed a kiss over his lips.

His groin hardened and the desire to have her now, on the lawn, in front of Nick, Mara and the wide blue sky overwhelmed him. "You realize we have an audience?"

He nodded toward his best friend and his assistant. Although in truth, Vaughn didn't know whether they were watching or engaged in their own version of foreplay.

"Why don't we go somewhere we can be alone?" Annabelle's eyes glittered with excitement and he wanted nothing more than to agree.

Unfortunately he couldn't. "I need to go home and shower." He leaned forward and nibbled on her mouth. "You can join me," he suggested.

"Actually I have a better idea." She stepped back.

"What?"

"It's all here." She held a piece of paper in her hand and playfully turned it from side to side.

He tried to grab the sheet but she snatched it away, still teasing.

"Are you coming, Annabelle?" Mara asked.

Vaughn glanced over in time to see Mara sweep a

hand down Nick's cheek and walk away, his friend's hungry eyes following the movement.

Nick had it bad. Not that Vaughn was one to talk.

"I'm coming," Annabelle told Mara.

"Where are you going?" Vaughn asked her.

She pulled on the waistband of his shorts and dropped her note into his pants. She was all sex appeal but in her eyes, he thought he caught a glimpse of something more. Something that made his breath catch and his heart nearly stop.

"Meet me tonight," she said in a husky voice.

He caught her wrist in his hand. "What do you have planned in that mind of yours?"

She grinned. "Something just for you in a place where we're guaranteed not to be interrupted," she promised him.

"Last taxi is pulling out now." Mara's voice interrupted them.

Annabelle waved goodbye to Vaughn with a wiggle of her fingers and a seductive twist of her hips as she took off with Mara.

Nick let out a slow whistle. "Who'd have thought wine coolers could have such a potent effect on women."

Vaughn laughed. "I take it Mara was flashing her wares at you?"

Nick looked up at the heavens. "That's one way of putting it."

"You trusting her now?" Vaughn asked.

"I'm trying."

"You?" Nick asked.

"I've got no reason to worry about that. Annabelle's job will be done and she'll be gone soon."

Nick kicked his sneakered foot against the dirt. "Yeah sure, buddy. That's what we tell ourselves when we're trying not to fall too hard." He slapped Vaughn on the back. "Just be careful, okay?"

"You looking out for me now?"

He smirked. "Actually you can take care of yourself just fine. It's Annabelle I'm worried about."

But Vaughn caught the lie in his friend's gaze.

They parted ways in the parking lot, Vaughn's mind on the note in his shorts from Annabelle, when a distinctive blue Chevy pulled into the space beside him.

His day went from promising to crap in seconds flat. He opened his car door anyway, intending to appear rushed and annoyed. Which he was, as his parents climbed out of their car.

"Hello, Mom. Dad." He propped his arm on the window and waited for them to come to him. He'd been dodging their calls and expecting this visit since the vandalism at the lodge hit the local news.

"Hello, Brandon." Estelle stepped forward, Vaughn's father at her side, and an awkward silence followed.

"How'd you find me here?" Vaughn finally asked.

"According to most everyone in town, if you aren't home and you aren't at the lodge, you're on the field coaching misfits," Theodore said.

"I doubt those were anyone's words but yours," Vaughn muttered. "But the point is the same. Everyone in town knows where your son is except you."

"Brandon, Theodore, please, don't do this," Estelle

said, interjecting between them. "We came to have a pleasant conversation."

"Which we tried to do on the phone except you've been ignoring our calls," his father added.

Vaughn pinched his forehead between his fingers. "I've been busy."

"Trying to get that godforsaken lodge up and running. We know." Theodore waved a hand dismissively. "Why coach here for nothing when you could have a prestigious job at the college?" his father asked.

Surprisingly his mother shot Theodore an annoyed look. Standing up for Vaughn? Doubtful.

"Brandon, the publicity surrounding this venture is all negative." His mother shook her head. "Your father and I only want what's best for us all. Take the coaching job and let this pie-in-the-sky dream go."

She reached out to touch his arm, but he stepped out of reach, the back of his legs hitting the inside of the car. "The lodge is my dream," he said through clenched teeth. "Just like pro football was my dream. But my dreams don't mean anything to either one of you. Only Dad's dreams do." He shook his head in frustration. "I'm not taking the damn coaching job and Dad can just tell the board that I said to shove it. You're both just going to have to deal with that."

"I told you this trip would be a waste of our time," Theodore said to Estelle.

She shot him a pleading glance and for the first time he saw a glimpse of a caring woman. Too bad the caring was all about them. And *they* excluded their only son.

He watched them walk back to their car and drive away.

Settled in his vehicle, he slammed a hand against the steering wheel, his parents disapproving faces in front of him. They never gave their support, he knew they never would and yet he wished for it anyway. Like a kid in a candy store, they reduced him to a needy state and he frigging hated how it made him feel.

He shifted in his seat and got stabbed in the gut. He couldn't help but grin as he pulled Annabelle's forgotten note out of his pants. He shook his head, laughing, his mood immediately lightening. Leave it to Annabelle to come up with such a unique method of delivery.

He unfolded the paper and read her hastily written words. "Peace, quiet and space. Meet me at the lodge for all three and more. A."

Her timing was impeccable, he thought. She seemed to know what he needed even before he did. And tonight he needed her.

CHAPTER FOURTEEN

VAUGHN DIDN'T KNOW what Annabelle had planned for tonight but his adrenaline was pumping big-time anyway. He'd returned home, showered and now he was heading for the lodge. He walked out of his bedroom and found Yank waiting for him, suitcase in hand.

"You're leaving?" Vaughn asked, surprised.

The older man nodded. "I'm not getting any work done here and I can't keep avoiding Lola forever."

Vaughn chuckled. "If you want to try, you're welcome to stay here."

Yank's expression softened suddenly. "You're a good man and I've missed you," he said, taking Vaughn by surprise.

"I missed you, too, Pops."

Without warning, Yank pulled Vaughn into a bear hug, squeezing him tight. The gesture meant even more because, like Vaughn, the other man wasn't big on expressing emotion or his feelings.

"At least we've started making up for lost time," Vaughn said, stepping back. He eyed Yank carefully, wondering how far to push, then decided to go all the way. "You can't really get back time that's long gone, Yank. Go home to Lola and make things right."

"When you're single too long you get set in your ways."

Vaughn snorted. "You've been set in your ways since the day you were born. Lola knows everything about you and loves you anyway."

"You deserve someone like that," Yank said, pinning him with his blue-eyed stare.

"Yeah, in another lifetime maybe." Thoughts of Annabelle drifted through his mind. She was waiting for him, but she'd understand if he was held up giving advice to her uncle.

"Did I tell you I met your parents while I was in town getting coffee?" Yank asked.

Vaughn stiffened. Now that was one scenario he hadn't counted on. "How'd you know it was them?"

"I was flirting with that pretty girl behind the counter and she laughed 'n said I reminded her of you only older. I said that's because you're my boy." Yank grinned, practically beaming at the notion.

Damned if a lump of appreciation and love didn't lodge in Vaughn's throat. He couldn't speak right now if his life depended on it.

But Yank had no such problem. "That's when I heard it. The snooty voice sayin', *I beg your problem? Brandon's our boy.* I turned to see a woman dressed haughtier than Lola at her prissiest and a man in argyle. From your descriptions in the past, I knew they were your folks."

"And they actually claimed me?" Vaughn asked wryly.

Yank nodded. "Long enough to put me in my place and then once Joanne introduced us, to blast me for encouraging your interest in sports. Like you were a little kid they could mold in their image." Yank shook his head sadly. "I'm sorry they never came around."

Vaughn cleared his throat. "Me, too."

Before either man could say more, Vaughn's cell phone rang, interrupting them. Annabelle was right. There was always one interruption or another around here. No wonder she'd opted for privacy at the lodge. A place he was heading to now.

"Listen, Yank I'm late for an appointment."

"Hot date?" the other man asked.

Vaughn's gaze darted from his. "Sort of."

"Annie must be busy working, so tell her goodbye for me and I'll see her in New York for the party."

"Will do," Vaughn said, feeling somewhat guilty for not telling Yank the truth. But what could he say? *I'm sleeping with your niece?* With a shake of his head, he pushed his uneasiness away and grabbed Yank in a bear hug. "Take care," he said to the other man.

"You, too. See you in a few days."

Vaughn nodded and while Yank headed back to face his problems in New York, Vaughn took off for a promising evening with Annabelle.

AS ANNABELLE LOADED the animals into Vaughn's SUV for her trip back to New York, her heart pounded in her chest and regret filled her. She found it hard to leave Vaughn behind, especially with their night at the lodge so fresh in her mind. She'd intended to take him away from all the pressures in his life and bring him to the one place where he could be himself. Instead she'd found a place where she felt more herself as well. As they'd laughed, playing twenty questions about each other, she'd realized he already knew the answers. The man understood her insecurities and admired her strengths in a way no man had before.

They'd shared the dinner she'd brought along with a bottle of wine and watched the sun set beneath the tree they'd settled under. It was another perfect memory to add to the others. Which only cemented this separation as a darn good idea. She didn't need to get any more attached to the man than she already was.

Their time together had been intimate and special, leaving Annabelle with her needs sated, both physical and emotional. Oh yes, she thought. Distance was very necessary right now. Better she turn her attention to the family fun fest that awaited her. She'd promised her sisters she'd come a couple of days before the party to help with the last-minute details and to shop for something to wear.

"Tell me something," she said as she slammed the trunk of Vaughn's truck closed and tried to sound nonchalant.

Vaughn was lending her his vehicle. He planned to drive down with Nick and Mara the day of the party, so he wouldn't have to leave the lodge for too long a time.

"What?" he asked.

"If this party is something we throw every year, why does it seem to get more complicated and make me more nervous each time?"

He walked her around to the open driver's side door and paused, one hand on the window. "Maybe because this year you invited an extra couple of dozen people?" He brushed her hair off her face. "Which you didn't have to do but I appreciate anyway."

"I know. That's why I did it. For you."

He smiled that killer smile. Not the sinful grin that made her knees melt or the sensual twist to his lips he used on many people but which meant nothing. No, he smiled the one-hundred-percent genuine smile focused on her alone. The one that made her feel alive, special…and even loved. Yet he'd promised her everything but.

Loved.

She blinked into the glare of the morning sun. The morning after she'd spent the night in Vaughn's bed, his arms wrapped tight around her, her animals surrounding her, and when all had been right with the world. Because she was in love.

Love.

Oh, no. She was obviously a complete idiot, she thought. Because she'd gone and done it again. She'd fallen in love when she'd sworn she would keep her heart under lock and key. And she'd fallen in love with Brandon Vaughn of all people, the egocentric, football jock who couldn't see beyond his own self-importance.

Hah. She wished those words were true. If only the description she'd thought pegged Vaughn was accurate, her heart wouldn't be in jeopardy right now.

"Are you okay? You spaced out on me for a minute."

She pasted a sunny smile on her face. "My mind's

already on the trip and everything I have to do once I get to New York," she lied.

"Then you should get going."

"I should."

But he didn't step aside, still blocking her access to the driver's seat.

"What are you doing?" she asked.

"Say goodbye, Vaughn," he said, his voice dropping a husky octave.

"Goodbye, Vaughn," she heard herself repeat, mesmerized by his voice. His compelling gaze. By him.

He leaned in closer. "Goodbye, Annabelle."

I'm going to miss you, she thought but didn't say so out loud.

And when his lips closed over hers, she thought he'd miss her, too.

AFTER GREENLAWN, New York City felt like another planet. Annabelle walked into Barney's to meet Lola and her sisters to shop for outfits for the party. What would normally be a near orgasmic experience for her, since she loved shopping in the extreme, felt like a chore because it didn't involve Vaughn. She knew she had *it* bad.

"Annabelle, darling!" Elizabeth, her personal shopper, met her before she'd reached the cosmetics counter not three feet from the door.

"Hi," Annabelle said, greeting her with a warm, brief hug.

"So good to see you! It's been way too long, so either you're cheating on me or you've repeated the outfits in your closet one too many times," Elizabeth chided.

Elizabeth had dressed Annabelle for events from black tie fund-raisers to afternoon picnics and lawn parties.

Annabelle laughed. "I'm not hitting other stores, I've just been busy."

"Well," she said, linking her arm through Annabelle's, "let me show you some of the special things I've pulled. I spent hours choosing just the right outfits for each one of you so Lola, you and your beautiful sisters will all stand out from the crowd."

"I'm sure I'll love everything," Annabelle murmured.

Elizabeth steered Annabelle toward the private back room. "While we're waiting for the others, tell me who you're working with now."

Annabelle forced a smile. Normally she loved indulging the other woman's taste for gossip about the athletes she worked with, though she never revealed anything Elizabeth couldn't find in the papers. But everything Annabelle felt for Vaughn was fresh and new. Most of all, her feelings and emotions were too private to share.

She hoped her sisters would get here soon and deflect interest off of her. Thankfully within minutes her wish was granted. Lola arrived, followed by Sophie who had a cell phone tucked against her ear and a pad and paper in hand, then Micki who predictably grumbled about having perfectly fine clothes in her closet and wasting her time shopping.

Elizabeth had her hands full getting Sophie's attention between phone calls, and Micki's fondness for pants drove the saleswoman insane. Then there was Lola who shocked Elizabeth by waving a dismissive hand at all of the conservative clothing the other woman had picked based on her past choices.

"Think Sophia Loren," Lola repeatedly said, sending Elizabeth back to peruse her inventory.

Micki shot Annabelle an amused look. "Thank God she didn't say Cher," Micki said, laughing.

By choice, Annabelle went last, content to watch her family and the chaos surrounding them. Normally this was when she was happiest, watching her family interact, laugh and act just like she expected. Normally this made her feel safe and secure. Normally she wasn't thinking about Brandon Vaughn.

Somehow he'd come to mean something to her beyond a fun time in bed. She'd come to understand what made him tick. Knowing that, she chose her outfit carefully with Vaughn in mind and holding on to the knowledge that she had to make a lasting impression because too soon, the police would find the saboteur and Vaughn wouldn't need her for damage control. She'd be able to do her PR from the office and her time with him would come to an end.

ANNABELLE HAD ONLY BEEN gone for two days. Not even a full forty-eight hours and Vaughn's entire mood had changed and not for the better. He was anxious and edgy, and lonely in a way he'd never been before.

Vaughn used to like peace and quiet. He used to enjoy solitude and privacy but no longer. For someone who'd always lived alone and loved it, after having a brief taste of not just company, but what felt like family, he hated knowing he was walking into an unoccupied house. Everything felt empty without Annabelle's vibrant smile and quiet understanding.

Even the silence echoed. Hell, he had to admit to himself, he actually missed the damn cat.

At least the lodge was proceeding quietly for a change. He threw clothes and a few other needed things into a duffel bag and glanced at his watch. Almost time for Nick to pick him up for their overnighter in New York.

Almost time to see Annabelle.

"I THINK THE ONLY TIME Tavern on the Green glitters more is during Christmas in the city." Annabelle plucked a mimosa off a passing cocktail waitress's tray. She turned back around to Sophie and felt the shimmer of air on her bare thighs when her short pleated skirt lifted slightly, then dropped against her legs.

She'd liked the flirty sensation so much, it had been the main reason she'd picked the first thing Elizabeth had shown her. That and the fact that her sisters had begun to focus not on each other but on *her,* and Annabelle hadn't wanted to talk about her relationship with Vaughn. Not even with those closest to her.

Sophie smiled. "You're biased because this is *our* party."

"And what a party it is." Annabelle glanced around the Terrace Room that The Hot Zone had rented for their summer event.

Dazzling Waterford crystal chandeliers hung from

a hand-crafted plaster ceiling, and surrounding them was a glass pavilion overlooking a private garden that they'd rented out as well. To top it all, they had a panoramic view of Central Park on a clear sunlit day.

She took a sip of her drink and licked the fruity taste off her lips. "A good number of Vaughn's foremen and employees showed up," she noted. She was pleased to see them soaking up the festive atmosphere, including the disc jockey playing hits for those who chose to dance.

She'd wanted his employees to take a break from the daily grind, to enjoy good food, drink and a day in Manhattan, and to head home happy to be working for Brandon Vaughn. She'd accomplished her goal and she raised her glass in the air in a silent toast to a job well done.

Sophie's glass clinked against hers. "We just had to switch from the Park Room to this one in order to accommodate the extra people. Luckily this one was available," Sophie said. "So. Where is Brandon Vaughn? I'm dying to meet him."

"He's not here yet."

"Maybe he got caught in traffic. What time did he start the drive?" Sophie asked.

"He didn't say." In truth, Annabelle hadn't asked him.

She hadn't spoken with Vaughn at all in the two days since she'd left town. When she'd called, she'd either missed him at home or at the office. What little business she'd done for the lodge, Mara had been able to handle. Was this how it was going to be from now on? Annabelle wondered, as she polished off her drink.

"I don't remember you as a guzzler." Randy Dalton,

Annabelle's ex-boyfriend and Sophie's current client came up beside them.

Annabelle narrowed her gaze.

Sophie did the same.

"Shut up, Dalton," both sisters said simultaneously.

He stepped closer to Annabelle. "You know I'm sorry, darlin'," he said in that good old Texan accent that used to make her weak in the knees. Now it just made her sick.

"Sorry you cheated? Sorry you got caught? Sorry you dumped me? Or just plain sorry for living, Randy?"

Sophie choked and Annabelle was sure her sister was trying not to laugh.

"Come on, Annabelle. We had absolutely nothing in common and you know it. So it ended sooner rather than later. *I'm sorry.*" He placed a hand beneath her chin. "Forgive me?"

Annabelle looked into the eyes of the man she once thought she'd loved. Those feelings paled in comparison to anything she felt for Vaughn. Dammit, she thought and tried to swallow down the fear *that* particular thought caused her.

Before she could accept Randy's apology or even tell the two-timing snake he'd never meant that much to her, either, someone smacked his hand away from her face.

"Stay away from her, Dalton."

Randy stiffened, poised for a fight just as Annabelle realized she recognized that voice.

"Vaughn," she said, so happy to see him, her soaring emotions should have been illegal.

"So this is the infamous Brandon Vaughn." Sophie's

voice filled with awe. "I've been dying to meet you." She held out her hand. "I'm Sophie Jordan, Annabelle's middle sister."

"The brain and the busybody all rolled into one package," Annabelle said, grinning.

These two important people in her life shook hands, then Vaughn turned to Randy, a scowl on his handsome face.

"I take it you two don't need introductions?" Annabelle asked the men.

"I recognize him from newspaper photos," Vaughn said, his disgust evident. "That's enough for me."

"Man, you're uptight." Randy shook his head and laughed, breaking the testosterone-filled tension. "I know you're retired, but you should really think about still working out. It relieves stress."

"I'll keep that in mind," he said to Dalton, then turned to Annabelle. "You seriously were involved with this guy?"

Annabelle groaned. "How'd you know that?" Because for all the things she and Vaughn had confided in one another, Randy's name had never come up. Just showed how insignificant a part he'd played in her life, Annabelle thought.

"I read the papers."

"And do you always believe everything you read?" She tipped her head to the side and said, "You've had enough experience with reporters to know their stories don't always give the most flattering of portrayals."

"She's got a point," Randy said.

"Shut up," Annabelle muttered.

Vaughn pulled her away from Randy, closer to his side. “I know better than to believe the rags but the fact remains you two were an item, he hurt you and now if he doesn’t stay the hell away, I’m going to hurt *him.*”

Annabelle’s eyes opened wide, shocked at this display of primitive emotion.

“Come on, Randy,” Sophie urged. “Let’s go get a drink.” She pulled at his hand, then gave Annabelle a look of apology. “We’re still working on his foot in mouth problem,” she explained. “Nice to meet you, Vaughn. Maybe we’ll get a chance to talk later.”

In Sophie-speak, Annabelle knew that meant Sophie wanted to grill Vaughn about his feelings. For Annabelle. And that would not be happening, Annabelle thought and glared daggers at her sibling.

“Or not.” Sophie grinned and grabbed Randy’s hand. In fact, she laced her fingers through his in an intimate, comfortable manner as she led him away.

As a waiter passed, Annabelle placed her empty drink on his tray.

“Your sister and Dalton look like they’re an item,” Vaughn said.

Annabelle burst out laughing. “No, Sophie just knows how to work an idiot like Dalton.”

Vaughn met her gaze. “If there was something going on would you be jealous?” he asked, surprisingly real questions in his gaze.

“Heck no!” she answered honestly. “Believe me Randy’s my—”

“Ex. I know.”

She grinned. "Very ex and it's nice to see *you* again," she said, changing the subject. "Make that *very* nice."

Vaughn's smile reached his eyes, as he answered. "It's damn good to see you, too."

"Do you mean that?" she asked, knowing her insecurity was obvious and not caring. "Because if I didn't know better, I'd think you were avoiding my calls."

Vaughn reached out and cupped her cheek in his hand. That was Annabelle, he thought. Astute as always. He *had* been avoiding her, hoping his need for her would disappear.

Seeing her now, he knew that would never happen. For better or worse, most probably worse, she was a part of him. "I mean it," he said gruffly and to prove it, he lowered his mouth to hers.

As he slipped his tongue inside her parted lips, the kiss felt like he'd come home after being away for far too long. Though he was mindful they were in public and her family and invited guests surrounded them, he still poured everything he felt into the one kiss. It seemed to go on and on, neither of them wanting to part again.

"Excuse me." Lola's voice interrupted them.

Annabelle jumped back and as if she were a teenage girl caught making out with her boyfriend, she wiped her mouth with the back of her hand.

Her gaze darted between Vaughn and Lola. "Caught me," she said, laughing.

"Yes but that isn't why I'm bothering you. I need to talk to you and your sisters."

Vaughn immediately recalled the conversation Annabelle had overheard between Lola and her uncle. The one that had caused her to break down. He knew she was hoping that Yank would come around and admit he loved Lola, but the older man was as stubborn as they came. Vaughn didn't hold out the same hope. The possibility of Lola's leaving still remained.

Annabelle's glance darted around the room. "Can we do it after the party?" she asked, ever the professional.

But Vaughn heard her voice crack and saw the struggle to remain composed. She'd already assumed the worst.

Lola grasped both her hands. "I suppose we can, but it's important."

Annabelle nodded. "Okay," she said in a whisper.

"I'll let Micki and Sophie know not to rush out after the party ends." With a last squeeze of Annabelle's hand and a slight nod acknowledging Vaughn behind her, Lola strode off to find Annabelle's sisters.

"Lola was always good at reading my emotions." Annabelle turned to Vaughn. "And just now, I know she picked up on my feelings. She knows I'm upset." Annabelle bit down on her lower lip. "But she chose not to tell me everything will be okay."

"That's because she knows you're strong. You can handle whatever it is," Vaughn said thinking of Yank's degenerative condition.

"I'm going to strangle my uncle." Annabelle shook her head, frustrated.

"You can't change how Yank feels."

"But he loves her! And he's still obviously going to let her just up and leave us!" Her voice rose along with her obvious panic.

Vaughn wrapped a strong, supportive arm around her shoulders. "First, it's his choice to make and second, you're not twelve anymore. Lola might leave The Hot Zone but she'll always be a part of your life. You know that, right?"

Annabelle nodded and drew deep, calming breaths. "I'm sorry I'm acting like a child." She squared her shoulders and lifted her chin.

He was proud of her. "That isn't what I said. Your emotions automatically regress back to your childhood. I'm sure that's normal when you've suffered the loss of your parents. I just want to make sure you view things in their right perspective now."

Annabelle treated him to a grateful smile. "I don't know what I'd do without you," she said and pulled him into a hug.

He inhaled her fragrant scent and emotions swamped him. He refused to answer that comment. He didn't know what he'd do without her, either, but like Yank, everyone had decisions to make.

"So what do you say we enjoy this party and worry about what Lola intends to do later?" Worry about what *he* intended later. He smoothed his hand over the back of her hair, trying to calm her.

"I say it's a deal." She picked up another mimosa from a passing tray and downed it in one continuous gulp.

He wanted to stop her but he sensed she'd need it

for the night ahead. And he'd be there after Lola dropped her news.

There was nothing that could keep him away.

CHAPTER FIFTEEN

AFTER THE PARTY ENDED and the last guest walked out the door, Annabelle joined her sisters as they filed into the small office lent to them by the manager. The cold furnishings didn't bode well for the discussion to follow, Annabelle thought, because Lola wouldn't insist on a family meeting unless something was very wrong. Something beyond her being just ticked at Uncle Yank. And after what she'd overheard at the house, Annabelle knew that something might send her packing for good.

Fear like icy shards of glass spread up Annabelle's spine. "Well that was a fun party," she said, breaking the silence that had surrounded them.

Micki raised an eyebrow. "For you, maybe. You had your super hunk to hang all over and Sophie had Randy the jerk to fawn over her."

"Something wrong, Micki?" Sophie asked, concern in her voice. "Man trouble?"

Their youngest sister shook her head. "No trouble. Everyone likes me," Micki muttered, her tone full of sarcasm and pain. "I'm good old Micki. Ever reliable Micki."

"You sound like a commercial for Eveready batteries."

"Or Timex watches. Micki takes a licking and keeps on ticking," Micki said, trying to make a joke.

Annabelle wasn't buying and from the quirk of Sophie's eyebrow, neither was she. "Talk to us, Mick."

Lola stepped forward. "Come on, sweetheart. You need to unload."

Micki eyed the pitcher of water on the side table. "Anyone want a cold one?"

"Stop changing the subject," Sophie said.

"What do you want me to say? I'm more like the poster girl for Friends than anyone's potential lover and I don't see that changing. Ever."

Though her sister looked pretty in a long ruffled skirt and tank, in her eyes, Annabelle saw frustration and pain.

"You just haven't met the right man to appreciate all you have to offer," Lola said in her calming, motherly voice. "But you will. Which actually brings me to my point for calling this meeting."

Annabelle held her breath.

"As you girls know, I've made myself indispensable to Yank over the years. Always at his beck and call, always there to think so he doesn't have to, and always there to be taken for granted." She met each sister's gaze in succession, as if giving them an opportunity to speak or contradict her opinion.

No one did.

"So what are you saying?" Micki asked, her eyes wide.

"The time has come for me to take a stand. I'm leaving."

Sophie stepped forward, while Annabelle, even though she'd had warning that this was coming, felt paralyzed by Lola's words.

"Leaving how?" Sophie asked, her *I'm smart and therefore untouchable* facade shakier than Annabelle ever remembered seeing it.

Lola placed a comforting touch on Sophie's hand. "I'm leaving The Hot Zone and in doing so I'm leaving Yank."

"But—" Sophie said, shocked by the news.

"But—" Micki yelped at the same time, also clearly upset. "You can't!"

Only Annabelle knew not to attempt to change Lola's mind. Her stubborn uncle had been given plenty of warning. Dancing with the young wives of his clients today hadn't shown Lola she meant a damn thing in his life. Annabelle swallowed hard, then did the most difficult thing ever, second only to acting strong for her sisters when her parents' died.

She walked toward Lola and set the proper example. "I wish you luck," she said, then gave the woman, the closest thing she had to a mother, a long, tight hug. Her light perfumed scent was as comforting as an embrace and Annabelle knew in that moment more than ever that she would miss seeing her every day.

Then one by one her sisters came forward and did the same.

As Lola embraced each girl she loved desperately, she sniffed and her eyes filled with tears. "You're all the best. And I want you to remember that. Also remember this doesn't mean I'm leaving *you.* I'll always be just a phone call away," she promised them.

Lola never wanted to lose touch with these wonderful young women, even if seeing them would arouse painful memories and thoughts of things she should have done differently. And she suspected that it wouldn't be easy to see the girls *and* avoid the subject of their uncle. Still she intended to stick by her decision.

Now she had one other thing to address with them. "I know I'm leaving The Hot Zone in capable hands but there's something you girls need to know. About your uncle." She eyed each of them, wondering how they'd take the news.

She wished she could protect them the way she had when they were little, monitoring their choice of television shows and playmates, bandaging their cuts and kissing away their pain. Adult reality wasn't as simple.

She'd struggled with this revelation. Perhaps it was Yank's information to divulge, but darned if she'd leave the girls in the dark. The Hot Zone was their business and Yank was their only real family. They deserved to make informed choices.

Each would react in their own way, of course. Sophie would analyze but hold her feelings inside. Micki would hover and try to make things better. And Annabelle would internalize the situation, equate Lola's leaving with her parents' deaths, and do everything she could to make peace within their little unit.

Lola shook her head sadly, knowing Annabelle

would probably hurt the most. No, that was wrong. All the girls would be in pain. Only Annabelle would also suffer the accompanying fear.

"Lola?" Micki asked. "What's wrong?"

"Tell us," Sophie encouraged her.

Annabelle remained strangely silent.

Lola drew a deep breath. "Your uncle's been keeping some important information from you and I've decided it's time to come clean."

"The hell you will," Yank bellowed from the doorway.

Lola tensed. She hadn't counted on him joining them but she should have anticipated it anyway.

"Who let you in, you old coot? You have no right to sneak around and listen to other people's conversations." Lola forced herself to meet his gaze. "Why don't you just turn around and take your gyrating hips out the door?" With that, she pivoted around, turning her back on him.

He deserved her cold shoulder. His actions today had merely cemented her resolve to leave and she didn't mind telling him off now. She certainly wasn't worried about holding on to her pride. In an hour, she'd be gone and Yank wouldn't care whether she'd bared her soul or not. But at least she'd leave with the knowledge that she'd done all she could to be up-front and honest and to try to save the life she loved.

"I'm talking to my family," she added for good measure.

"Family?" Yank snorted. "This is *my* family."

His words cut deep, but she held on to her resolve.

"Well these girls are mine, too, and I can have a private talk with them if I choose. Unless you'd like to be the one to tell them everything?" Lola challenged him.

Yank Morgan could bluster and storm around. He could resist her charms and her body if he wanted, but no way could he ever resist a challenge.

Silence reigned. The girls had stepped back toward the wall, giving them their own private arena to play this out. Even Brandon, who'd come in behind Yank, stayed in the shadows. But he met her gaze and gave her a silent nod of encouragement. Brandon was such a good, decent man.

But he'd never known trust and understanding. Would he ever realize Yank considered *him* family? Always had and always would. And then there was Vaughn and Annabelle. What a couple they could be. Lola shook her head, knowing she didn't have time to dwell on them now.

She faced Yank, possibly for the last time. "You're as scared to tell them the news as you are to face the truth," Lola goaded him. "And you're just as scared to make a commitment and I've had enough. Of everything." All the frustration she'd held inside, all her fear for him, all the love he'd never let her show—she'd kept everything bottled up inside and now the cork came loose and her emotions spilled out in mean-spirited accusations.

She hated how she'd been reduced to this level, and that was yet another reason she was finished with this man who didn't love her back.

"Girls," she began, "your uncle—"

"Is going blind," Yank said, rising to the occasion as she'd predicted. "I'm gonna be blind as a bat one day and there ain't nothing you can do about it."

Stunned silence filled the air around them as the girls digested Yank's version of his situation. Which wasn't completely accurate, but that had been Yank's attitude since they'd gotten the diagnosis. Defiant and angry. And hopeless. Unwilling to do anything the doctor suggested to help his situation.

"He's exaggerating as usual," Lola explained to the girls. "But there are issues that will need to be dealt with and since I won't be here, you all need to know everything."

"Harrumph."

"The diagnosis?" Annabelle was the one to ask, ignoring her uncle's grumblings.

"Macular degeneration," Lola said.

Sophie narrowed her gaze. "It's the leading cause of blindness in people over age fifty-five, right? I watched a segment on the Science Channel."

"That's right. But there is help when it's caught early. The reason you girls need to know this is you need to make sure the business doesn't suffer." And she'd taken steps to make sure The Hot Zone stayed as strong as ever. Lola might be leaving physically but her heart would always be here. "I have a plan."

Annabelle stepped in closer as did Micki and Sophie. Yank merely continued to scowl. He probably still didn't believe she was going anywhere. But he'd know as soon as he returned to the office and saw her empty desk.

"What do you have in mind, Lola?" Annabelle asked.

"A merger with Spencer Atkins and Associates. Spencer's already agreed."

"Over my dead body," Yank shouted and stormed out the door without looking back.

VAUGHN SLIPPED OUT of the office where Annabelle's family was arguing like crazy. He'd listened to their dynamics with mixed feelings. On the one hand, he recognized the sounds of arguing. Lola and Yank's bluster resembled the fights he'd had with his father every year. The reason never mattered. The lack of harmony did. His own family never quite connected and the bickering was something he could relate to.

But on a stronger, deeper level, Vaughn felt Annabelle and her sisters' pain on hearing about their uncle's illness. He felt for Lola and understood the hurt she was suffering by being excluded from a family she considered her own. He could empathize so well. Even more, he envied their closeness and caring despite Yank's gruff, obstinate exterior. Even when they weren't getting along, Vaughn knew their love overrode everything else.

And that's when Vaughn had suddenly experienced a sharp, knifelike pain that made him feel like an outsider, much as he did in his own family.

So he slipped back into the hall.

He caught up with Mara and Nick just as Nick was placing his cell phone back into his pocket.

Vaughn knew at first glance something was wrong. "What is it?"

Nick glanced at Mara. Mara looked at Nick. Neither met Vaughn's gaze.

"Fire," Nick said at last, his face pale. He didn't have to say it was at the lodge.

The implication was obvious and Vaughn's stomach plummeted. "How bad?"

"The firefighters are working now, but it doesn't look good for the north end. We need to get back right away," Nick said.

Vaughn gaze shot to the closed office door where Annabelle remained with her sisters and Lola. Yank, he noticed, had found the nearest bar and was nursing a drink. "Yeah. Let me just leave a message and we're out of here." He headed for the old man.

"Don't you want to tell Annabelle yourself?" Mara asked.

Vaughn shook his head. "I'll let Yank know." He couldn't allow himself to see her right now. Because as far as Vaughn was concerned, his obsession with Annabelle had caused him to leave the lodge at a crucial time. With dire consequences.

He'd abandoned his lodge when he knew somebody was out to get him and destroy his dream. And he'd left for a goddamn party to be with a woman who represented everything he wanted but would never have. No. He couldn't let her stand in the way of the one dream that just might come true.

Mara followed him and placed a hand on his shoulder. "You couldn't have prevented the fire, you know," she said, reading his mind.

"But I could have been there when it happened."

And he should have been.

SINCE ANNABELLE had had private time with Lola while she'd stayed at Vaughn's house, Annabelle let her sisters talk with her now, while Annabelle headed straight for her bullheaded uncle.

She found him at the bar, talking to the same bartender who'd served at their party. She glanced at his half empty glass. "Scotch?" she asked.

"Is there anything else?" He downed the glass and pounded it on the table.

The bartender complied by pouring him more. "Miss?" he asked Annabelle.

"Club soda with a wedge of lime, please."

"Sissy drink," Uncle Yank muttered.

"Yeah well I'm a girl so what do you expect?"

He shrugged. "I raised you girls to have balls."

"And thanks to Lola we have feminine sides, too. And because of you both we have big hearts. So what happened to yours?" she asked, not disguising her real feelings.

He slid the unfinished drink across the bar, then turned to face her. "It takes more heart to let someone go than to make them stick around and suffer."

She pursed her lips in thought. It was probably best not to remind him he'd strung Lola along for years without giving her hope of anything permanent. After all, it had been Lola's choice to remain at The Hot Zone despite her unrequited feelings. Apparently now Yank was finally taking into account how his self-centered attitude might affect Lola, too late to do any good.

"That's the dumbest thing I've ever heard," Annabelle

finally said. "If you love someone and they love you, nothing else matters." Wasn't that the reason wedding vows contained the words, *for better or for worse?*

"I'll always be here for you," she assured him. "And if you let her, Lola would be here too." Annabelle rose to her feet and hugged her uncle tight.

"Where are you going? We have Lola's dumbass business proposition to discuss."

Annabelle recognized the subject change. Her uncle's eyes were moist. Maybe on some level, she'd gotten him to think. But she wasn't about to discuss The Hot Zone's future when they were all so emotional or her uncle was on his way toward getting drunk.

"I'm going to find Vaughn." He'd promised he'd be there for her after the family fallout and she needed him now.

"He's gone," Uncle Yank said.

Annabelle turned around fast, certain she'd heard him wrong. "What did you say?"

"Vaughn's gone. He asked me to relay the message." Uncle Yank stared at his drink once more.

"What message?" she prodded.

"Something about having to leave because there was a fire at the lodge." Yank took a solid gulp. "Guess everyone's having a crappy day," he muttered.

He didn't know the half of it.

ANNABELLE HEADED BACK to her apartment, Micki alongside her. No sooner had she unlocked the door and stepped inside than Boris attacked, jumping up and down on his hind legs, his tail wagging like crazy.

"There's nothing like a doggie greeting," Annabelle said as she scooped the white ball of fluff into her arms.

Micki laughed. "I hear you. Find me a man who'll lick my face and breathe in my ear and I'll die a happy woman."

"It's good to know you want so much out of life." Annabelle's grin dimmed. "What's bothering you, anyway? You seemed uncharacteristically grumpy back there."

Micki was the happy-go-lucky sister who rarely complained. It was unusual to hear her gripe, especially after a party.

She shrugged. "I'm just getting tired of being alone, you know? Maybe it's an early midlife crisis. It'll pass, I'm sure."

"Well I'm here for you no matter what."

"And I'm grateful for it," Micki said.

"Speaking of grateful, I don't think I've thanked you for taking care of the apartment for me while I was gone."

Micki swung her lithe body onto the comfy couch Annabelle had purchased from a Pottery Barn catalog. "Not a problem, sis. What's a little plant watering, right?" she said with a touch of sarcasm as she gestured around the living room, her sweeping arm encompassing Annabelle's vast collection of beloved plants. "Anyone ever tell you this place looks like the Garden of Eden?"

"Hah, hah. Is that your way of saying I owe you?"

"Just a little." She squeezed her fingers together.

"Next time you might want to consider getting a live-in plant-sitter."

"Is there really such a thing?"

Micki rolled her eyes. "I was joking."

"I know." Annabelle joined her sister on the couch and released Boris so he could jump into Micki's lap. "And it looks like I'm going to owe you some more. I might have to go back to Vaughn's."

"Annie," Micki groaned, leaning back against the couch. "Do you realize how many times I have to refill the watering can to feed these thirsty monsters?"

"Did you try talking to them? They're usually much more pleasant if you sing 'You Are My Sunshine' while you're pouring water and misting their little leaves."

"Misting?" The color drained from Micki's cheeks. "You never said anything about misting!"

"Joke," Annabelle said, chuckling. She'd missed spending time with Micki while she was away. Nothing beat hanging out with her sisters. Unless she counted hanging out with Vaughn.

She thought about the fire at his lodge and she shivered.

"Whew." Micki wiped a hand over her forehead. "You're really in love, aren't you?"

What had they been talking about? Annabelle tried to remember. Oh, yeah. Her plants. "I love all living things," she said to her sister. "I can even tell you where I got each one of these babies and how long I've had them."

"Impressive," Micki muttered. "But I was talking about Brandon Vaughn. The big, sexy guy in the tan chinos and black Polo shirt today. Remember him?"

"Vividly." Annabelle sighed. From the moment she'd realized Vaughn had not only received more horrible news about the lodge, but that he'd chosen to leave for home without her, she'd been torn up inside.

On the one hand she told herself that by letting her handle her crisis while he took off to handle his, he'd done the only practical thing. On the other hand, he could have told her in person if for no other reason than he was paying her to handle public relations. And a damaging fire would desperately need PR. Yet he hadn't come to her.

And her gut told her that his reasons had nothing to do with business or with allowing her personal space. His avoiding her had everything to do with creating distance between them.

"Hello?" Micki tapped on Annabelle's head with her knuckles. "Where did you go?"

Annabelle kicked her feet up on the table. "No place pleasant."

"Let's start at the beginning, shall we?" Micki suggested.

Annabelle nodded. "Might as well."

"You love him?"

She nodded, refusing to meet her sister's knowing gaze. "And before you say a word, it's not the same as the other times." She knew her sisters thought she gave her heart too easily and too fast, and maybe in the past, she had. This time was different.

"How do you know?"

"I could name a bunch of reasons," Annabelle said.

"Like?" Micki scooted closer. "I really want to know."

Annabelle let her thoughts drift to Vaughn and how he made her feel. "Like how when I'm with him I know I'm safe. I'm not so focused on the past and what I don't have in my life. And it isn't all about sex." Even though that was incredible. "It's so much more than that. But there's one more reason I know this is more real than ever before."

"You've got me hooked."

Annabelle forced herself to meet her sister's gaze. "Because I care more about what he needs than what I want. How else would you explain the fact that when I should be in Greenlawn doing my job, I'm home debating with myself whether or not he wants me there?"

Micki nodded. "Like I said, you're in love with him. So are you going to sit home and feel sorry for yourself or are you going to go after the one person who actually completes you in this damn lonely world?" Micki asked as she absently scratched Boris's scruffy head.

Annabelle rolled her eyes. "Someone's been watching *Jerry Maguire* again."

"And a certain someone else seems to be too afraid of abandonment even to try and tell a certain sexy ex-football player how she feels." Micki raised an eyebrow, subtly daring Annabelle to face her deepest fears.

Annabelle had risen to every obstacle life had thrown her way. Micki was right to challenge her now.

Annabelle scooped Boris out of her sister's arms and stood. "We're going back upstate," she told the squirming dog. "And Micki's going to plant-sit while we're gone."

CHAPTER SIXTEEN

THE MORNING AFTER the fire, the dank smell of smoke still permeated Vaughn's office just as it did in his dreams. The officials pinpointed the source of the fire as a lit cigarette and if not for the previous incidents of sabotage, this would merely be classified as an unfortunate accident. But it was anything but an accident.

Meanwhile nobody was admitting to smoking or seeing anyone light up on the premises. They didn't have to. Detective Ross had just turned to Vaughn and asked one question. Did Laura smoke?

She hadn't when Vaughn had met her. She'd started later on. The detective had immediately set out to find Laura's whereabouts last night and it turned out she didn't have an alibi. Agitated from the credit problems she was having, Laura said she'd taken a sleeping pill and crawled into bed. Alone. All night long. The police continued to follow up leads but Ross was convinced Laura was the culprit.

Vaughn couldn't buy into the theory. Divorce and ugly words were one thing. Outright destroying him was something else and Vaughn just felt sick.

"Earth to Vaughn."

He turned to see Annabelle standing in the office doorway, a breath of fresh air in an otherwise sooty, smelly place. She wore her trademark miniskirt but, thanks to the combination of construction and fire damage, she'd traded her flimsy sneakers for bulky sheepskin boots. In pink to match her bright lipstick and skirt. Enjoying the combination, he let his gaze travel downward. Damn but she had sexy legs no matter what she wore.

And he vividly remembered those long limbs wrapped around him as he drove deep inside her body. He shivered at the memory and a sudden realization struck him. He'd never have enough of her.

Ever.

Though he recognized his obsession with Annabelle had taken him away from the lodge at a crucial time, he couldn't deny he was glad to see her now. So much so that even Laura's potential betrayal didn't affect his trust of or feelings for Annabelle.

"Hi there." He welcomed her with a big grin.

"Mind if I come in?" She didn't smile in return.

He shook his head. "Not at all."

"Where is everyone?" she asked as she stepped inside and glanced around the otherwise empty office.

"Nick's with the insurance guy and Mara's home sick today."

She placed her purse down on Mara's desk. "I dropped Boris off at the house. I didn't want him inhaling the smoke."

"Not a problem."

She seated herself at the desk farthest from him and

he suspected she was taking her cues from him. His biggest one being that he'd left her alone in New York City after promising he'd be there for her after her family meeting. He'd gone over that move in his mind and still wasn't sure whom he'd been protecting, but he suspected if he looked deeply enough he wouldn't like what he saw.

"Look, Annie—"

"What's the damage assessment and what do the police say?" she asked, briskly cutting him off.

He cleared his throat. Talking about the lodge hurt badly, the pain slicing through him each time he thought about it. It hurt almost as much as her cool demeanor did now. "The bad news is that the north section is completely destroyed."

"Oh, Vaughn." She reacted instinctively, the sympathy and caring in her gaze and in her tone overwhelming. Touching. Comforting in a way he needed badly. She rose from her seat and he could almost feel her arms around him. Then just as suddenly she sat down, obviously rethinking her decision as she clasped her hands tightly in front of her.

Something inside him froze as he realized he'd caused the change. He'd pushed her away. Leaving her in New York had seemed prudent at the time but he hadn't expected to feel so empty now.

"What's the good news?" she asked, all business.

Thrown by his emotional reaction to her distance, he decided business was best. "As you can see, no damage to the main part of the lodge. We'll have to rebuild what's been destroyed and we'll lose a good number of bookings as a result, but because there are rooms in the main section, too, we can still open on time."

"That's fantastic!" she said, her voice rising, her pleasure obvious.

He was nearly drawn in by her enthusiasm until he realized she'd grabbed a pad and a pen and had begun to take notes and scribble down ideas. Deep in PR mode, she'd found a damn good way of avoiding discussing anything personal between them.

She glanced up. "Any solid leads on who might have started the fire?"

"The police think Laura's the best suspect. She has no alibi."

Annabelle frowned. "I don't know. That sounds like an awfully flimsy tie in to me."

"Yesterday I'd have agreed with you. Today I'll grasp any lead or possibility if it means this being over." He swept his arm around him.

She nodded in understanding.

"It's like this person is either a genius or so damn lucky it defies description. Either way he—or she—is winning." He slammed his hand against the desk as he'd done too many times before.

"Interesting analogy." She cocked her head to one side. "Do you look at everything in terms of win or lose?"

"Pretty much."

"Do you think the person responsible views things the same way?"

"Meaning?"

She tapped the pen against the desk. "Well, it's similar to Detective Ross's theory. Laura wouldn't want you to win while she's suffering defeat." Annabelle paused in thought. "I just wonder if whoever's doing this thinks maybe you took something away from them and so they're trying to take something from you in return."

He frowned. "If that's the case, Laura or not, I'm definitely being hit where it hurts."

As she listened to Vaughn's reply, she wondered if the lodge wasn't just his most obvious weak spot, but his *only* one. Certainly nothing else in his life mattered to him as much as the lodge.

Did any*one* matter as much? Could anyone?

She licked her glossed lips, trying not to let her emotions show as she performed her job. After all, her reasons for being in Greenlawn revolved around Vaughn's need for PR support. When that need ended, she would return home to New York since any supplemental work could be accomplished from there.

She'd waited until this morning to return because professionally, that was the smartest time to begin work. Though she'd taken Micki's advice and not run from her feelings, the initiation of anything personal between them would have to come from Vaughn. She'd met him halfway by coming here at all.

She reached into her bag. "I've prepared a press release I need you to okay." She handed him the paper with the words she'd come up with while working late into the night. "If you have any changes, let me know."

"I will. Thanks."

She rose from her seat and pulled her keys from her purse.

"Leaving so soon?" he asked, sounding surprised.

"I assume you've done no food shopping since I've been gone?" The fridge was near empty before she'd left for New York.

"That would be a good assumption."

"I figured as much. So even though it's not in my job description I'm going to see to it you're well fed." She could also use some breathing space that didn't include the smoky air and Vaughn's imposing presence.

She couldn't be surrounded by the devastation from the fire and not be compelled to take him in her arms and tell him she understood his pain. That she'd be there for him always. Suddenly she understood why Lola had decided to pack up and leave. Except Annabelle refused to devote a lifetime to unrequited love.

Vaughn made her want on so many different levels she couldn't name them all. He also knew how to withhold, thereby deepening her yearning. His parents had taught him not to count on anyone and to withdraw when things were tough. She hadn't had parents to teach her a damn thing.

She wondered where that left them now.

AFTER LEAVING THE LODGE, Annabelle stopped at Vaughn's to pick up Boris. She placed him in his carrier and headed for town. Now that she had her car, she also had the freedom to explore and she took advantage.

She passed the high school and its legendary football field, since renamed Brandon Vaughn field. She drove by Vaughn's parents' house and was struck by the fairytale quality of the house and its surroundings, the white picket fence, daisies blooming all around and the veranda with a porch swing built for two. How could two people, two *parents,* live in such a perfect place to raise a child and turn his life into an unhappy, unhealthy nightmare? she wondered sadly.

Instead of making a right turn, which would take her directly into town, she drove the long way around the outskirts just so she could pass Vaughn's present residence. The house he'd purchased so he could have peace, quiet and space. But the house gave him none of those things and merely reinforced all that was lacking in his life—unlike the warmth of the lodge, which filled at least a portion of the aching emptiness he had deep inside.

She thought she understood him a little better now. The desire to keep himself apart from the family that hurt him had led him to buy on the outskirts of town. The never-ending hope that those parents would come around kept him from making his home somewhere far away. But he'd chosen the most unwelcome home he could find and had done nothing to make it warmer. Not, she suspected, because he didn't know how, but because never having experienced love, he was too afraid to embrace it. She pulled into the parking lot of the supermarket, no closer to figuring out how or if Vaughn would ever come around.

Before she'd barely stepped out of the car she heard someone call her name. She glanced over her shoulder, shocked when she realized Estelle Vaughn was waving and striding toward her, a welcoming smile on her face.

"Looks like things are about to get interesting," she whispered to Boris whose head stuck out of the carrier so he could look around.

"Miss, um...Annabelle, I'd like to have a word with you."

Annabelle turned and waited for the other woman to walk over. "What can I do for you?" she asked Vaughn's mother.

"Would you like to get a cup of coffee?" she asked, taking Annabelle by surprise. "There's a place just around the corner. My treat."

She added the last quickly, as if she was afraid Annabelle had been about to say no.

"I suppose food shopping can wait." She treated his mother to a welcoming smile, hoping to ease her obvious discomfort. "I hope you don't mind Boris here." She swung around to show the dog's sweet face.

"Oh! Well, no. Not at all." She reached out tentatively.

"Go on. He doesn't bite."

Mrs. Vaughn patted Boris on the head and he responded by attempting to crawl out of his carrier.

"Stay," Annabelle said.

Five minutes later, she found herself seated in Cozy Cups across from Estelle, as she'd asked Annabelle to call her. Joanne was obviously attempting to listen shamelessly but incoming customers kept her too busy to remain near their back table.

Annabelle wrapped her hand around the frozen

Macchiato she'd ordered and waited to hear what Estelle had to say, but the other woman merely sat and unnecessarily stirred her coffee, staring into the dark liquid.

Annabelle decided she had no choice but to break the ice and begin conversation. "Nice weather we're having," she murmured politely.

"Is Brandon okay?" Estelle asked right after. "I woke up this morning and heard the news of the fire. I've been trying to reach him all morning. Nobody's picking up the phone at the lodge and I've left half a dozen messages on his answering machine at home. I've been worried sick and so has his father."

You see, Annabelle silently said to Boris. *I told you this was going to be interesting.*

"He's fine. In fact he was nowhere near the fire because he was in New York City at my firm's party last night," she assured Vaughn's mother.

"Oh thank goodness." She looked visibly relieved, her shoulders relaxing and her tension easing a bit.

"If it makes you feel any better, I doubt Vaughn's been home much since last night and the lines are down at the lodge. The phone company hopes to have things up and running by tomorrow at the latest." Though Annabelle doubted Vaughn would make any effort to return his parents' calls regardless.

The other woman nodded, obviously grateful for any information.

"Have you tried his cell?" Annabelle asked.

Estelle shook her head. "I don't have the number." Obviously embarrassed, she didn't meet Annabelle's gaze.

Annabelle poked her straw into the creamy liquid in front of her while she tried to figure out how much to pry into Vaughn and his parents' relationship. Since his mother had sought Annabelle out, she decided to dig deeper than she probably should.

"Pardon me for commenting on something so personal, but it seems to me you care about Vaughn a lot more than you let on."

"Of course I care!" Estelle said. "He's my child."

"Then why not show it?" Annabelle couldn't help but challenge Estelle's assertion, but she softened the blow with a personal revelation of her own. "My parents died when I was twelve," she began.

"How awful!" Estelle patted Annabelle's hand awkwardly, then withdrew her touch.

Obviously maternal caring wasn't her forte. Annabelle wondered if she even realized her shortcomings.

"I'd have given anything to have my parents around while I was growing up," she continued. "Instead I had my Uncle Yank and Lola, two people who did their best to compensate for my loss and give my sisters and I lots of love and attention."

Estelle's eyes brightened with curiosity. "You have sisters?"

"Two. We're all very close."

"Theodore and I couldn't have any more kids after Brandon." Estelle's voice dropped to a whisper.

Annabelle wasn't sure whether to offer condolences or thanks that they couldn't subject another child to neglect the way they'd done to Vaughn.

"I'm not used to explaining myself to anyone, but

you seem genuinely fond of Brandon and for that reason, I'm going to try."

"I do care about your son."

Estelle drew a deep breath before beginning to talk. "I'm not sure if you know this but I'm what you'd call from the wrong side of the tracks. My father ran off and my mother cleaned homes for a living. When I met Brandon's father he was studying to be a professor. Imagine my shock that he fell in love with me! I was so grateful I promised myself I'd do everything I could to support him and make certain he succeeded."

"Because if he succeeded, you succeeded," Annabelle guessed without much difficulty.

"Exactly. With Theodore I have respectability, a solid home, and the love of a good man. Everything I was denied growing up."

Annabelle noticed she didn't mention a loving family or a wonderful son but she refrained from commenting.

"Then Brandon was born and he was the most wonderful child." Love sparkled in her eyes at the memory.

"Until he started school?" Annabelle guessed.

Estelle blushed and at least had the grace to look ashamed. "I didn't know anything about dyslexia or learning disabilities. The teachers said he was antsy, that he didn't pay attention. As he got older, his grades were poor."

"And he was a disappointment to his father." Annabelle pushed aside her cup. The sweet drink would only make her feel sicker.

Estelle inclined her head. "Theodore never understood Brandon. He was an academic while his son was an athlete. The two never mixed."

"Did Theodore even try? Did *you* try to find a common bond between father and son?"

She shook her head. "I'd carved out my path a long time before. I was the supportive wife. I guess I let being a mother come second and I failed at it." Her voice dropped an octave, her ever-present pride nowhere to be found.

On impulse, Annabelle reached out and took the woman's hand. "Look, it's not my place to judge the past. But you seem to care now. Maybe it's not too late to take steps to repair your relationship."

Heaven knew, Vaughn would benefit if his mother took even baby steps toward a normal family life and offered some sort of acceptance from at least one of his parents. Not that Annabelle expected him to welcome any overture immediately, but anything good in life took time.

"Every time I try he closes me out."

"I'm going out on a limb here, but did you ever think of accepting who he is and what he wants out of life?"

Estelle leaned back in her seat, silently thinking for a moment, and then sighed. "You're a wise woman and I hope my son realizes how lucky he is."

Annabelle murmured a thanks and opted not to touch the statement. Her problems with Vaughn weren't anything a conversation could solve.

As Estelle rose to leave, Annabelle popped the top off the drink and let Boris lick the frothy top. As she was getting ready to leave, she caught sight of the construction crew from the lodge coming in for their coffee, Roy at the head of the pack.

"He wasn't at the party," Annabelle realized aloud.

"Excuse me?" Estelle turned.

"Oh. Nothing important. I just realized that Roy wasn't at my firm's party in New York City." She explained to Estelle why she'd invited Vaughn's work force and the woman seemed impressed with her way of thinking.

"Would you like to walk out with me?" Estelle asked.

Annabelle shook her head. "I think I'll let Boris finish the drink while I talk to Joanne for a bit."

"Well I'm so glad we had this opportunity to chat. And I appreciate your honesty, young lady."

Estelle walked off, leaving Annabelle alone.

She patted Boris on the head. "Will wonders never cease?" she asked aloud. She'd never thought Estelle would come around and she prayed Vaughn could find it in his heart to do the same.

Not in the mood to talk to Roy, Annabelle started for the door but he called out her name, giving her no choice but to acknowledge him.

"Hi, Roy." She waved and kept walking.

"Don't go. At least let me buy you a drink for the road. The boss would never forgive me if I wasn't nice to his lady. Besides it's hot out there and something cold will wet your whistle."

Annabelle had no desire to have a drink or anything else with Roy and since the rest of the men had been served and since left, she wasn't about to hang around with just him.

She shook her head. "No, thanks, I just finished an iced coffee."

Unfortunately he didn't take a hint and strode up to her, getting into her personal space. "So how's it going?" he asked.

"Fine." She forced a smile. "Why did you miss our party last night?"

He glanced from side to side and looked uncomfortable as he fumbled for an answer. "I—uh—"

"Was your wife under the weather?"

"My son, actually. Injured his wrist playing ball at the last practice," he said, warming to his subject. "Vaughn said Todd's a natural just like Vaughn would be a natural college coach. He'd guarantee my boy entry into the pros, that much I know."

"Vaughn's the best," she agreed, but she was unable to get his first statement out of her mind. His reason for missing the party was a bald-faced lie. "I saw the last football practice. Nobody got hurt."

Roy paled and glanced at his watch. "I gotta get going. Work calls."

She nodded in understanding. "You must be busier than ever between the last break-in and now the fire damage."

"Like I said, busy, busy." Roy stepped backward in a sudden rush to leave.

Since she hadn't been the one to initiate the conversation, Annabelle let him go. She stopped at the counter for a brief conversation with Joanne before heading outside.

Just in time to see Roy puffing on a cigarette beside

his car. And for a brief second, his gaze met hers. Right before he dropped the butt and ground it out beneath the toe of his boot.

ANNABELLE'S THOUGHTS spun more quickly than the tires on her hooker mobile. Roy. Cigarettes. Fire. She needed to talk to someone about her suspicions, but immediately dismissed Vaughn from her list.

He had enough on his mind without having to cope with her half-baked assumptions about his head foreman, too. And surely that's all they were—ridiculous assumptions about a lecherous but otherwise harmless man. Still, needing someone to bounce things off of, she drove directly to Mara's apartment and began to bang on her door.

She heard sounds from inside but nobody answered. She knocked louder.

"Okay, okay, maybe I should just give you a key after all." Mara yanked the door open wide. "Annabelle," she said, clearly surprised.

"I guess you were expecting Nick?"

Mara ran a hand through her disheveled hair. "Yeah. Well no I wasn't expecting anyone, but with all the banging, I thought he'd come back. Never mind. Come in." She waved Annabelle inside.

She walked into the small but pretty apartment with enough windows to provide lots of sunlight and enough plants for Annabelle's liking. "I'm sorry to barge in when you're home sick but it's important."

Mara shook her head. "It's just a cold. I woke up with it this morning. But between the fire, the smoke and all, I thought I could get more paperwork done here. What's up?"

Annabelle twisted her hands together, feeling ridiculous. "It's about the fire. The marshalls said it was caused by a cigarette, right?"

Mara nodded.

"Let me ask you something. Did you know Vaughn's ex-wife?"

Mara shook her head. "They didn't live in town but from what I understand, she was a mistake he hates to talk about. Why?"

"The police think she could be a suspect but I have another idea I need to run by you."

"Shoot."

"If you count everyone we sent invitations to, who didn't show up last night?"

"Hmm. Let's sit down a minute so I can think. Want something to drink?"

"No, thanks."

Mara poured herself a large glass of orange juice and joined Annabelle at a small white kitchen table. "It's hard to know since it was so last minute. There were no place cards and no official RSVP was required. Off the top of my head, the only two noticeably missing were Roy Murray and Fred O'Grady. Fred's wife went into labor and the only time Roy's predictable is when he's hitting on women or pushing his son's athletic agenda."

Annabelle nodded. "See? That's motive right there," she said, her voice rising.

"What's motive? And for what?" Mara sneezed.

"Bless you."

"Thanks." Mara grabbed a tissue from the box she'd been carrying around with her. "Have Kleenex will travel," she said laughing. "Now talk to me. What are you thinking?"

"You have to promise not to laugh."

Mara nodded. "Swear."

"Well, I ran into Roy at the coffee shop. I wanted to leave, he tried to buy me a drink, I said no, but he made me stay and talk. Until I mentioned he'd missed the party. Then he couldn't wait to be gone."

Mara rolled her eyes. "There's no doubt about it, Roy's an odd duck."

"But there's more. He lied about why he wasn't at the party and when I walked outside he was grinding a cigarette butt into the ground." Her stomach jumping, her nerves rioting, Annabelle tapped her fingers against the Formica tabletop.

"Look, I understand why you're upset, but with Roy it could be as simple as the fact that he was cheating on his wife last night and doesn't want to get caught." Mara paused to blow her nose. "Rumor has it Roy's wife told him if he strayed again, he'd be out on his ass and she'd file for sole custody. And you know how much his son means to him."

Once again, Annabelle's hunch was strengthened. "That's just it! If the lodge were destroyed, Vaughn would be free to take the coaching job. It's Roy's dream for his son to go pro and he thinks the boy needs Vaughn to do it."

Mara frowned. "Even without the lodge, Vaughn

wouldn't take that job. He'd rather help in his own way."

"You know that. I know that. Any sane person knows that, but is Roy sane?" Annabelle pressed her fingers against her pounding temples. "I just don't know what to do with this theory of mine. I'm afraid the police will laugh me out of the building, and Vaughn and Nick have enough on their plate without me adding stupid ideas to their list of problems."

"Obviously you don't think it's all that stupid or you wouldn't be this upset," Mara said softly. "And really how much more lame is your idea than blaming Vaughn's ex-wife?"

Annabelle bit down on the inside of her cheek. "If I do something about it and I'm wrong, I've accused an innocent man. Innocent of arson, anyway. His cheating is a foregone conclusion. But if I'm right about the fire and I say nothing, the lodge is still at risk."

Mara touched her hand. "The lodge is at risk until *whoever* it is is caught," Mara reminded her.

She rose and shook her head. "It's probably my imagination acting overtime. I'm going to go."

Mara stood. "Annabelle, wait. You're upset. Let's talk some more."

"You need your rest. Besides, Roy was going back to work. I can talk to him there. I need to get a feeling one way or another before saying anything to Vaughn. Besides both Vaughn and Nick are watching everyone right now. It'll be okay," she said as much for Mara's benefit as her own.

"Well I'm here if you need me."

"Would you watch Boris for me?"

Mara nodded.

"Thank you. And don't worry." Annabelle forced a smile. "It'll be okay," she said, hoping to convince herself and relieve the gnawing gut feeling that just wouldn't disappear.

CHAPTER SEVENTEEN

VAUGHN RUBBED HIS FISTS against his burning eyes. He hadn't slept in over twenty-four hours and was so exhausted he could barely concentrate. Yet hours after Annabelle had left his office, he still couldn't stop thinking about her. He had financial statements to go through, he would have to put thousands of his personal money into the lodge to keep it afloat, and yet the only thing on his mind was Annabelle.

She never ceased to surprise him. From showing up here this morning, to covering any emotional reaction to his disappearing act the night before, to making sure he had food in the fridge, the woman simply blew him away. So much so he hadn't had the heart to tell her he wouldn't be home to share meals because he planned to live, eat and sleep at the lodge until the culprit was caught. He'd just have to arrange to have the contents of his full refrigerator delivered to him here. As for Annabelle...

He reminded himself he couldn't afford any more distractions if he didn't want to end up bankrupt, his dream gone up in smoke. Literally.

"The insurance adjuster thinks we'll recoup enough to rebuild," Nick said as he strode into the office.

Vaughn glanced up at his partner and friend. "That's good news. In the meantime I've arranged to liquidate some stock and CDs to cover us until the money comes through."

Nick nodded. "I've done the same."

Vaughn blinked, startled. "You already put in the amount of cash we agreed upon. I'm not going to let you—"

"Shut the hell up, will you?" Nick shoved his hands into his front pockets. "We may not be equal in all things, but I can damn well help out my partner in a crisis. It's *our* investment," he reminded Vaughn.

Not wanting to insult his best friend and too grateful to speak anyway, Vaughn merely nodded.

Nick headed for his desk and they worked in silence for a few minutes, until Vaughn couldn't hold in his thoughts any longer. "What did you mean when you said we may not be equal in all things?"

Nick didn't lift his head from the paperwork in front of him. "Never mind that."

Vaughn thought back over the last few weeks. To things Nick and Mara had said and done, and to Annabelle's accusations against Nick when she'd first come to town. "You can't possibly think you aren't my equal in all ways, Nick." There weren't many people Vaughn would give life and limb for but Nick was one of them.

Nick tossed down his pen and glanced up. "Do you not realize? You're a living legend. In the eyes of the ladies and this town, you're the man."

Vaughn couldn't help but smirk at the ridiculous

irony. He was a man who looked in the mirror and saw inadequacy day in and day out. Football had been his only salvation and those days were long gone. He didn't know how to explain any of this to Nick though. "I'm nobody's hero. Just ask Estelle and Theodore," he said wryly.

Nick grinned. "Hell, if *you* thought or acted like you were God's gift, I wouldn't be in business with you. I wouldn't consider you like a brother. Now can we drop this? I feel like a whiny kid and that does nothing for my self-esteem."

Vaughn let out a laugh. "We're a pair."

"That we are."

Both men turned at the sound of footsteps just outside the door. "Oh good, you're both here." Mara burst in, out of breath at a dead run.

Nick stepped forward, catching her before she practically fell. "I thought I told you to stay in bed," he said, his gruff voice barely disguising his concern.

She rolled her eyes. "This is important."

"Ever heard of a phone?" Nick growled.

"It's not working," Vaughn and Mara reminded him at the same time.

"Have either of you seen Annabelle?" Mara asked.

"Not me," Nick said.

At the sound of Annabelle's name, Vaughn cocked an eyebrow, on instant alert. "She went food shopping last I heard. Why?"

"Well she came by my apartment earlier and she was very upset. She had this theory about the sabotage and the fire. It involved Roy." Mara went on to explain

Annabelle's hunch regarding Roy, backing up her instinct with motive and opportunity.

Vaughn knew the man also had easy access to the job site.

"Why didn't she come to me?" he asked aloud.

Vaughn didn't think the theory was as far-fetched as Annabelle might believe. In fact the more Vaughn mulled things over, the more he realized that Roy as the culprit made more sense than Laura if only because he had opportunity. Then again, the man's only crime they knew of was cheating on his wife, which was a far cry from arson.

"Annabelle didn't go food shopping," Mara said, interrupting his thoughts. "When she left my apartment a little while ago, she said she planned to talk to Roy. She asked me to watch her dog so she could come here."

An uneasy feeling trickled along Vaughn's nerve endings. He strode to the window and glanced out to the parking lot. "Damn. Her car's there. Where's Roy scheduled to work this morning?"

Mara checked her clipboard. "Pre-fire he was overseeing the repairs to the last round of sabotage. Today things are so off schedule, he could be anywhere."

Vaughn began barking out orders. "Nick, check the north section. I'll take the main section. Mara, you stay here. And call the police. My gut tells me not to blow this off as some sort of asinine theory."

ANNABELLE FOUND ROY in the main section, working with the men who were repairing the damage. He stood by a stack of boxes he was opening with a box cutter. She stepped carefully into the construction area, grateful she'd worn her Ugg boots instead of heels. As she marched in, all appraising eyes turned her way.

Used to attention, she trained her gaze on her target. "Roy, I'd like to have a word with you."

He glanced around at the stares of the other men. "Take a break, boys. The pretty lady wants to talk to me."

The room emptied out. "What can I do for you?" he asked, stepping too close to her.

The stench of cigarette smoke and body odor assaulted her but she didn't want to risk offending him by backing off. "I just thought you and I could finish our conversation from this morning."

"I don't have anything else to say." He folded his arms across his chest.

"That's not like you. How about we talk about your son?" She chose his favorite topic, knowing he'd couldn't stay silent for long.

"What about him?" Roy asked warily.

"I thought we could revisit how much he'd benefit from Vaughn's taking that coaching position."

Roy tossed the box cutter onto a windowsill and Annabelle breathed easier. He rolled his head from side to side as he contemplated her topic. Finally he nodded. "So I'm not the only one who thinks it. Vaughn's life is football. He ought to make coaching a full-time job."

"So you thought you'd make your point, right?" she asked gently, hoping Roy was more delusional and misguided than violent. "You thought if you could just get Vaughn frustrated enough to give up on the lodge, he'd come to his senses and coach."

Roy narrowed his gaze.

"I *know,* Roy. When I saw you smoking, it all clicked into place."

"You're just a dumb broad and you don't know what you're talking about." He spat on the floor by her feet.

She stepped backward. "Unfortunately for you, I do. What do you think would happen if I gave the police the cigarette butt you crushed outside Cozy Cups and they compared it to the one they found at the fire's point of origin?" she asked, hoping she sounded sure of herself when she was anything but.

For one thing, she hadn't picked up Roy's butt this morning, and for another, she had no idea how a fire marshall determined what started a blaze. She didn't even know if they'd found the actual cigarette butt at the lodge. The only thing she was suddenly certain of was Roy's guilt.

His current pale coloring confirmed her already strong hunch. "Talk to me, Roy. Because you seem like a decent man. You love your son and you want what's best for him. Nobody can fault you for that."

His hands shook as his bravado and arrogant demeanor began to falter. "I didn't mean for it to go so far."

"I know you didn't." She reached out a hand but he didn't take it.

"Do you really understand? 'Cause all I meant was for little things to happen. Like missed deliveries, people not showing up for work. Even cutting the wires before the inspection was ingenious, wasn't it?"

"I'm not sure I'd call it that," she murmured.

Roy wasn't really listening. Though his expression was sheepish, his eyes glittered with barely veiled pride at his plan. "I knew I could get the place up and running again after that damage but I figured I wouldn't have to. That Vaughn would see he was meant to coach and that the lodge was nothing but one big hassle and not worth the headaches."

Annabelle nodded. "But it didn't work, did it? Vaughn was more dedicated to his dream than you thought, so you decided to torch the whole thing and end it once and for all?" Her mouth ran dry at the thought.

"Hell, no!" Roy said, actually affronted.

From the corner of her eye, Annabelle saw Vaughn approach and quietly enter the room. She couldn't signal him to remain silent so she kept focused on Roy and prayed Vaughn would stay in the background.

"What really happened last night? Tell me so I can help you."

Roy's hands waved fast and furious as he tried to explain. "It was supposed to be a small fire. Just a warning. A final frustration. But the wood's dry and it caught faster than I thought. By the time I got to my car to call the fire department from my cell phone, the north side was nearly gone and the fire engines were roaring in." He shook as he explained. "I never meant for it to be so bad. I felt so guilty and—"

Vaughn chose that moment to move forward. His boots creaked against the floorboards.

Roy lurched around, took one look at the man he admired staring at him as if he were pond scum, and all Annabelle's hard work drawing him out vanished in an instant.

In the second it took for Annabelle to look from Roy to Vaughn and back again, Roy had reached for his box cutter and pulled her tight against him.

She froze at the realization a frightened man had a blade against her throat.

"I never meant it to go this far. I swear I didn't." Roy's voice shook and Annabelle didn't know whether it was his sweat or tears she felt against her skin.

Vaughn raised both his hands in blatant supplication. "Do not do anything stupid, Roy."

"You mean don't do nothing dumber than what I've done so far? Tell me you didn't hear everything. That this bitch didn't set me up by bringing you here."

"I didn't!" If anything she'd gone out of her way to avoid telling Vaughn until she was sure.

"Shut up." Roy pulled her tighter against him. "I gotta think and I can't think when you're talking. It's like my wife. Talk, talk, talk."

"I agree with you on nagging women, Roy." Vaughn looked paler than Annabelle felt at the moment. "Come on. We've known each other a long time and you'd never intentionally hurt anyone."

She felt Roy nod but he was tense and his knife was still against her throat. She shut her eyes and assessed her situation. Her legs were too close to Roy for her to get a good kick in. She had one arm locked between her body and Roy's.

"I'm so sorry," Roy muttered. "One day I think you're incredible for all you do for my kid and the next

I'm so jealous I could spit because Todd loves you and can't stand being around me." He'd begun to ramble.

Vaughn still stood, hands in front of him. "That's not true and you know it. All kids go through a period when their parents embarrass them. I remember it, don't you?"

Roy was silent.

"And I understand Todd because I'm dyslexic, too. Did you know that?" Vaughn asked Roy, admitting his biggest weakness to this man. "And I'm sure that's why he thinks he can talk to me. But it doesn't leave you out in the cold, Roy. You're his *dad*."

"I am, aren't I?" Roy asked, sounding almost dazed.

With the man's focus on Vaughn, his idol, Annabelle took a deep breath for courage and with her hand, she grabbed him by the balls and squeezed hard.

He yelled in pain and Annabelle let her body go slack so she fell out of his arms and to the floor at the moment he let her go.

VAUGHN'S GAZE NEVER LEFT Annabelle's and though she caught him off guard, he dove for Roy, knocking him to the floor and wrestling him for the weapon. He'd taken control of both the box cutter and Roy at the same time the police barged in. They quickly took over, leaving Vaughn free to go to Annabelle.

She glanced over his shoulder to where the police were subduing Roy with handcuffs and reading him his rights. "Don't hurt him," she called as the police led him away.

"Don't you think you ought to be worrying more

about yourself than Roy?" Vaughn asked her as he pulled her to her feet. "And what the hell were you thinking by confronting him alone?" he asked her, all the fear he'd felt on seeing Roy grab her descending upon him.

"I know how much damage he caused but he isn't dangerous. He just needs psychiatric help." She stared at him, those deep blue eyes begging him to understand.

He doubted he could invest that much faith but he wasn't about to argue over it either. "You call holding a box cutter to your throat not dangerous?"

"I think he just panicked. And I—"

"Didn't believe in me enough to come to me with your theory? You didn't think I'd trust you or your instincts?"

She shook her head. "Don't be ridiculous. I didn't want to burden you with a crazy notion that might not be true. You had enough to worry about, what with the police suspecting Laura, her asking you for money, and the lodge still at risk." Annabelle sighed and lifted her hand to her neck.

For the first time he realized she'd been grazed by Roy's blade. He reached out and touched a finger to the reddened skin bruising her flesh.

"He hurt you." The thought caused anger and a primal feeling of possessiveness to sweep through him. As if no one had the right to touch this woman but him. Ever. Such an instinctive desire to protect and to cherish was as alien to him as love.

Love.

Love?

"I'm really okay," she said, unaware of the emotional turmoil taking place inside of him.

"Vaughn?" Nick interrupted, coming up beside them. "The cops want a word with you and Annabelle."

"Not now. She was hurt and shook up. I'll bring her by to talk to them later."

"But I'm fine," she insisted.

He ignored her protests and grabbed her hand. "We're going home." He wanted, no needed, to see for himself how fine she was.

ANNABELLE HAD NEVER seen Vaughn in such an intense, dark mood before. And though she won the argument and they gave their statements to the police before leaving the lodge, she let him take charge afterward. Despite that she was more than okay, he insisted on leaving his car and driving hers back to his house for her. If she didn't know better she'd think the incident with Roy had shaken him up more than it had her.

They drove home in silence and Annabelle assumed he was contemplating the unexpected resolution to his problems. A man he'd trusted had turned on him.

But at least now he was free to finish the job at the lodge without worrying about sabotage or delays—and without the need for further crisis management from her. Beyond a statement that they'd succeeded in catching the culprit as they'd anticipated they would all along, Annabelle's job here was complete. If Vaughn wanted basic PR for the lodge, she'd be happy to continue working on his behalf but she didn't need to do that from here. Her heart squeezed tight as she accepted the fact that it was time to go home.

They walked into the house and Vaughn kicked the door closed behind them. Because things had wrapped up so quickly, she hadn't had time to run a few more ideas by him and she wanted him to know there was so much more he could do to make his dream for the needy kids a success.

He'd been so quiet, so withdrawn, she hadn't looked at him straight on since they'd arrived here and was almost afraid to do so now.

"Listen, I had one more idea I'd like you to let me implement," she said, talking fast and not turning to see his face. "Since I doubt the college will release the names of its students for a mailing, I've put together a letter and a brochure suggesting your hotel for their lodging needs during the school year. You can ask the college to send it out with their welcome package to the families."

When he didn't answer, she forced herself to turn and face him, possibly one last time. He stood leaning against the wall, studying her in silence. He still had that dark, brooding look and she couldn't see past the mask he'd put in place or read the emotions deep inside.

Her heart pounded fast and furious and her chest hurt at his lack of expression. Was he pulling back because their work and time together was over and he didn't know how to tell her to leave?

Without any clue from him, she grasped on to her business proposition. "If you don't like the college letter idea, we can just call it a day—"

With a low growl from deep in his throat, he stepped forward and, shocking her, he pulled her into his arms.

Once again Annabelle didn't argue with the man. After all, these were probably the last moments with him that she'd have. So when his lips came down hard on hers, Annabelle shut her eyes and gave herself up to sensation. She wanted to feel everything he did to her and imprint it on her memory, to last her for years to come.

He brushed his lips back and forth over hers, tantalizing and arousing her with each seductive caress, but the teasing wasn't enough. She thread her fingers through his hair, tugging his scalp and pulling him closer until he backed her up against the wall. His body flush with hers, her breasts pressed hard against his chest while his solid erection thrust between her legs.

She sucked in a breath and rolled her hips from side to side so his hard member created friction that built, waves of desire rocking her body. He thrust his tongue inside her mouth, mimicking the action they both so desperately desired while his hands wreaked havoc with her breasts. Over her shirt, beneath her shirt, she couldn't keep track of all the sensations buffeting her body.

She wanted him now and began to tug on his jeans in an effort to free him so he could push inside her and fill her the way she wanted. Needed.

"Slow down, baby," he murmured as his lips slid over the sensitized skin of her cheek.

She shook her head. "The hell with slow." She reached between them and pulled her T-shirt over her head and tossed it onto the floor.

His heavy lidded gaze met hers before traveling lower. As he took in the lace covering her breasts and taut nipples, his pupils dilated and his eyes glazed over. She had him now and while he watched, she reached up and released the front clasp of her bra, then slowly, teasingly parted the cups, revealing her full, aching breasts for him to see.

"You think you can tempt me into moving at your pace?" he asked in a voice gruff with desire.

She straightened her shoulders, thrusting her breasts toward him. "I don't know. Can I tempt you?"

He cupped her breasts in his hands, his warm flesh palming her heavy mounds and then he lowered his mouth, encircling one nipple with his tongue. His touch reverberated between her thighs, the emptiness more engulfing than ever before.

With deliberate care, he teased her with his teeth, then with his silken tongue slowly lapped at the same place he'd grazed. Different textures, different feelings, but one thing never changed. He took his time, until her hips bucked and she writhed with the need to have him fill her hard and fast.

"You made your point," she gasped. "You have way more control than I do."

He raised his head, his dark gaze meeting hers. "That wasn't the point I had in mind."

She leaned her head against the wall, trying not to weep or beg. "Then what was it?"

"That I can't resist you. *All* of you." He picked her up in his arms and carried her down the hall to his bedroom.

After laying her on the bed, he pulled off first one

boot, then the other. Next he slid his hands beneath her short skirt, letting his palms skim her thighs as he hooked his fingers in her panties and pulled them down and off her legs.

"I'm really not into slow, either." He stood beside the bed and undressed quickly before rejoining her on the mattress where she'd propped herself against the pillows. Then as if to prove his words, he moved between her thighs and lifted her, unveiling her to his heated stare.

Her own gaze was just as hot as she took in his erection. Long and hard, the head of his penis was poised at her moist entrance. She pulsed there, dewy and empty, her desire for him surpassing the physical. She was in love with him. But she feared if she said the words aloud, she'd scare him away for good.

She was an open, honest person, as she'd told him from the beginning, and she didn't plan to leave without making her feelings known. But she wasn't about to frighten him off before she'd expressed those feelings in the ultimate act one more time.

His hands pushed her skirt up higher. His palms then encircled her thighs, his deep stare never leaving hers at the same time he thrust deep, giving her absolutely everything she physically needed.

Emotionally she wondered if she was always destined to lose.

Buried deep in Annabelle's body, looking down at her beautiful face, Vaughn understood that he'd never made love before. Not like this. The distinction between that and sex had never been so great. But he knew he couldn't handle that emotion at the moment when the rest of his life was in pure upheaval.

He pulsed inside her, feeling her slick walls around him. He needed her now and she was here, alive, unharmed and all his. Lacing his fingers through hers, he raised her arms above her head and eased himself out of her body, then in. Out and in. Until they picked up the rhythm that was all their own and he lost himself in everything that was uniquely Annabelle.

Afterward they slept, woke and ordered in dinner, and made love once more. To Vaughn's relief, not once did Annabelle look for any sort of deep discussion or insist they dissect their feelings.

As she slept beside him, he felt the clock ticking away. Now that Roy had been arrested, there was no need for Annabelle to remain in Greenlawn. Though he'd need her expertise to get the lodge up and running, there was no unknown crisis to contemplate dealing with the next morning. She could treat him like any other client and return to work from her Manhattan office. The thought caused his stomach to twist in tight knots.

If he'd read the emotion in her eyes correctly, there was every possibility that with one word from him, the right word, Annabelle would stay by his side. But he needed to have the courage to believe. Believe someone like Annabelle could invest in him for the long haul and not be disappointed in the end. Obviously much of his past still haunted him but Annabelle wasn't just anyone and his heart told him to trust in her. He just didn't know if he could believe that deeply in himself.

ANNABELLE DRESSED and stood beside a sleeping Vaughn. Her bags were packed and loaded in her car. The animals, including the cat who loved to sleep on Vaughn's pillow, waited for her to start the long drive back to Manhattan.

Her heart pounded hard in her chest as she leaned down and brushed a kiss on his forehead. A deep sleeper, he rolled over but didn't wake up. She smiled and studied his profile for the last time.

He was such a good man. He'd even bared his greatest embarrassment to Roy in an effort to make the man understand why Todd would bond with Vaughn more than his father. He'd done it to save Annabelle's life. She'd loved him before and she loved him even more now.

Unlike the other relationships where she'd invested emotion but gotten nothing back in return, Annabelle couldn't regret a minute of her time with Brandon Vaughn.

But during their brief relationship she'd learned much about herself, not the least of which was that no matter how much she loved, she wasn't going to follow in Lola's footsteps. She wasn't about to spend her life pining for a commitment from someone who felt too unsure to provide one.

She reached out and stroked his cheek. "I love you."

She thought he smiled or maybe she just wished he had. Either way Annabelle had enough self-respect to walk away now with her head held high.

She could survive without Vaughn, even if she wished she didn't have to.

CHAPTER EIGHTEEN

VAUGHN AWOKE and discovered Annabelle was gone, leaving him alone in his large bed and even bigger house. He couldn't think of a day that had started worse. The words *I love you* rang in his ears, but he didn't know if they were real, a figment of his imagination, or part of a foolish dream.

He stormed through the house in a foul mood. He checked her room only to find she'd packed and taken everything that belonged to her. Natasha the rabbit was gone as was the cat who'd begun to curl up on top of Vaughn's pillow whenever he was around. A quick phone call told him Annabelle had even stopped by Mara's to collect Q-Tip, a sure sign she didn't plan on coming back.

He ought to be pleased that his life was back to normal. He had a truckload of work ahead of him if he wanted to step up the construction schedule. He'd never make up the time lost caused by the fire but at least he wasn't waiting for the next incident of sabotage. And he no longer had Annabelle here as a tempting distraction.

Vaughn's head pounded and he slung back two aspirin, then called Nick for a ride to the lodge where he'd left his truck. Half an hour later, the doorbell rang and though Nick was early, Vaughn went to let him inside.

Instead he had a shock waiting for him when he opened the door. Estelle stood on his front step with a bag from Cozy Cups in her hand.

His headache increased. "Hello, Mother. What brings you by?" Because Estelle's visits were few and far between. To come bearing food was even more unusual.

"I heard about the awful incident at the lodge. That dreadful man pulling a knife on poor Annabelle. She must be so shaken up. I came to see how she was doing. And I brought both of you breakfast." She offered him the bag, shifting from foot to foot, clearly as uncomfortable as he was with this surprising visit.

"Annabelle's gone." Certain Estelle hadn't planned to stay long, especially now that she knew he was the only one home, he didn't ask her to come in.

"Oh my, she went to work already? She's certainly made of strong stuff."

"Annabelle's gone back to New York." He ran a hand through his hair. He was exhausted and his mother was the last person he wanted to deal with at the moment. "Look, I don't know what your angle is or what you want with Annabelle, but she isn't here, so you can turn around and go home."

Estelle drew a visibly deep breath. "But *you're* here and I'd like to come in and share breakfast," she said, her voice trembling.

Vaughn narrowed his gaze. She wanted to have breakfast with him? "What's going on?"

She blinked. "Did Annabelle tell you we had coffee yesterday?"

He took the news like a punch in the gut. "No, she didn't. But we didn't have the chance to talk much." They'd done everything but talk.

And like a fool, he'd been ridiculously relieved at the notion. Yet he didn't miss the irony that Annabelle apparently talked in depth to his mother, a woman who'd never bothered to talk much to *him* at all.

Vaughn studied Estelle, really seeing her for the first time. She seemed more subdued, less uptight and arrogant than usual. What had caused the change, he didn't know but something made him step back and gesture for her to come inside.

Feeling awkward—he couldn't remember having breakfast with her as a teenager—he poured two glasses of orange juice, the only drink left in the house since Annabelle had never made it to the store. Then he sat down across from his mother.

"The fire changed a lot of things," Estelle said at last.

Vaughn raised an eyebrow but didn't reply.

"We—and I do mean *we*—panicked. Your father and I couldn't reach you by phone. He drove up to the lodge but you weren't there, either. At that point the firemen didn't know if you had been inside." She spoke, her voice low and subdued.

"I wasn't in town. Annabelle's firm threw a party and I was in Manhattan."

His mother nodded. "Annabelle told me. And I realized I didn't even have your cell phone number. What kind of mother am I?" She didn't meet his gaze.

Vaughn didn't know how to answer her question. "We don't understand each other, that much is a fact. And I'm not sure you ever bothered to try. Or to accept that I wasn't the kind of son you wanted."

The words burned the back of his throat but he forced himself to say them anyway. Not with hatred or anger this time, but as a means of baring his soul and maybe cleansing himself of the bad feelings he'd harbored for so long.

"That's all true," she admitted, shocking him. "Your father had dedicated his life to academia and I'd dedicated my life to him. An athlete wasn't... didn't—"

"Fit into your plans," he finished for her. "Neither did a kid with a learning disability, but that's what I had. That's who I was," he continued, his voice rising as he spoke. "It's not a goddamn choice I made to make your lives more difficult." He slammed his hand against the tabletop and started to rise.

Then catching sight of his mother's glassy eyes and hearing Annabelle's voice in his head saying, *give her a chance,* he forced himself to remain seated.

"I was wrong," Estelle said. "*We* were wrong. We didn't know any better. I'm not making excuses, Brandon. Your father was raised that way by his father before him and you've seen where my parents came from. I was lucky to get out and not end up washing someone's toilets for a living like my mother did." She reached for a napkin and blotted her eyes. "But as I said, we were wrong and you paid the price. So did we, missing out on celebrating all your achievements and accomplishments because we had tunnel vision."

He pressed a hand to his pounding temples. "I don't suppose I made it any easier," he admitted. He'd been a pain-in-the-ass kid from the moment he'd realized he didn't understand school and never would.

Amazingly she laughed. "No, you didn't. But it wasn't your job to make our lives easier. It was ours to be more accepting. Now I'm not saying peace can come overnight or that we can all just wave a wand and forget the past and our differences, but I was hoping maybe we could try. You know, make a start toward trying to be a family."

Damn, but he just didn't know. Old habits were hard to break. Old resentments even harder.

"I don't know where to go from here," he admitted.

"I'm just glad we made a start." Rising, she offered him a tentative smile. "I'm glad I took Annabelle's advice."

Her words caught him up short. "What advice?"

Estelle shook her head. "Nothing specific. Just some words on how to bridge the gap between us. She's a very special woman, Brandon."

They hadn't discussed girls when he lived at home and he felt ridiculous starting now. Especially since he'd let this particular special woman walk out of his life without a word from him to try and stop her.

He started to lead Estelle to the door when he paused by the kitchen counter and scribbled on a sheet of notepaper.

"Before you go," he said, feeling more off-kilter than he could ever remember. "Take this."

She accepted the paper and looked at him questioningly.

"It's my cell phone number."

Her look of gratitude said it all.

THREE DAYS AFTER leaving Vaughn behind, Annabelle sat in her office sorting through a stack of messages and piles of important documents. For an hour, she tried to concentrate but thoughts of Vaughn and their time together continued to intrude. Missing him was enough to distract her but the thumping that had started from her uncle's office next door was driving her insane.

The entire atmosphere here had changed because, true to her word, Lola had packed up and gone, leaving The Hot Zone in the hands of temporary help. There never would be a good time for Lola to quit and without her presence, the office felt vacant and empty. At her desk sat the third temp in as many days. Competent or not, each woman had quit after one of Uncle Yank's yelling tantrums.

Another loud thump sounded from her uncle's office. Annabelle picked up the phone and buzzed for their new assistant but nobody answered. She tried Sophie next.

"What's up, Annie?"

"That's what I want to know. Can you come in here?"

Sophie entered the office seconds later and shut the door at the same time another loud, jolting sound came from next door.

"That!" Annabelle pointed to the wall adjoining her and Yank's office. "What the hell is going on in there?"

Since Lola's departure, which had coincided with

Annabelle's return, Yank had been more out of sorts than usual and Annabelle had no intention of checking things out on her own.

Sophie shook her head. "You really don't want to know."

"Yes, I do. Just break it to me gently."

Before Sophie could explain, Annabelle's office door opened and Micki stormed inside. "I can't take it anymore!" she screamed.

Since Micki's office bordered Yank's on the other side, Annabelle didn't have to ask what her sister meant.

"Shut the door and join us," Sophie said, then turned back to Annabelle. "Uncle Yank is in his office and he's practicing."

"Practicing *what?*" Annabelle asked, wincing even before she heard the answer.

"Being blind. He's got a bandanna tied around his eyes and he's trying to see if he can navigate his office."

"Oh my God." Annabelle laid her head down on her desk and groaned. She raised her gaze and looked at her sisters. "Wait a minute. I've done Internet research on macular degeneration. There are some very promising treatments and it could be years before he has a serious vision problem. Am I right?"

"Completely correct," Sophie said. "In fact, he may retain much of his peripheral vision. Right now he's operating on pure fear."

Micki nodded. "Lola's leaving didn't help, not that I blame her. The man's impossible! I think we should keep him blindfolded until he admits he needs and loves Lola. Then he'll be reasonable again and we can deal with his eyesight and the future of the agency."

Annabelle rolled her eyes. "If only it were that simple," she murmured. "Sometimes a woman's love isn't enough. Sometimes a man hasn't been given the foundation to enable him to express his feelings in return."

Sophie cocked an eyebrow, then strode over to Annabelle's desk. Leaning down, she got right into Annabelle's face. "Are you talking about Uncle Yank or Brandon Vaughn?" she asked bluntly.

Annabelle dropped her head against her desk once more. *"Argh!"*

"She's talking about Vaughn," she heard Micki say.

Annabelle peeked up from above her folded arms. "I really blew it this time. Me, Miss *I Can Handle Him Without Getting Attached,*" she said wryly. "Not a chance."

"I'm sorry, sis." Sophie shot her a sympathetic glance. "Can I take that to mean you're over Randy, though?" she asked, her expression showing she cared just a little too much about Annabelle's response.

Annabelle glanced from Micki to Sophie. "I knew it. Even Vaughn sensed it at the party. You *are* involved with him, aren't you? Sophie, are you insane? I couldn't care less about Randy but I'm worried about you." She cocked her head. "Besides I thought you didn't like athletes."

"I don't." Her sister glanced at her long fingernails. "That's what makes him safe."

"Sophie," Micki groaned.

"What? Did you think I could be around all these guys and never, well, you know."

Annabelle glanced at her sisters, grateful for their closeness, even grateful for their disagreements. As long as they had each other, they could weather outside storms.

And Vaughn was Annabelle's most turbulent.

Another loud crash followed. They forgot the girl talk and ran for Yank's office. Annabelle got there first and opened the door to find he'd knocked his private black phone off its special stand with a cane he held in his hand.

"Dammit!" He ripped a ridiculous-looking pink bandanna off his eyes and tossed it to the ground. Blinking as his eyes adjusted to the light again, he looked at the girls. "To hell with the cane. Annie, call and get me one of those Seeing Eye dogs," he yelled at her.

"This is ridiculous. You don't *need* any of these things," Micki yelled as if he were losing his hearing, not his eyesight. "You need Lola!"

"I don't need anyone. Annie, you gonna get me a dog or what?"

She rubbed her hands against her pounding temples. "You hate dogs that shed," she reminded him, buying time.

"I just read about a new breed," Sophie said, spouting from memory at a really bad time. "It was bred for blind people who have allergy issues but still need a canine companion."

"Uncle Yank isn't blind," Annabelle reminded her. "And we're going to set up appointments with specialists to understand his condition before we do anything drastic." Like get the man who couldn't make a commitment a dog that he'd have to take care of for a good ten years or more.

"What's the breed called so I can look into one myself?" Uncle Yank asked.

"It's a Labradoodle," Sophie supplied with a smile. She often got so caught up in her explanations that she forgot the important things going on around her. Like the fact that they didn't want to encourage their uncle's behavior.

This time Annabelle leaned backward, so she could hit her head against the wall in complete frustration. Because despite the utter family chaos surrounding her, one important question floated in her brain.

If Vaughn were here, what would he do in order to get through to Uncle Yank? It seemed no matter how hard she tried, all roads led back to Vaughn. Too bad those roads seemed to be full of potholes, including the fact that he hadn't called her. And she didn't know if he ever would.

EVERYTHING WAS frigging perfect, Vaughn thought. So perfect that the construction and reconstruction crews didn't need him to oversee every small step anymore. In the one short week since Roy's arrest, everything that had been failing before fell into place now.

Laura had called to thank him for helping to bail her out of the financial mess she'd gotten herself into. She wasn't even upset that the police had grilled her and looked into her business. She was just grateful everything was over now. She even accepted his criticism on how she'd screwed up the bars and his advice on how to whip them back into shape. *You're smarter than I gave you credit for, Brandon,* she'd told him. Unbelievable.

Then there was Todd. The kid was devastated about his father's involvement in the lodge's problems and even more messed up now that the man was being evaluated by a psychiatrist and would probably do time either in a hospital or jail. Vaughn had made it his mission to see that Todd remained on track both for football and his last year of high school. After all, that's what had motivated Roy, no matter how misguided he'd been.

But with everything running smoothly now, Vaughn could actually afford to take time for himself. And what did he normally do when he had free time? He picked up the phone and dialed Nick's cell.

The phone rang and rang and just as he was about to hang up, Nick's voice came on the line. "What the hell do you want, Vaughn? And it better be important."

"Did I catch you at a bad time?"

"Uh, you could say that."

Vaughn heard giggling in the background and Mara's distinctive whisper to Nick.

"I don't suppose you want to go get a beer?" Vaughn asked, feeling like an ass and an unwanted third party at the same time.

"Give me the phone," Mara said in the background.

What sounded like a wrestling session followed as Nick and Mara struggled for control of the receiver.

"Vaughn?"

"Hey, Mara. I guess we know who's gonna wear the pants in the family."

"Ha, ha, ha. Now shut up and listen. How are you?" she asked.

He scowled. "I'm fine."

"Oh, really? Is that why you're calling Nick to go for a beer at seven o'clock on a work night?"

"What the hell's wrong with that? We always go for a beer after work."

"That was before Nick had me in his life. What, or should I ask who, exactly do you have in your life, Vaughn?"

For the love of— "Put Nick back on the phone."

"I can't. He's busy." She giggled and whispered something that sounded like "Cut that out."

"I get the point, Mara. Nick's whipped now. No more boys' nights out." Vaughn paced his small kitchen.

"I'll ignore that. I'm serious. You've got your lodge and your volunteer work and the kids you help practice on the side, but what's your personal life consist of?"

Before he could answer, Mara kept right on going. "In other words have you spoken with Annabelle?" she asked, getting to the crux of things.

"Way to tread lightly," Nick called out in the background.

"Well have you?" Mara asked Vaughn.

"No," he grumbled, more irritable now that she'd pointed out his life's shortcomings.

Mara groaned. "You're an idiot, Vaughn. And if you aren't careful and you don't do something soon, you're going to end up alone."

Vaughn let out a hard exhale. "Jeez, thanks for being a friend."

"I am your friend and you know it. I love you and I don't want to see you screw up the best thing to happen to you. She's special, Vaughn."

He raised his gaze to the ceiling. "Now you sound like my mother," he muttered.

"You've been talking to your mother?" Mara asked sounding stunned. "Nick, Vaughn's been talking to his mother!"

"Don't go hiring a skywriter to announce it or anything."

"That's a fantastic idea!" Mara's voice rose in excitement.

"Hey. Don't get carried away."

"Both of you listen. We should hire one of those airplanes with a banner to advertise the lodge! I'll put it on my list of things to do."

He nodded. "Sounds like a plan. Since you two are busy, I'm gonna let you go."

"Promise to think about one thing for me. If you're talking with your mother, you've made strides you don't even realize. And remember, you're just as special as Annabelle is," Mara said.

An awkward silence followed.

"So don't let her get away," Mara said before Vaughn heard the click ending their connection.

And leaving him alone.

So alone, he climbed into his truck and took a ride to the football field where it had all started. His career. His life. It was the place he'd first found something he excelled at and where he felt worthwhile.

During and after a game, the cheers of the crowd had

always sustained him, but never enough to compensate for the fact that his parents weren't in the stands. He thought he'd come to terms with that. Just as he thought he'd come to terms with misjudging Laura and how she'd belittled his abilities. But had he come to terms or was he still running away?

He couldn't believe the way he'd come full circle. He'd made peace with everyone from Yank to Laura, and had even made strides with his parents. He'd suffered through an awkward family dinner, one where everyone had discussed what was going on in their lives and actually acted interested in each other's answers. Both his mother and father had proclaimed to accept the lodge as Vaughn's dream for the future.

A dream, he realized, that wouldn't mean a damn thing to him if he had to live it alone. Without Annabelle.

Yet to bring her into his life, he had to know he believed in himself. That he *had* come to terms with everything. Which meant an end to the running. Running from both the boy he'd been and the man he'd become.

He parked his truck and walked to the field which was as empty as his house felt with Annabelle and her pets gone. As he stared over the vast landscape, he couldn't help but take Mara's words to heart.

Was he just as special as Annabelle? Worthy of her love and spirit and generosity? He didn't know if he'd ever completely believe in himself that way but, dammit, *she* did and for Annabelle, for them, he had to try.

ANNABELLE WALKED into her uncle's office. He greeted her with a loud catcall, followed by a frown. "Go home and change. No niece of mine is going out of the house dressed like a damn floozy."

Annabelle grinned and twirled around. "What's wrong with Oscar de la Renta?" she asked of her pale pink, strapless cocktail-length dress. "Sarah Jessica Parker wore this dress. I saw the picture in *Vogue* magazine."

He snorted. "I don't care if Sarah Bernhardt wore the damn thing. You'll have the young buck drooling. The twins are fallin' out, for God's sake," he muttered, speaking of her breasts.

If she hadn't grown up with his frank talk, she'd blush now. "I have a very supportive bra. It's fine. Can we change the subject, please? So tell me, have you spoken to Lola?" she asked him.

"Have you spoken to Vaughn?" Uncle Yank shot back.

"Nice comeback," she said through clenched teeth. "I came by to look through the list of people who'll be at the event tonight. I like to know who I can hit up for client coverage."

Tonight was a party hosted by Oakleys and covered by Entertainment TV. She'd gotten a ticket to the A-list event for a new client she'd recently taken on—a young baseball player who'd been brought up from the Minors and who would benefit from meeting key sponsors. He'd asked her to join him.

At first she'd declined. She was through with men and though she'd sung this tune once before, she meant it even more now. Because now she understood the difference between ego bruising and devastating heartache.

Thank you, Brandon Vaughn.

But she wasn't an antisocial person and she wouldn't be happy sulking in her apartment every night. So here she was, covering her hurt by attending a charity event with a client. The man wanted arm candy and arm candy was what she did best. In the meantime, she'd make and renew contacts to help all clients of The Hot Zone.

A win-win situation if only she weren't so unhappy inside.

"What are you doing here so late?" she asked her uncle.

He glanced down. "I got nothing better to do."

Annabelle knelt beside his chair. "Call her. All Lola wants is you. That's a simple, easy thing to give if you feel the same way in return."

He patted her head like he used to do when she was a little girl. "When'd you get to be so smart?"

"Same time you got to be so stubborn. Just think about it, okay? Lola doesn't want perfection. She just wants you." Hearing her words, Annabelle laughed and jumped back before Uncle Yank could react to that comment.

"I love you, Annie," he said gruffly.

"I love you, too."

His smile faltered as he said, "If Vaughn hurt you I'm going to go after him with my Mickey Mantle Louisville Slugger."

Annabelle shivered. Vaughn had swallowed too much of his pride and made too much progress with her uncle to lose ground because of her.

She shook her head. "Vaughn's fine. The job ended and I came home. That's that."

"Bull. I know something was going on between the two of you."

Not for the first time, Uncle Yank actually made her blush. "Well I was the one that ended it, not him," she lied. "If anyone's hurt, it's Vaughn not me."

Uncle Yank nodded slowly and Annabelle hoped he accepted her answer.

He might never know it, but Annabelle considered that fib her farewell gift to Brandon Vaughn.

CHAPTER NINETEEN

VAUGHN SHOWERED, changed and drove into Manhattan, arriving late at night. He'd long since finished with the city scene but just knowing Annabelle was here gave him a jolt of anticipation and excitement. For the first time in his life, he allowed himself to admit that he needed someone and he was damn well going after her. But he had one obstacle to overcome first.

He stopped at Yank's New York apartment, then the old guy's favorite sports bar and even Lola's place, with no luck. Finally he pulled into The Hot Zone's building, and seeing Yank's vehicle in his VIP spot, Vaughn headed up the elevators. He didn't know why the older man would be here so late at night but he figured that, like Vaughn, Yank was running from his fears.

The elevator doors opened and Vaughn stepped inside. The reception area was lit with its fluorescent lights but devoid of people. The other offices were dark except for Yank's, squelching the hope he might find Annabelle here as well. Vaughn supposed it was for the best though. He had business to take care of here first.

He rapped on the door to make Yank, who was

dozing with his feet propped up on his desk, aware of his presence.

Yank snapped to attention. “I’ve never seen those panties before,” he said as he dropped his legs to the floor and sat up straight in the chair.

“Sounds to me like you got caught cheating once or twice in your life,” Vaughn said laughing.

“Oh, hell. I was dreaming.” The other man ran his hand over his scruffy beard. “Every man’s worst nightmare, you know? It’s come more often lately,” he muttered.

“It’s guilt,” Vaughn said with certainty. “You let the woman of your life walk out and you can’t live with it.”

Yank waved for him to come in and have a seat. “I’m gonna assume that’s yourself you’re talking about, my boy.”

Vaughn let Yank appraise him with those all-knowing eyes. “You’d be right,” he admitted.

“I knew Annie was lying through her pearly whites.”

“What’d she say?” Vaughn asked as he leaned forward in his seat.

“That you didn’t hurt her, she hurt you when she dumped your ass back in Greenlawn. But I knew better. I could see in her eyes she was protecting you, not that you deserve it you lowlife, sorry excuse for a—”

Vaughn held up a hand to stop him. “I think we’ve been here before. And I’m not going to argue with you this time either. I just want to make things right.”

“Just how do you propose to do that?” Yank asked.

“By going after Annabelle. But I had to come to you first.” Embarrassed but certain, Vaughn shoved his hands into his jeans pockets. "You're like a father to me and I'm sorry I screwed you all those years ago. I'm grateful to have you back in my life now. To prove it, I'd do anything you asked of me except for one thing. I can't leave Annabelle alone. I love her, I need her and I want to marry her," he said in a rush, getting the words out before he lost his courage.

Yank rose and strode up to him, glaring. "You won't leave her alone. Well isn't that swell."

Vaughn's mouth grew dry. The last thing he wanted was to make a choice between his mentor and the woman he loved but there'd be no contest as to who would win. Unlike the beginning of their relationship when he'd sworn to himself he'd keep his hands off Annabelle, Vaughn refused to walk away from her now.

"I have one question," Yank said, sounding good and pissed.

"What?"

"Who the hell *asked* you to stay away? As I recall, I told you my niece needed a good man. One who'd care for her and not abandon her because that's her greatest fear." Yank shoved Vaughn's shoulder with one hand, pushing him hard. "When I said those words I meant that *you* were that man. But true to form, you didn't see yourself that way. Never have, never will." He snorted and shrugged. "Actually that's probably what makes you such a decent guy."

A good man. Vaughn shook his head in disbelief. "Are you saying you *want* me with Annabelle?"

"Give the man a cigar," Yank said laughing. "It takes you a while but at least you aren't permanently dense.

So are you going to sit here talking to me all night? Or are you going to rescue Annie from that baseball player who isn't out of diapers yet?"

Vaughn narrowed his gaze. "What baseball player?"

Yank shrugged. "All I know is she was dressed to the nines and her twins were hanging out."

"Twins?" Vaughn asked but he was afraid he already knew what Yank meant.

"Um, juggs, boobs, breasts, for God's sake," Yank muttered. "This is my niece so can we keep it clean?"

Vaughn rolled his eyes. He'd seen Annabelle dressed for big-time events and knew exactly what her uncle meant. "I'm guessing she's gone out with a client, so just give me the address, okay?"

He remained calm because he knew better than to think Annabelle would go out with another guy so soon after leaving him. But that didn't mean he liked her attending anything with another man, especially with her twins on display.

Yank handed him a sheet of paper with the address. "Go get her, *son*."

Vaughn choked up. He'd waited years to have Yank call him that again.

Yank pulled him into a bear hug and when Vaughn stepped back, he grabbed Yank's arm. "I love you, Pops, and I want you to enjoy your life, not sit around alone at night feeling sorry for yourself. So if I'm going to go after Annabelle, you'd better go after Lola."

Yank shook his head. "I had my chance years ago and I blew it."

"Stubborn old man. I'll deal with you later," Vaughn promised. "Right now I have a lady to rescue."

And that lady had captured not just his heart but everything Vaughn was.

As he headed back for his car, he replayed his talk with Yank in his mind, one part in particular. His heart pounded hard in his chest as he recalled Yank telling him that Annabelle had defended him to her uncle.

Vaughn couldn't get over that fact. She'd told Yank she'd broken up with him when it was completely untrue. Yeah she'd left him in Greenlawn, but he knew damn well it was because she wanted to avoid an awkward goodbye, because she also knew he wouldn't be asking her to stay. At the time she'd have been right. Yet knowing Yank would skin him alive if he knew Vaughn had hurt her, Annabelle had looked out for his relationship with her uncle anyway.

Vaughn hadn't been looking for proof of her love or commitment to him. He'd come to New York without either and he would have laid his soul bare for her and risked all the protective barriers he'd spent years erecting on pure hope alone. He still planned to do just that, only now he had some proof that Annabelle loved him as much as he loved her.

He just hoped love was enough and that he hadn't finally, irrevocably pushed her away for good.

KEEPING A FAKE SMILE pasted on her face was getting more difficult by the minute. The charity event wasn't the problem. Annabelle liked mingling with other industry professionals. She enjoyed meeting the athletes, models and actresses also attending the event. She also liked the fact that Oakley sportswear and sunglasses was sponsoring such a good cause—the Lighthouse Foundation. And she was definitely enjoying the champagne punch. Unfortunately it was her client, Russell Bruno, who had her on edge.

The man had huge teeth—made brighter thanks to the contrast with his black tuxedo jacket—a huge smile and an even bigger ego. To make matters worse, he also had large, groping hands and he liked to settle his palm on her ass. Clearly the man didn't understand the term *professional association.* She was tired of it and tired of him. So tired she was ready to go home.

Unfortunately she'd let Russ, as he liked to be called, pick her up from The Hot Zone and now she was stuck here until he was ready to leave. But she was loathe to call his attention to her since he was finally, blessedly involved in conversation with someone else. A pretty brunette soap opera actress who was obviously impressed with his physique and pretty-boy face.

Annabelle motioned to the bartender and he refilled her punch but before she could take a sip, she yawned and a loud sound escaped from the back of her throat by mistake.

Russ turned around fast. "Oh, I've been ignoring my date." His attention back on Annabelle, he shot a regretful glance at the other woman by his side.

"Not a problem for me," Annabelle muttered.

Russ chuckled, clearly not taking her seriously. "I get carried away telling the story of how I was called up from the Minors, but I'm back now," he promised

Annabelle and followed up his comment with a bold slide of his wandering palm from her back to her bottom.

His other female companion took off in a huff.

Russ let out an exaggerated exhale of relief. "I thought she'd never leave. I'm so sorry, sugar."

Annabelle gritted her teeth but kept a smile for appearances. First thing tomorrow she was informing her sisters that this stud muffin was officially Annabelle's ex-client and could be shuffled to the new PR person The Hot Zone had yet to hire.

In the meantime, he was still her problem. "Russ, either you take your hand off my ass or I break your arm. The choice is yours," she said with saccharine sweetness.

"You heard the lady, Bruno."

Uh-oh. Annabelle knew that voice as well as she knew her own. Her heart soared but she immediately squelched the emotion, reminding herself she had no idea why he was here.

"Brandon Vaughn, well I'll be damned!" Russ quickly removed his hand and extended it so he could greet the football legend.

But a quick glance at Vaughn's strained expression and Annabelle knew this wouldn't be an easy, friendly how do you do. "Russell Bruno meet Brandon Vaughn."

She performed the perfunctory introductions but doubted it would make Vaughn soften.

She was right.

He ignored Bruno and his outstretched hand. "Time to go home, Annie."

She raised an eyebrow. Going home, and with Vaughn at that, seemed like the best idea she'd heard all night. However she wasn't about to let him show up out of nowhere and call the shots as if he owned her. Especially after he'd been silent and out of her life for the last week.

He certainly knew how to make a re-entrance. Wearing denim jeans, a black T-shirt and sport jacket, he was completely underdressed compared to the tuxedoed men surrounding them. Still he was the sexiest, most gorgeous sight Annabelle had ever seen.

He was also royally ticked off.

Beside her, Russ began to sweat and he glared at Annabelle. "I thought you came with me. I mean if I'd known she was with you, man, I never, not even as a professional courtesy, which this date was. Not that it was a date at all," he said, rambling.

"Do you always park your hand on a lady's ass, Russ? Or is it just your way of finding common ground?" Vaughn asked.

Annabelle stifled a laugh.

"I've really got to get going." Russ glanced at Vaughn. "Good to meet you, man." He took off at a near run, never looking back.

Annabelle lifted her eyes toward the chandelier on the ceiling. "Another man who backs off at the mere sight of Brandon Vaughn," she said in disgust. "What am I—back in Greenlawn?"

Vaughn's gaze devoured her, his eyes glittering with so many mixed emotions she couldn't read them all. She'd start with basic understanding.

"What are you doing here?" she asked him.

"Can we discuss this somewhere more private?" He tilted his head, indicating the television cameras and reporters circling the room. Certainly some of their encounter had already been caught on tape.

She didn't care. He'd put her through the ringer and she wasn't about to make this easy for him. "Before I go anywhere I want to know why you're here."

He shrugged out of his jacket. "I had a feeling you weren't going to make this easy, not that I deserve it. Isn't it obvious what I'm doing here?" he asked. "I came to see you."

He took his sport jacket and lay it over her shoulders so the broad garment draped her back. Then he pulled the lapels together in front in an obvious attempt to cover her cleavage.

Leaning forward, he whispered in her ear. "You're gorgeous, sweetheart, but I'd rather you save the show for me and me alone, if you don't mind."

"What is it with men and their obsession with breasts?" she asked, realizing he'd obviously gone to visit with Uncle Yank before coming here. How else would he know where to find her?

She stepped out of his grasp. "It'll be a cold day in hell before you see these babies again, Vaughn. That is unless you have some fancy footwork to show me that'll compensate for the hell you put me through."

He treated her to that sexy, cocky grin she'd come to adore. "I'm known for my footwork, love."

Her heart tripped at his word choice and her gaze flew to his to judge if he meant the word or if he'd tossed out a flippant term of endearment. But his expression wasn't giving anything away.

She swallowed hard. "Start showing me and you'd better not put that foot in your mouth."

"Not here." He wrapped his arm around her and led her toward the door but they didn't make it far before Entertainment's star reporter cornered them with her cameraman and microphone.

"Brandon Vaughn, what an unexpected surprise. Are you and Miss Jordan an item?" Vanessa Fulton leaned toward them as if she were about to get the scoop of the year. "Come on and give my viewers something to discuss over the water cooler tomorrow."

Annabelle stiffened as she waited for his answer. She expected a defensive word or a terse "no comment." Instead Vaughn's grin was as big as his colossal ego. Or at least the ego he used for public appearances, Annabelle thought. Unfortunately for her she'd gotten to know the real man, the vulnerable man, and *that* had been her undoing.

"You're going to have to ask Ms. Jordan the current status of our relationship. I'm open to whatever she desires," Vaughn said, obviously playing for the camera.

The louse.

Annabelle had seconds to contemplate her options. No publicity is bad publicity? Not a good choice because that mantra had come back to bite her with Randy Dalton. Instead of the wounded party, she'd come off as the spoiled, jilted brat. Discreet silence? Also not a possibility since it'd leave the viewer in control of perception and result in Annabelle looking as if she were Vaughn's latest conquest of the moment.

Perception, she thought to herself again. *That* was the key. She smiled big and wide for Vanessa and her viewers. "You heard the man. He's open to anything." She winked at the reporter in a woman to woman sort of way.

Then she gave the perception that *she* was one hundred percent in control by hooking her finger into Vaughn's belt buckle. "If you'll excuse us now, we have important issues to discuss." And with that, she pulled Vaughn toward the door, leading him by the front of his pants, laughing as the swinging ballroom doors closed behind them.

"That was low, Annie," he said in her ear.

She shrugged. "Next time wear a tie."

Vaughn growled. He was finished playing games. He lifted her around the waist, tossed her over his shoulder and refused to put her down until the valet brought his truck around. He buckled her in and locked the doors, including the childproof locks so she couldn't run out on him.

Late at night, no traffic. Man, sometimes he loved New York City and how close everything was, since not five minutes later, he pulled up to her apartment building. Fate was definitely on his side as a parking spot waited out front. He pulled in, then strode around to help her out.

He couldn't read her mind, but he knew she was less than pleased with him at the moment. He wasn't pleased with himself and wouldn't be until he had her alone in her apartment where she could yell, he could talk and they both could lay things on the line.

She stormed into the building and he followed her into one of the elevators. “Aren’t you going to thank me for saving you from Bruno’s wandering hands?”

She hit the eighth-floor button. “I could have handled him.”

“I know,” he told her.

That seemed to take her off guard and she glanced at him warily.

“It’s just that I couldn’t handle that SOB’s hands on you. He’s lucky his arm’s still in its socket,” Vaughn muttered.

They stepped out of the elevator and she stopped at the second door on the right.

“Tell me one thing,” she said as she turned the key in the lock, then glanced over her shoulder at him. “What the hell gives you the right to act as if you have any rights over me at all?”

He leaned an arm against the wall beside her. From his perspective he had a clear view between her breasts, inside her dress. His heart pounded in his chest as he realized how badly he wanted what she’d just said. The right to claim her, all of her, as his own.

“Nothing gives me that right. Not a damn thing. At least not yet but I’m hoping by the time I’m through talking, you’ll give me that and more.”

She pushed the door open and whispered in a shaken voice, “Come on in.”

He took that as a positive sign and followed her inside. Leaving nothing to chance, he kicked the door closed behind them, then immediately turned the lock and slid the chain through the holder.

Boris greeted him, coming to a skidding halt at his feet and jumping up and down on his hind legs begging for attention. Vaughn couldn't believe how damn happy he was to see the fuzzy mutt.

He knelt down and patted him on the head. "Hey, Q-Tip, how're you doing?" he asked. "I missed you, boy."

As Vaughn rose to his feet, he glanced at Annabelle. Shoulders stiff, she walked to a large couch and shrugged his jacket off her shoulders, acting as if she didn't have a care in the world.

He knew better. He could almost hear her thinking, "What about me? Did you miss me, too?" Very soon she'd have her answer.

He drew a deep breath before joining her in what looked like a garden rather than a living room. He was surrounded by plants, by the cat who was curled on the windowsill, by the rabbit who stared from inside the cage. By everything that was important to Annabelle because these things gave her unconditional love. The love her parents' deaths had denied her and the love she'd been seeking all her life. Vaughn knew this because they had that in common.

He paused in front of her and took her face in his hands. Her eyes were wide, her cheeks damp and her hands, though clutched in front of her, were shaking.

She was afraid to believe. Something else he understood because he'd been there too.

He brushed a stray tear with his thumb. "I'm not going anywhere ever again," he said, his gaze never leaving hers. "I know this, I'm sure of this and I wouldn't be here unless I had no doubts." He tried to answer her unasked questions.

"What changed?" she asked him. "Because I can't let myself believe. I can't open up and trust—"

Her voice caught and he felt as if his heart were being torn apart, so deeply did he understand her fears.

She grasped his wrists hard. "I lost my parents. I lived in fear of being separated from my sisters. In the middle of the night, that fear still lives inside me. And though I told myself I'd been in love before, it was all an illusion until I met you." She bit down on her trembling lower lip.

"Go on." He needed her to be so honest, there could be no misunderstandings, no leaving ever again.

"I love you. I said it before I left, but you were half asleep."

She squeezed him even tighter, probably stopping his circulation. Which was okay since he knew she'd get his blood flowing again soon. "I thought I dreamt the words."

She shook her head. "You didn't. But saying them while you were asleep was safe. Saying them now is the biggest risk I've ever taken. You have my heart, Vaughn and if you abandon me or leave me, I'll hurt you worse than I hurt Roy and if you remember, he doubled over clutching the family jewels."

Vaughn smoothed his thumbs over her cheeks, caressing, soothing, silently asking her to believe in him.

He was rewarded when ever so slowly she loosened her grip on his wrists.

"It's funny—" he began.

"I'm not laughing." But her gaze seemed lighter, more open.

"It's just that I came here thinking I'd be the one to slice open a vein and beg you to take me back, but here you are as scared as I am of being left behind." He shook his head at the unexpected way this evening was playing out.

"Vaughn?"

"Hmm?"

Annabelle smiled. "It'd be a good time for you to open that vein about now."

Grinning but knowing he wasn't out of the woods yet, he pulled her down to settle on the couch with him. "I love you, Annie. And I only let you go because it was easier than facing myself."

She threw herself into his arms and kissed him hard on the lips. Kissed him for a good long time until, finally, she pulled back, but her arms remained hooked around his neck.

"Tell me more. Tell me something I don't know. Tell me how we got to this point because I never thought it would come, you know."

He completely understood. "My mother came by looking for you. She had breakfast in one hand and a peace pipe in the other. So to speak, anyway."

Her mouth opened then closed again.

It was good to see he still had some surprises left for her. "She said you'd helped her approach me. I'm grateful for that. I'm grateful you protected me from your uncle even when I hadn't done a damn thing to deserve your faith."

Her eyes opened wide. "You know about that?"

Vaughn shrugged. "Your uncle isn't the discreet type. Anyway, I'm not really sure I can give you an explanation as to what changed except I missed you like crazy."

"I missed you, too."

He glanced into her warm, welcoming eyes and decided she was right. Now was the time to open that vein. "I'm still not sure I believe I'm worthy of you, but *you* seem to think I am and that's all that counts. Besides, without you, the lodge, my dream—it all meant nothing."

"Oh, Vaughn."

"And now that Nick's tied up with Mara, I had nobody to hang out with after work."

Laughing, she pushed him against the couch so they lay down, their bodies aligned. "I love you, Brandon Vaughn."

Knowing he'd found love and complete acceptance at last, he relaxed. His heart pounded hard in his chest but it was from excitement and desire, not anxiety over the future. Not anymore.

"I want to open up my huge house and fill it with our babies. We can live in the city and make the house our summer home. Or we can sell it and live wherever you want. Because I love you, too, Hot Stuff. And I always will."

EPILOGUE

YANK GLANCED AROUND the grounds of Vaughn's lodge, which had been open over six months now. The place was destined to be a huge success, filled with kids and laughter and love. Which meant he and his stinking bad mood ought to stay far, far away.

"You need to get your act together, Uncle Yank," Micki said, brushing by him and giving him a kiss on the cheek. "Nobody likes a sourpuss."

"And I don't like Spencer Atkins all over Lola." He pointed to the blanket they'd spread underneath a huge tree where they sipped champagne and held hands. Made a man want to puke, that's what it did.

"As I recall you let her go. Did you think she was going to crawl into the woodwork and die without you?" Micki pursed her lips. "It isn't too late to get her back, you know. It's not like they're married or anything. At least not yet."

Yank straightened his shoulders. "What's that supposed to mean?"

Micki shrugged. Always the coy one, she treated him to her dimpled grin. "I'm just saying that Vaughn and Annabelle got married this past June and now here we are in July and love is in the air." She swept her arm around to where many couples surrounded them. "You just never know, so if you don't like your life as it stands, you need to do something to change it. Now."

She strode off before he could remind her to do the same. After all, it wasn't like *she* was coupled off yet. None of the damn men she'd met and none he represented were good enough for his littlest niece. At least none he'd found yet.

And then there was Sophie, his Miss Know It All niece who bombarded him with daily advice and articles on his eyesight, who insisted on being the one to take him from specialist to specialist. She shouldn't be focusing on her uncle, she should be finding a good man to settle down with. But how could she have time for a relationship if she was so busy taking care of him? Yank and his condition were nothing but an excuse for Sophie to avoid a serious commitment.

Just like *he* was using his eyesight as an excuse not to deal with his feelings for Lola? He shook his head. He didn't want to travel that road, but how could he not when she was cavorting with Spencer, his best friend and biggest business rival, right under his nose?

Before Yank could figure out how to fix his messed up life, the sound of Vaughn's voice over a microphone caught his attention and he joined everyone gathering at a makeshift stage. He stood on the fringe of the crowd and waited.

"It's time to announce the recipient of the first Brandon Vaughn Scholarship," Vaughn said. "The winner will receive a five-thousand-dollar grant to be used at the college of his or her choice."

A round of applause followed.

"Hi, Uncle Yank." Sophie sidled up to him and put an arm around his shoulder.

"Hiya, honey."

"Did you see that Vaughn's parents are here and they're actually smiling?"

Yank scowled. "I still don't like 'em but I admit they're trying to act human," he muttered.

Sophie laughed.

"I'm going to let the person who came up with the scholarship idea announce the recipient," Vaughn said. "So I'm going to ask my beautiful wife to do the honors. Annie, will you join me up here?"

A second round of applause interrupted the action on the stage, then Annabelle spoke.

"The recipient isn't just a fantastic football player and someone who's struggled to overcome educational challenges this year, but he's someone who's had emotional hurdles as well and he's overcome every one. Please give a big congratulations to Todd Murray," Annabelle said, clapping and then hugging the guy who ran up to the podium to accept the award.

"That's the kid whose father damn near burned this place down, isn't it?" Yank asked.

Sophie nodded. "Roy's in a psychiatric facility but Annabelle and Vaughn said Todd's worked hard to make him proud anyway. He really deserves this."

Yank assessed the kid's height and build the best he

could judge from a distance and with his sight. "Maybe I'll be representing him one day."

"I sure hope so. Which reminds me. Have you given any more thought to the procedure the doctor told us about? You're at an early enough stage of the disease to be a perfect candidate," Sophie said and he heard the hope in her voice.

Yank patted her cheek. "We'll talk," he promised.

Sophie glanced at the stage and Yank followed her gaze. He couldn't see clearly but he was certain the two shadows sucking face were Annabelle and Vaughn.

"Annie looks so happy," Sophie whispered, sounding completely thrilled for her sister.

One of the things Yank adored about his nieces was how genuinely they loved each other, even if occasionally they fought the good fight. They were wonderful girls.

"I always knew Vaughn was the right man for Annie. They fit each other, you know?" Yank asked.

Sophie inclined her head. "I sure do. Just like you and Lola."

Yank cursed. "Not you, too."

"Forgive me for just stating the obvious. How long before you cave in? The only reason you let so much time go by at all was because she went on a cruise, spent time visiting an old friend in London, and then the three of us agreed to keep tabs on her for you," Sophie said.

"And fat lot of good the three of you did me. Lola ended up working for Spencer Atkins!"

Sophie shrugged. "You only asked us to make sure

she was safe and happy. You didn't say anything about keeping her away from other men."

Yank stiffened. "There've been other men?"

Sophie hugged him tight. "You really need to get your act together, Uncle Yank," she said, repeating Micki's advice, then took off to go talk to Annabelle.

Yank looked around for Lola and Atkins but they'd packed up and gone. The woman had him tied up in knots and had since she'd left him. He'd expected her to come back, but she'd stayed away.

Damn women. *Can't live with 'em, can't live without 'em.*

His nieces were wise women and they were right. Yank could no longer put off admitting that he had to make a decision about Lola. And he'd be damned if he'd let Spence Atkins have *his* woman.

* * * * *